I0847479

MIDNIGHT RADIO

MIDNIGHT RADIO

PROLOGUE

Just after midnight, April 14, 1942
Aboard the USS Jesse Roper

The midnight watch of the *Roper* had come on a few minutes early. It was their custom, in order to acclimate to the pitch black that the Atlantic threw at them. With not even a sliver of a moon present, the ocean and night sky met in an invisible horizon all around the old ship. The sailors hurried to their positions.The sooner they all got to their posts, the sooner the last watch could leave for their bunks. The crew was fortunate in that they had only been steaming from the port in Norfolk, Virginia since 0600 the morning before.

Normally the crew would have visions of good times recently passed in the bars of Norfolk and Virginia Beach. The crew aboard the *Roper* would usually spend time with the men of the other three destroyers tasked with defending the Atlantic coast from an onslaught of Nazi U-boats. While most of the US Navy was being used in defense of the large convoys heading from New York to England, the entirety of the lower east coast had protected, if protected was even the right word, by four outdated World War I era destroyers. The ships, the *Roper*, the *Jacob Jones*, the *Herbert*, and the *Dickerson*, all tied up at the same slips in Norfolk, and regularly shared the skilled ratings from one ship to another as they were needed. All the destroyers were undercrewed, but every crew member was well trained and diligent. Most of the crew members had trained together before being assigned to their respective ships, and many were close friends.

That was what made it even more horrible for the crew of the *Roper* when the *Jacob Jones* had been sunk by a German U-boat. All but eleven of the crew of the *Jones* died from the attack.

Reeling from the loss of a month earlier, the *Roper* steamed out on patrol, called "hunting U-boats" by the Navy brass, but more accurately described as "chasing U-boats" by the sailors. Most of their patrols involved steaming toward ships already torpedoed and sinking, aflame with the crews in the water or on life rafts. They did more rescue than hunting.

When the ship did come across something, a strange shape detected by sonar as the sound lashed out into the cold waters, it was always a wrecked ship, another loss to the Nazi drumbeat of U-boats along the North Carolina coast. Never sure of what they might find, and always on edge after the loss of the *Jones*, the *Roper* would throw depth charges over. The high explosives would sink and detonate, but whatever damage they caused did nothing to change the fate of the shipwrecks already at the bottom of the Graveyard of the Atlantic.

The sailors of the *Roper* would often struggle with the day to day activities. They were always chasing, never catching. The diligence began wearing thin over the continual calls to General Quarters. The inability to rest frayed the sailors as the shorthanded crews went four hours on, four hours off. Depth charges and alarms continually sounded, all while the crew kept running thoughts in their heads of their late friends on the *Jacob Jones* lying dead at the bottom of the ocean. Would this tour be any different, they all wondered.

Ensign Kenneth Tebo took the midnight watch for the first night shift of the *Roper*. The night was perfect. Dark skies were clear with nothing but bright starlight across the ocean. To the west, a thin flash of light, followed a slow heartbeat later by another, meant that little Bodie Island Lighthouse was signaling that the ship was in position off the Carolina coast. The ocean was nearly still, with only soft waves churning the tiny phytoplankton to life as the microscopic creatures lit up with agitation. The bridge was near dark as well, with soft lights coming from the dials and screens, including the new radar detection unit that had just been installed on the previous port. Above Ensign Tebo, soft and almost noiseless, spun a big wire cage, endlessly looking with radar out over the flat ocean. No ship had ever detected a U-boat with radar before, and the ensign wondered if the new technology would actually help.

Huddled over the screen was the radar technician, still tired, waking up and trying to focus in the dark night on the continual circling beam on his screen, hypnotic, ever-present, unchanging…

A green blob appeared on his screen, something on the surface. It could be anything, he thought, a derelict merchant, a fishing trawler, perhaps a small Coast Guard boat.

It could also be a U-boat.

He reported his contact to Ensign Tebo.

Things started happening fast on the *Roper* after that. The sound operator, locked away with headphones squeezed close enough to his ears that they hurt, reported the sounds of screws turning, a sure sign this was a submarine. Within the same moment, the deck crew, edgy, anxious, always looking for the torpedo running toward them, spotted the wake of the mysterious craft, a foamy white line that billowed in the dark sea, aided in its visibility by the glowing plankton churned in its wash.

The ship's commander, Lt. Commander Hamilton Howe, was awakened. The *Roper*, too, was awakened, with speed put to her to chase down the phantom, if she really was a Nazi U-boat.

That question was answered quickly as the crew saw a torpedo speed out of the gloom. Its propeller churned the ocean like a blender, making a comet's tail in its wake, barely under the water and meant to strike just below the waterline of a ship to split and flood the destroyer.

It passed to the port of the *Roper*, a close call and unfortunate miss by the captain of the U-boat, but fortunate for the US ship.

Lt. Commander Howe now knew he was dealing with an enemy combatant. Even in the dark, they both had sent greetings.

There was no need for subtlety. He sounded the alarm for General Quarters and the *Roper* came alive, ready for payback.

The *Roper*'s spotlight now reached out across the waters, trying to find the Nazis in order to give her guns a target. Sonar lashed out, the neverending *pongpong* sound that submariners fear. When the U-boat was found, Commander Howe gave orders to commence action on the U-boat, freeing his crew to fire upon the enemy.

The *Roper*'s gun crews worked feverishly. The light from the spotlight leaped out onto the sub, revealing the conning tower, the deck, and most importantly, the large German 88 deck gun affixed to the submarine. The big 88 could easily punch a hole into the destroyer, or could pump round after round down the ocean into her boiler, magazine, quarters, and bridge. The ship would be sunk or dismantled, if the *Roper* didn't get into a firing position and bring to bear her more powerful and numerous armament.

The *Roper* was armed with large 50 caliber machine guns, as well as a pair of 3 inch 50 caliber deck guns. All had been left loaded and armed as soon as leaving the safety of Norfolk. The gun crew of the big 3 inch gun on the foredeck of the *Roper* swiveled their gun to take aim on the U-boat, as the enemy crew began the same task hundreds of yards away across the ocean. As soon as the *Roper*'s gun was on target, the gun captain ordered to fire.

Click.

The gun misfired. Across the ship, due to the weapons being left in loaded condition, the salt and sea took action against the guns and ammunition. The machine guns jammed and misfired just as the big deck gun froze as well. The German sailors and captain would be wondering just why the destroyer hadn't opened fire, but did not stop to count their blessings as they cleared the barrel of their own 88, and began the laborious act of shoveling the shells by hand up and out of the hatches on the U-boat.

A young seaman pulled the bolt on his 50 caliber machine gun and squeezed the trigger mechanism. Absolutely nothing happened. The young sailor, only 19, with the *Roper* being the first boat he had ever been on, knew only the basics of gun safety and firing the big machine gun. He had no idea how to clear the jam. Chief Bosun's Mate Jack Wright was the old salt of the ship. His boys were his charge, and he didn't want anything to happen to them. He saw the Nazis getting closer to firing on his ship, his crew, and knew he had to do something. He pushed the young sailor aside and cleared the jam, pulling the chain of shells through until there were clean, unexposed shells in the machine gun's action. Then he let loose hell upon the Nazis.

Wright traced his bullets as they flew, letting them walk up the water in loose splashes until they hit the U-boat. The big 50 ripped into the Germans. They saw it all coming and could do nothing but be torn apart by the blasts meant to tear airplanes from the sky. The distance was great enough that the sound from the 50, a dull and loud tapping cough in sets of three or four, would be silenced just long enough for the shells to go downrange and ring into the conning tower of the U-boat with an ominous hollow gong. Passing through the Nazi sailors did nothing to change the tenor of the song the bullets sang.

The bridge continued its demand to fire the big guns in order to destroy the U-boat. One machine gun would not stop the threat. The only thing that slowed the constant orders to fire were the interspersed swear words, becoming more vociferous and creative with every second that the U-boat still floated.

Coxwain Harry Heyman heard the vitriolic demands from his position aft. He had only been named gun captain two days ago, and had not even a day at sea to get used to the command. He wondered why the other guns weren't firing. From the stern of the ship, he had no clue that the weapons had all misfired. He just knew that as the *Roper* turned starboard, his gun would soon be clear to fire. The big 3 inch deck gun twisted under the force of the crew spinning it toward the target. As soon as he had a target, Heyman ordered his gun to fire.

There is a magical strange silence right after a gun fires. The initial concussion is less than most civilians would imagine it would sound. It is a loud and short cough. But the recoil makes the entire ship shudder, especially at the stern, as the gun shakes through the ship. Everyone onboard the *Roper* knew she had gotten her big guns involved now. The shell flew at a high rate, with a flat trajectory as it came from the low deck of the destroyer to find its home on the barely floating U-boat. The shell is too fast to be seen, but it still leaves an imprint on the viewer. It flies and reaches out. It almost seems like there is time to move or dodge the shot.

Then it strikes, and all around, the world is split open.

Heyman saw his shot, a single blast, strike home perfectly, below the conning tower, just at the waterline.

By the time the geyser of water had finished falling, the captain and crew of the *Roper* could see that the U-boat had stopped dead in the water and had begun sinking. Lt. Commander Howe ordered a torpedo in the water, but the submarine was already disappearing. They all watched it go under, stern first, as the U-boat flooded from the gaping hole on its side. German sailors, the ones still alive, attempted to abandon the submarine into the cold Atlantic waters.

Unsure of whether or not the U-boat had been sunk or was still functional, as well as receiving a possible sonar signature of a second U-boat, the *Roper* had to cease any operations of rescuing the sailors in the water. Circling around, still chasing ghosts, Lt. Commander Howe did what he had to do. He ordered arrays of depth charges to be fired in the last known position of the U-boat. The *Roper* had passed through the survivors on their initial evasion, but could not respond to the calls in German and English for help. After the firing of depth charges, and with no success in finding any debris from a sunken ship, the *Roper* again passed by the Germans in the water. This time, there were no calls. The ocean remained silent.

It took time to bring support in the form of air cover. The *Roper* collected most of the bodies after daybreak, searching the dead sailors' pockets for any identification or intelligence. The Germans were determined to be from the U-85, one of the many submarines that had prowled the Atlantic coast. They gathered the sailors bodies in a heap, unceremoniously laid on the deck. The crew of the *Roper* didn't feel any joy at the actions. Sinking the U-85 had brought about a small measure of revenge, for the *Jones* and her crew, as well as the countless ships and passengers lost over the past months. But the sailors aboard the *Roper* mostly looked on with sadness. The Germans, dead, torn, bloated, and waterlogged, still looked a lot like them. The only difference was the uniforms, the beards of the U-85 sailors, and the fact that the Germans were dead and the Americans were alive.

Noticeably absent from the dead was the U-boat's captain, Gregor Eberhard.

1

Wednesday, May 14th, 1985

Steve Brodie watched his footprints disappear into the darkness behind him as he jogged across the beach of the Cape Hatteras seashore. They either disappeared into the darkness or were washed away by the tiny waves that rushed the shore. Steve ran at an even pace, just fast enough for him to clear his head of all the thoughts and concerns, "Not worries," he convinced himself. It was late into the evening, with only a thin sliver of orange twilight still burning in the sky over the sound waters to the west. The sky above and over the ocean was already an inky purple, with stars beginning to dot the oncoming night.

Steve felt more at home in the darkness. It hid him from the others on the island. He enjoyed running, especially on the smooth beach when no one was out. Running had become popular about ten years earlier, though Steve had only recently taken it up. It was mostly a stress relief, a needed exercise for him to move, and not feel trapped in his own skin.

Looking back over his shoulder, he saw his footprints as they barely registered in the firm, wet sand. The sand gave way begrudgingly, as if his feet were too light to make a mark. The soft low waves quickly raced up behind him to erase any mark he made. Farther in the distance, the beam of Cape Hatteras Lighthouse circled out to the sea. As a beacon, it was no longer needed as a maritime aid. Mariners might still see it, but they had long ago developed more sophisticated thechnology that kept them away from the sharp and haunted shore. Locals found comfort in the light, he knew. But the area just offshore had not been nearly as safe in the past, he had discovered as he learned more and more about his new home.

Perhaps, it only served as a warning, Steve thought.

Steve had only recently moved to Buxton from Asheville. A move from the mountains to the coast of North Carolina would have been hard enough, but he was local to neither. He was local to nowhere, he realized. A vagabond, even though he moved only occasionally, he had no defined home, not for years, and his family, what little he had once had, was long gone.

Hatteras Island was as far away from everything as Asheville had been. When Asheville was a city wrapped in winter, sitting in a valley surrounded by frozen mountain peaks, Hatteras blew gales intermixed with unseasonably warm breezes. The island was as far from the rest of the world as Steve could get. It wasn't just the middle of nowhere, but more the end of nowhere. It was a backvelt or hinterland that gave forth no detail on any map. Now in May, the winds only whispered of a summer breeze, and the waves lapped softly at the ocean's edge. If he had looked for a better place which to escape, he couldn't have found one.

He had only been on the island for two weeks. Steve had tried to learn what he could of the area, as sparse as it was. As he ran, he looked out at the darkness over the Atlantic Ocean. He had learned the nickname of the waters was the Graveyard of the Atlantic, a rather ominous moniker for a beach community. The coast earned the name honestly, as the churning Atlantic had been known in the past to take ships by the thousands into her dark depths, and relinquished the dead bodies begrudgingly. He had wondered why they didn't popularize the more sparkly colorful nickname

Diamond Shoals. Steve was told by a knowledgeable local that the name came from the diamond shaped underwater dunes offshore that would reach up to crush ships' hulls as they were pushed too close to shore during spring storms.

"Graveyard of the Atlantic would have to do," Steve thought.

Steve picked up his pace. He needed a little physical stress on his body to take the place of the mental stress his mind had been under for the past two weeks. He was tired, tired of unpacking haphazardly. He still had boxes he hadn't opened yet. His house wasn't yet a home, and it seemed scattered, with old scents running through it that could not be rid of no matter how many open windows he had. It had smelled of stillness, old cooked food, and the bodies of people who must have lived there years ago. Steve didn't relish the mundane work he still had to do. Running let him escape his life back at his house. Again he looked back, checking the distance he had already covered. By now the big stack of the candy striped lighthouse had disappeared into the night. He saw only the light appearing from the beacon as it rotated across the dark sky.

Steve ran in comfort at a higher speed, even with his feet slipping on the unstable and angled shoreline. He could run for miles easily at this pace. The ocean air wrapped around him. The sunset dipped away; soon he would be fully in the dark, and he liked it that way. No distractions, no one to see him and stop him. On Hatteras at least the small population lent itself to space and privacy. The air from the ocean was laced with the aroma of the sea. It was full of salt and the sordid rot of dead and dying detritus, all rich and intertwining. Steve could smell his own sweat as his body worked harder. Sea grass on the dunes past the soft beach sand waved in the darkness at him. Their own scents came in rushes of green sweetness.

He made good time on the beach. "I must have covered two miles or more by now," he thought as he glanced back at the diminishing tower light. Even at that distance, the tall Cape

Hatteras Light still gleamed well over the low dunes. He would have to run for an hour to outrace that light, he thought.

"And then," he huffed slightly at this high pace, "I still have to go back," Steve realized as he thought about where he had left his Jeep at the parking lot near the light. "Just a few more miles," he compromised with himself. His need to run and have a moment of freedom battled with his needs for organization, structure, a deep root from his past.

Both are part of my past, he thought.

Part of me now. Still.

One more mile, a fair compromise, both sides of him agreed, and his mind rested while his legs and lungs and heart did the work this time. He let himself take in the natural world around him. The smells especially, with the salt air, what everyone agreed to be a healing magic of some kind, coating over his sticky skin. The salt seemed to be everywhere, and everyone liked it. Steve rubbed the back of his neck, feeling the sweat, the grit from the sand, and the thin rime of the ocean under his long blond hair.

For his first time since he moved to the island, still new to the coast and this life, he felt a little comfortable. The distractions left his head, and he focused just on his breath, his speed, one foot in front of the other.

That was why he didn't notice what was in front of him in the darkness until he stumbled right over it.

At first, he only knew something was there. It was a dark shape on a dark shore in a dark night. Just a vague lump laying on the beach. His foot caught on something soft and fleshy, making him stumble.

At first, he thought it was a dead shark or porpoise that had washed up on shore, but then he smelled it.

Even with the salt air and ocean water covering it, Steve recognized the smells of death immediately. It was large, a body of some kind. This was no mere dead fish he had stepped on. Feeling the soft spongy flesh under his foot, through his shoe, it was still a surprise for him.

He immediately knew it was dead, whatever it was. Only a feeble brush of his hand as he knelt by the corpse told him the body was cold. The temperature of the water was the same. Possibly warmer.

Steve reached into his pocket for a small flashlight. He didn't bother to steel himself for what he would see. It was dead, whatever it was, shark, porpoise, and the only thing Steve could do for it was to push it back into the ocean. Or leave it there. A feast for the fish or the land crabs, neither would probably be choosy. When he turned on the light, it cast strange shapes and shadows over the object laying in the sand. Steve had seen death before, worse than this, but it didn't make what he saw any better.

The body was that of a young woman. Or at least most of her.

Her arms were cut off at her elbows, exposing worn and soft flesh and muscle, with a jagged stump of white bone.

Worse than that, her head had been cut off.

There was barely any neck protruding above her shoulders. Only a chipped piece of spine stuck out above a raw pink stump. The body was soft all over, bloated but strangely clean. She had obviously lost most of her blood from the wounds, which left her skin alabaster pale.

The rest of her body was there, but it had none of the strength that life would provide. It laid almost shapeless in the wet shore. The body, without a pulse or breath, shared no normal position that a living person would have.

This was definitely abnormal.

Steve looked at the dead body, then looked around him, wondering what had happened to her. Why was she just left on the beach like this? Did she fall off a boat and get cut up by the propeller? Instinctively, Steve looked up and out to sea. Far off, he saw the moving lights of a distant ship, some freighter bound northward. Hardly likely to lose a woman and have her wash up here.

He looked down again, at the wounds. They were horrific, but with the ocean washing over her, the body had been cleaned of blood. She almost looked porcelain smooth. The water had already begun to fill and bloat her. Her skin was tight and pale. One knee was decidedly twisted unnaturally under another leg.

The wandering tide still lapped at her legs and Steve's feet. He couldn't leave her there to be washed out back to sea. Setting his mind to the task, holding his breath, he wrapped his arms under her truncated shoulders, hoping to pull her to drier land.

His hands slipped on the body. Unable to hook himself under the arms with the elbows and forearms missing, he slipped and sat in the soft sand, his legs spread out above her, on each side of where her head should have been. It was like looking at a car wreck, he thought, as he stared into the dead woman's neck. He shook it off and tried to dig his hands into her soft flesh and pull. As he dragged the corpse above the high tide line, he noticed how clean the cut was for the poor woman's decapitation.

It was a quick realization that someone had probably cut her head off. Steve realized there would be little way to identify the woman, with no hands and no head. She had been killed, dismembered, and left on an empty beach in hopes the body would wash away to join the others buried deep in a watery tomb and forgotten in the Graveyard of the Atlantic.

Steve stood up and looked around. How long had she been there? Suddenly, his body became wary of just how open and exposed he was. He turned off his light, then moved away from the body and knelt. He listened, willing his own heart to slow so its pounding would not drown out the ocean and any other sound he might hear along the beach.

He waited and waited, with no sign. Nothing else moved. Far away, along the thin ribbon of Highway 12, cars passed occasionally in the darkening evening. There were no sounds of a vehicle starting and driving away, nor were there the soft pads of feet running. Steve listened intently to see if he could hear them in the sand.

Steve glanced at his watch. The telltale radioactive glow of yellow green showed the time. He wondered how far the light could be seen, if there was a maniacal murderer somewhere in the sand, looking for another victim. The glow barely made it to Steve's eyes, though. He had little to worry about. He could barely make out the striped ribbon that was his watch band for outdoor use. The time glowed feebly, saying it was 8:45 p.m. Sunset was 45 minutes ago, and twilight had already burned itself down to a cinder, with night coming on full.

Steve had to get back to civilization to find help.

Civilization, he thought. "I don't even know if this place has a police force."

2

"You sure you ran this far?"

It was a question Sheriff Rodney Midgette almost regretted asking the young man next to him in the sheriff's county supplied Blazer.

The big off road vehicle churned and bounced through the sand as Rodney piloted through the beach with a deft skill, letting the truck coast and bite when it wanted to, and never letting the big, soft tires ever begin to spin or dig in any soft sand. After meeting the boy, "Better not call him that," thought Rodney to himself, and getting a brief description of what he said he found, the two had piled into the Blazer and driven off to the north from an access near the lighthouse. There was no way he was going to walk the beach at night, especially if the sheriff had to discover a dead body several miles up the beach.

Sheriff Midgette, short, round, rounder than he would like, definitely overweight, knew he looked like a stereotypical southern sheriff, with a bulging gut over his waist, and a pink face with a slightly balding head. He wasn't going to give this boy the satisfaction of blubbering out in some strange southern twang,

"Well… whutta you boys got goin' on round heah?" or some such nonsense.

He was already cursed with being overweight, something that his age and the job caused rather than diminished, and he knew no amount of situps would fully get rid of the big inner tube of a spare tire he had around his midsection.

Nor could he help his accent. He was born here, had learned to talk on the Outer Banks, and had developed the same patois everyone else on the islands had.

But he knew he was skilled at his job. He was a trained veteran of the sheriff's department, and when the last sheriff finally retired, he put his name and experience up against anyone and everyone during the election period. He was from Hatteras, Buxton, and had run on the idea that the region needed someone to represent them well.

But time, sitting in a car, or at a desk, and, he admitted, eating too much fried shrimp probably did a lot to get him into the shape he was in. That's why he dreaded the accusatory words as soon as they came out of his mouth.

The "boy," as he looked like he was nineteen, with blond curly long hair, was as fit as Sheriff Midgette wasn't. Rodney just didn't need this kid, young man, whatever, judging him any more than he should be judging the kid. Still…

"Yes," Steve answered, "it was at least two miles." The words came out confident, but at least not condescending. Sheriff Midgette looked over at Steve in the light of the dash. He wasn't positive if he believed the young man. Sure, people have occasionally died, it happened, and sometimes it wasn't pretty. Sheriff Midgette had seen the occasional dead body, but usually it was someone who was old, who passed on. What this kid described, well, he just wasn't sure.

But then, someone had reported a dead body, a dead, decapitated girl, and if he didn't go look for it, and it turned up somewhere else in a few days, well, there'd be hell to pay. "And I'm a poor man," Sheriff Midgette said to himself.

He had wondered if the boy, "young man," he repeated, had seen a dead fish, a shark, porpoise or whale even, or just a strange pile of seagrass in the dark. A cursory drive so far had turned up nothing, no body, no shark.

Sheriff Midgette saw Steve fidget a little. He seemed uncomfortable, maybe for being judged that he couldn't have run so far so quickly at night. He looked a little miffed, like the way someone doesn't like it when you say their food is just "good."

Sheriff Midgette huffed, still not sure that he was going to find a dead body. He at least hoped he wouldn't.

The magic wasn't on his side, however. Just over two miles out, as the sheriff took another phlegmatic breath, the body had appeared in his headlights.

It was worse in the yellowing light of the truck's lights. After being moved to higher and dryer ground, the body had been found by the land crabs that came out at night on the shore by the hundreds. They had already started to feast upon the remains.

"Oh, Gowddam," Sheriff Midgette cursed in his brogue. He slammed on the brakes, making the truck skid for a moment in the soft sand before rolling to a stop. There was more grunting, by the sheriff, the seat, the door, all unintelligible gibberish to Steve. To his credit, Sheriff Midgette began to shoo off the beady eyed creatures. Their sand colored carapaces and ivory white claws scampered away, but only far enough to be out of the bright light. They had gotten a taste, and wanted more of the poor girl. Sheriff Midgette only grunted. Steve couldn't tell if he was nauseated by the sight or just disappointed in the job the sheriff would now have to do.

In order to stave off the hunger of the ghost crabs, Sheriff Midgette removed a cadaver bag from the truck to place the body into. Steve helped unfold the stiff plastic. It was obviously old. There had been no use for it in the several years it sat in the back of the Blazer. It had probably sat in the vehicle he had before this one, with the sheriff before him as well, Rodney thought.

With no medical examiner or deputy nearby, Sheriff Midgette had little choice but to take help from Steve. He puzzled over how to get the body in the bag before ultimately deciding to pick her up and drop her in. He noticed how Steve didn't seem squeamish over a naked, headless, armless dead body. But then, he figured that Steve was probably thinking the same thing about him.

He started to take her shoulders, with a wordless grunt and gesture at Steve toward the woman's ankles. Sheriff Midgette realized then that Steve would be staring down between the legs of a naked dead woman. Steve looked at him and simply shrugged.

"How about we just roll her into the bag, huh, Chief?" It seemed like a simple solution.

Less simple was what happened next. There were three people on the dark beach. An overweight sheriff, a young blond man, and a corpse in a body bag. Sheriff Midgette wandered the shore, ostensibly looking for clues. Steve watched him, wondering if he may just not know what to do next. Steve was quickly surprised by the sheriff's investigative skill.

"So, ye say you found here, roight about there?" he pointed into the surf, where the ocean had wiped clean all message of imprint. He shone a flashlight around the area, finally taking in the body bag with its beam t the high tide line. "And drug her up here?"

"Dragged, yes," Steve said.

"Dragged."

Sheriff Midgette eyed Steve. He didn't like someone correcting him.

Steve just didn't like any implication that he would drug a woman.

"You ever see a dead body like this?" Sheriff Midgette asked.

3

"You ever see a dead body like this?"

Steve knew immediately what he was implying. A dismembered corpse had done almost nothing to make his gorge rise, no vomiting, no retching, no averting his eyes from the horrid jagged wounds.

"I used to live in L.A.," he said simply. Steve used the city as an excuse. Everything bad happened in Los Angeles and New York. The people there were used to it, jaded, uncaring, they had seen everything. It was true, that he had lived there, and hopefully it would be a good enough excuse for the backwater sheriff, Steve thought.

But he had never seen a dead body in L.A.

Asheville, yes, and then long before that.

Steve sat down on the beach to watch the light of Cape Hatteras spin its way rhythmically out to sea. He wasn't going anywhere unless he wanted to run off into the dark to get back to his Jeep.

He watched Sheriff Midgette look around while he waited. For what, Steve wasn't sure. There certainly weren't any clues to be found.

Which is exactly what Sheriff Midgette pointed out.

"No footprints," he said simply.

Steve said nothing at first. Then…

"Should there be?" Steve shrugged into the darkness. The sheriff was decent enough not to shine the light in his eyes. "I mean, you don't even see my footprints, except there," he pointed toward the dark shape, "where I pulled her. My footprints were washed away by the ocean."

"Yeah," agreed the sheriff. "But look around." He shone his light across the beach. The entirety of Cape Hatteras was around them in the darkness. "No one comes this far out here. They all go within a couple hundred feet of the lighthouse, or go down to Cape Point fer fishin'." The sheriff seemed to state the obvious to Steve. But then, Steve followed the beam of light toward the dunes behind him.

The beach was still wide, strewn with lines of shell hash, untouched by footprints. Then, beyond that, a white line of dry sand, a course powder of natural white in the flashlight, that Steve knew was really an ecru cream of broken shells and pebbles that had been pummeled by the ocean for years before being spit up to the shore. Rivulets of sand, minuscule dunes themselves, waved across the beach, only inches high. They stood clean and untouched by the foot of man. No person, tourist or local, had trod this beach. It looked so natural and unspoiled to Steve that it took him a moment to realize what the sheriff was saying.

"How did she get here?"

The ride back was eerily silent. Sheriff Midgette had decided it would take too long to wait for anyone to get to the beach where they were, so Steve had helped him unceremoniously stuff the corpse in the back of the Blazer. It was a discomfiting and quiet ride for both the passenger and rider, though fortunately for both the load they carried in the rear of the truck made no complaints.

"You sure are taking this well," commented Sheriff Midgette again.

Steve said nothing.

"You musta seen some things out in California."

"It was an interesting place," Steve tried to remain noncommittal. He didn't want to have to explain any more than needed to the sheriff, but he didn't want the lawman to be prying into his past more than necessary. "Let's just say, outside of tonight," he jerked a thumb towards the back of the Blazer, "I'm happy to be in a quieter spot of the world."

Steve gathered up an accusation of his own to change the tone of the conversation. "You get stuff like this often? That's pretty brutal, even for big city deaths." He hoped it sounded just challenging enough to get the sheriff to be on the defensive about his home, but the answer he got wasn't what he expected.

"Not in a long while," the sheriff said the word like "whoile," a part of his coastal dialect dripping through. "Local girl, about eight, ten years ago, came back from college, she got killed by a man, he thought he was her boyfriend, but she didn't have any of it. He got mad. I guess he figured if he couldn't have her, no one could. Done her in pretty bad.

"But... no," the sheriff paused with a nod of his head in the pale glow of the dash. The beam from the lighthouse swept across the windshield and Steve could see a small crease of worry in the sheriff's face. "Not like this."

The rest of the trip was in silence, with only the spasmodic melody of the Blazer's engine as it revved and bogged in the sand to serve as music for the two men. Even the police radio was silent. All the criminals were in bed by now, Steve thought.

Steve's late night was made later by not getting to work on time, but little could be done about that. Steve drove his Jeep back to his house. He needed to go home and have a shower. Any normal night's run would have left him salted, sandy, with a light sweat over his body, but tonight, with the mix of ocean water, the sad and soft flesh of the dead woman's remains, and the thoughts of the crabs as they nipped at her exposed wounds called for a deeper cleaning. His job would wait. He stared at the phone, wanting to make a call to say he would be in soon, but then he would have to explain things. It would be easier to wait, and just say it all once. Then he thought about making another call, and put that out of his mind, too.

His new house was new only to him, not the world. It was at least fifty years old, probably older. He had picked it out based mostly on its location, with barely a thought to the looks, though it was beautiful. The old houses of Hatteras, he still had not yet gotten accustomed to calling his home Buxton yet, were built simply, but solidly, with a mix of floor to ceiling woods, as well as thin rattling windows that either wouldn't open or wouldn't stay up without a stick. His home was strangely gingerbread house-like, with exquisite scrollwork across the front, but also with a warped and bulging porch that Steve knew he would trip on until he either fixed it or got used to it.

The land was what really sold it, though. By the 1980s, there started a drive to build bigger, maybe not better, houses along the shore. Steve had seen a few of these going up north in Kill Devil Hills, but Hatteras, "Buxton" he thought to himself, had not been touched. Yet. The land was once cheap and plentiful, as if the owners had no idea how to get rid of all of it. The properties were simply drawn in long rectangles, from the road all the way out to the sound. Steve owned a huge chunk of twisted live oaks that sheltered him from the sun all the way to a marshy brackish water beach and an old weathered dock that must have been built in the 1940s. The empty house next door to his north could have been in another county, it was so invisible through the trees.

To his south, on the map where he had looked when he chose this property, there was nothing. Just acres of trees and brush. It went out to a distant peninsula that stuck into the Pamlico Sound.

Unfortunately it was an older map, and didn't show the plans for a new development next to him. Through a thin screen of woods, at least five houses had already gone up, with a road that led out to the highway.

At the moment, however, only one part of his house interested Steve. The Outer Bankers had seemed to stumble upon something that he had never seen before, especially in cold Asheville. While his home was not so archaic as to not have running water and indoor plumbing, there was an outdoor shower. It was meant to allow people to rinse off the grime of a hard day's work, or shower away the persistent beach sand that clung to them up to the thigh.

"And hair," Steve scratched at himself.

The cold water poured out of a simple showerhead. It was clear, icy, with a metallic taste in his mouth that matched the clean, steel hard feeling the water had as it ran down his body. The water was fresh, from a deep well sunk into the property and brought up from an old pump. Steve let it just run down him for a moment, drinking a bit the hard water, letting it rinse the taste out of his mouth. Steve found the mixture of the dark shower on the outside of the house, along with the icy cool water, revitalizing and private. He could hide from the world, wash away his daily sins, and come out refreshed. He was surprised no one else in the rest of the state had outdoor showers on their houses.

A pair of toads hopped out from under the smooth wood plats that sufficed for a floor as Steve turned on the water. He felt bad about interrupting their hunting. The two had been doing their job of keeping the insect population down in this small area, and now he had come to interrupt their dinnertime. They wouldn't go far. Hunting was good here. They would be back when the water turned off.

He washed and then dried off quickly. The former owners of the house had left a few old towels, one of which Steve liked. It was thin, a faded blue, with a wonderfully scratchy surface that felt good on his skin as he rubbed it over his back. He felt his chin. The thin stubble wasn't long enough to need a shave yet, especially for his work. Tomorrow, definitely, but not now. Not yet.

Steve ran into his house to get dressed, then immediately left to get into his Jeep. He drove into the dark night to get to his work down in Hatteras from his home in Buxton. Steve has tried to understand the names of the towns and villages, some simply places, just segments of land. Buxton, near the light, Frisco, an area to the south. He had no idea what actually was there. Or how it got its name. Hatteras village, which was nowhere near his home and Cape Hatteras Lighthouse, was where he worked. It seemed important to the locals, but as he drove down the relatively straight road that passed through these village names, he still had no idea what they all meant.

At least he had become familiar with the straight and simple drive to where his place of employment, the old weather station, stood. Now though, the dark road with messy scrub brush on either side felt like it hid something lurking in the dark, in the mysterious woods that bordered the lighthouse and Park Service land. Or even just over his shoulder in the back seats. He felt a cold shudder as he glanced at his rearview mirror, but there was nothing there.

4

Tim Watkins sat at a small desk in the middle of the old Cape Hatteras Weather Bureau building. Outside of the ubiquitous desk calendar, which had dates filled in, crossed off, and scribbled over, the only things that sat on the cheap table was a pile of mail, two copies of *Billboard* magazine, and a paper bag with a pound of ground coffee and filters.

At one corner, a telephone sat, its lights on the different lines blinking like mad, though they made no sound right now.

There was nothing remotely weather related on the desk, nor in the room. Not even in the whole building, really, outside of an old barometer and thermometer on the wall.

Tim Watkins was no meteorologist, even if every person on the Outer Banks quickly became a weatherman or woman as soon as the first hurricane got close.

The Weather Bureau building had stopped forecasting the weather sometime around 1946. Before that, it had made its share of radio broadcasts, as well as picked up many distress calls. The old yellow and red brick structure had seen the tides change over the years, Tim was sure of that.

When it closed down in 1946, it sat empty for years until it was bought and used as a private home. It ended up in the hands of Tim Watkins after he had retired from his career up in Kill Devil Hills as a manager of the local radio station for the area. But the job had decided not to retire him. He purchased the old building partly because of its history as a broadcast location. When locals had expressed their desire to have a community radio station, one that could broadcast school news, local events, and play some music across the island, Tim jumped in. His DJ alias was quickly revived, and Chris "The Rock" Stone opened up WZHX, Hatteras On The X.

So a small tower went up, and Tim unpacked his collections of electricity, boards, turntables, microphones, and shelves of tapes and recorders. Additionally, his collection of new and vintage LPs travelled with him.

With the space to keep his records and all the electronics he had collected, Tim not only had a decent radio station, but a very tight recording studio with some state of the art equipment. The notoriety of his collection traveled across the state. Which led to a rather surprising phone call soon after Tim had advertised for some new jocks who would like to DJ part time, especially if they had music they could license.

Steve Brodie, *the* Steve Brodie, the king of radio, who was doing his shows out of Asheville, NC, after years of being famous for being a hitmaker in Los Angeles, had called, looking for a place to record his weekly Top 40 radio program, Rocksound.

For a while, Tim was in disbelief. This was the guy, *the guy*, bigger than Kasey Kasem, bigger than Wolfman Jack, and he was saying he wanted to move to sleepy little Hatteras Island and work with Tim at his little radio station. It took a couple long phone calls to even convince Tim that this was actually Steve Brodie, and not a prank.

Steve had explained he needed a good place to write a prerecorded show, where he could make tapes and then send them out every week to be pressed into vinyl, which would then be sent to radio stations across the country by the end of the week, where it would be heard by millions of listeners.

Steve had told Tim that he started working in radio because it let him work nights, away from others, in a little box with just a microphone. "LA seems like a big city," he had said, "but it gets small real fast when every rock band, record producer, and screaming fan wanted something from you."

He had moved his show to Asheville, and then, abruptly after two years, had moved once again to Hatteras.

Tim didn't know why, and he didn't ask. He was simply enjoying the ride two weeks in. Steve had even agreed to take the late night show on weekends, and said he would be willing to go longer once summer hit the island.

Every night that Steve came in, Tim wanted to ask the same question he did the first night, "What are you doing here?!"

He looked at the clock on the wall. Steve was late as Tim heard the crunch of tires on the gravel and shells in the small drive outside. It didn't matter. The radio station still was on the sunup to sundown broadcast schedule.

When Steve came in, Tim had the same reaction he had had the first time he saw Steve. In walked a young man, terribly handsome, long blond hair, looking somewhat like a quintessential California surfer dude, with bright blue eyes and muscular arms. If he walked in carrying a surfboard and wearing Jams, Tim would not be the least bit surprised.

But this time Tim noticed a less than colorful visage. He tried to ignore it as the phone distracted him when it lit back up again. He didn't bother to ask, "What are you doing here?" or even "Why are you late?"

What Tim opened with this time, as the phone blinked in the bullpen and at his desk in the hall, was, "Did you hear there was a murder on the beach?!"

Steve let out a sigh. It was not the response Tim was expecting.

"I know," Steve answered quickly, before Tim could start to wonder. "I found the body when I was out on a run. That's why I'm late. I was out with the sheriff recovering her." He spent a moment telling Tim a truncated version of what had happened, while muting some of the grisly details of the woman's condition.

"I wonder if we should go on air and report this," Tim noted that this was one of the main reasons that the radio station was created. He was there to help get news to the locals who couldn't get information over TV airwaves and didn't have cable on the isolated islands. "It's probably why the phone has been ringing off the hook," he said.

"Look," Steve fairly pleaded with Tim, "If you can, will you answer the phones? I really don't want to have to go through that with everyone on the island right now. Or just turn the ringer off?"

Tim reached for the phone, grabbing it behind the receiver and lifting it to turn the phone off. "We're not even supposed to be here, anyway." In the back of the old building, in the booth, a soft glowing light blinked on the phone there. The ringer was never on there so it wouldn't interfere with the jock when they were on the air live. "I'll go turn that one off," he agreed. Tim didn't have to think long about what it must have been like to find a body on the beach, especially in the condition Steve had said she was in.

"I got a bit of prep for tomorrow morning's show," Tim pointed to some tapes. "You need any help?"

Steve picked up a stack of his own tapes, along with a worn but neat brown writer's notebook. "I'm good, Skip," he said with a wan smile.

"Alright," Tim acquiesced, "I'll make you a pot of joe, though I wonder if you'll need it." Tim was amazed at Steve's ability to stay up all night. He knew Steve was a nightfly, a late night jock, the soft warm sound of a jockey that could tell you a story to keep you up or lull you into dozing comfort. It was Steve's forte, and the bane of Tim's existence. Tim had loved doing the morning shows, and now did the daytime push into evening, but the late night sound had always been tough for him, only getting tougher as he had gotten older. He was thrilled when Steve had first offered to come in and work the weekend overnight. Having someone work the night was great, but when it was Steve Brodie, Tim felt like a girl meeting a rock star. Because that's what Steve was in the radio world. He was Dr. Johnny Fever and Bruce Springsteen rolled into one.

5

In the recording booth, Steve gathered himself to get into his work mode, and get the image of a dead body out of his head.

He tore out the Hot 100 from Billboard Magazine and scanned to see what he would be talking about. The Top 40 hits would be no surprise to him. They would be the same as the week before, with only a few jumps and falls. First he scanned to see what new songs were on the charts. These would be lower, and he would find one he liked, not necessarily something he thought would chart, but just a good song. Phil Collins had a new song from his album. He had turned into a hitmaker, and MTV loved him. He needed no help from radio to promote his songs. Deeper down he saw Lone Justice, a local, "not local," Steve had to say to himself, band from LA that had been playing cowpunk for a few years. He loved the band, and they would steal the show when they performed. Ways To Be Wicked would be his Heat of the Week, the middle song that he predicted would be a breakout hit. Steve made a few notes about seeing them in LA at the Whisky A Go Go three years ago.

The rest was pretty much the same fodder, Madonna at number one, some mention of We Are The World, tie in Tom Petty's new hit with Lone Justice, definitely putting Nightshift by

The Commodores on there, he commanded to himself. He checked off the songs he wanted out of the Top 40, added a couple spaces for new songs or a retrospective, and went to work.

Steve benefited from two hours of work he had done the night before, where he recorded bits of color and the setup prompts needed to get his entire show in a good order. The bit of work from the night before made this evening, and now morning, go by a little bit easier.

Six hours later he had a rather tight tape. He had lead ins and stories about the bands, some fun anecdotes, and really polished intros and outros. "This is one of my better shows," Steve was wistful over thinking about how he could separate what had happened to him only hours before. He noticed in the final recordings the slight difference from his Monday recordings and tonight's. He put it out of his mind. He had to pack up his tapes to be sent out within the next two hours by a special UPS pickup. It would then be shipped to a record press near Baltimore, where the tracks would be converted to three LPs, along with a song lineup and time marks for the DJs that received the discs to plug in local ads for each station. The LPs would get pressed, packaged, and shipped out across the US to be played by stations all over the country by Saturday night.

By the time his tapes made it to Baltimore, Steve would be in a deep sleep in his dark house, while the rest of the world moved on. He wondered what would be happening on the island while he slept. He put the thought out his mind, as he had done time and time over that night. It wouldn't help wondering; he just wouldn't be able to sleep, and he'd be tired the next evening.

It was 4:30 in the morning, and the island slept while Steve had worked. Now he only had to wait until the pickup at 5 am. He poured out the undrunk coffee and set up a fresh pot. Tim would be in around 5:30, or sooner, to get ready for the 6 am morning show at sunrise. The two had not crossed morning paths in the two weeks Steve had been there. He was always gone by the time Tim came in.

Today, Tim got there early.

"I gotta get some news clips ready," he explained as he walked in to Steve thumbing through a worn copy of Billboard. "You hear anything more about what happened last night?"

Steve shook his head.

"No, of course not. You stay locked in that recording booth. I'm amazed you haven't slept in there."

Steve said nothing more than a grunt. Other voice track jocks sometimes put in ten hour work days over two days, sleeping in their own recording booths, in order to get their shows done. Steve wasn't going to end up sleeping at work. He didn't have that luxury, and had no desire to be asleep on some shiny worn couch in the back of a DJ bullpen.

"I gotta put together some sort of news brief," Tim struggled with having to do a quick and unplanned news article without much information. "I don't have much. I did get a word that the sheriff doesn't know what the cause of death was."

Steve snorted, then regained his discretion. It wasn't something to laugh at. "Having her head removed wasn't it?" he tried to take out the sarcastic laugh.

"No, maybe not," Tim answered cryptically. "I contacted the health department up in Manteo, I know someone there," all DJs knew someone, Steve noted to himself. "The one thing the medical examiner noted when they took in the body was that the body seemed to be drained of blood… I know, I know," Tim waved off the obvious comment, "No, I mean, he seemed to think that she should have had more blood, something about how it would pool in the body," Tim winced, realizing how he was talking, but Steve just listened. "Like, she lost blood before all the…" Tim just waved his hand around his own neck, unable to go on.

"You make it easy for a guy to get some sleep, Tim," Steve answered gravely. "Thanks a lot."

Undeterred, Tim seemed ready to continue. "Ya know, this happened here before."

Steve stopped his teasing and listened.

"Yeah, about, I dunno, eight or ten years ago, I gotta look it up, a girl here was killed. College girl, she came home for break. There was this local fellah, see, and he figured he was her boyfriend, even though she never really liked him that much. You know how some of these boys get, pushy, a little blind to the world, like they deserve something for their effort. Well, she told him where he stood, and it wasn't next to her. I guess this boy decided that if he couldn't have her, no one else could, either."

Steve immediately recognized the story the sheriff had told him earlier.

"Did her in pretty bad, too," Tim continued. "Still, I remember, there was a lot of talk about how she died, like, she was hurt up, but also like it looked a little like something else happened to her. Anyway, the boy kept saying he didn't do it, swore up and down, but nobody believed him. Said he was out working on a boat in the marina that night, but no one saw him. I think the locals figured he was either guilty of this or would be guilty of something real soon. Got sent away for life. I don't know what happened since."

"What was the something else that happened to her?" Steve was intrigued. Death around here had to be common enough that when something uncommon happens, people would notice.

"I think it was she drowned, or had water in her lungs. Something like that. I'll run up to Manteo this weekend and check the library, if you like."

Steve was about to say no, when a roar came up from the drive, as the big UPS truck hurried its way to the station. "We'll talk later, Skip," Steve tried to leave on a lighthearted note, but it fell hollow as he ran out the door with the tapes. He should have been out there waiting. "I gotta get some sleep."

Tim waved Steve off to run his last errand of the night.

"Good luck."

6
Wednesday, May 15ᵗʰ

The news of the murder and the state of the body quickly made its way across the island. The last people to hear of it would be the students at Hatteras School. Parents would speak of the crime in hushed tones the next morning, but it would be loud enough for the large ears of prying teens to hear. The stories would slowly make their way around the school, with changes being made from one student to the next, until the story was muddled and confused.

Jackie Wood heard more than most, and believed less than half of what she was told. The coconut telegraph that spread rumors across Hatteras was only made worse when placed in the hands of teenage boys, who would do anything to embellish a story. Lunchtime would give the students time to spread the story and make up what they didn't know to add to it. Teens who would normally compain of the smells and tastes of questionable cafeteria food suddenly had cast iron stomachs as they embellished the description of the dead body while they sat in loud, elbow to elbow groups and cliques. By the afternoon as school neared its end, numerous stories made their way across the high school side of Cape Hatteras School.

As kids gathered at the end of the day, they found their ways into small groups where they could gather and gossip.

"Did you hear?" Jason Todd Midgett commented in hushed awe and amazement, "that she was *naked*?!"

Jackie shook her head. She was amazed at the willful single-mindedness of the boys. That's all he took out of this. "You sound thrilled," she almost snarled, dripping with sarcasm, "Not the part about her being killed, or her head and arms cut off." The decapitation and mangling of a human body, no matter the state, slipped the mind of the teenaged boy. "You probably would have liked to see her, wouldn't you?" With a shudder of her eyes, she added quietly, "sicko…"

"My momma won't let me go out on the beach anymore, not at dark, least," added in Jackie's schoolmate, Tally Strickland. Tally was sixteen, with a car, a used one, but still, a sign of freedom and a bit of trust from her folks. Trust and freedom were going to disappear quickly for her and a lot of others, very soon.

"Not like I wanna go out there at night," Jackie added on. "I just wonder if they know who did it."

"Yeah, that's pretty sick," Jackie agreed.

Teenagers lived a life of almost superhuman ability to think that nothing would happen to them. Jackie and her friends, as shocked and mesmerized by the news, saw it as only a passing event, something that happened to someone else, not from Hatteras, so therefor it would never happen to someone from here. Especially not to them. A teenager was an immortal being as far as they were concerned.

7

Tim Watkins had done what he could to gather information on the murder, the nuts and bolts of what had happened. He began by putting calls from the radio station into his contacts and friends up in the northern Outer Banks, in Manteo at the *Coastland Times* newspaper and the radio stations there, along with calls to the health department, police, and sheriff's office. He thought about calling the state police, too. But when his phone didn't ring back fast enough, he had gotten into his car and gone up to Manteo to get answers a little more directly.

When he came back that afternoon, he didn't really like what he had gotten. Sitting alone in his office, he reviewed the information he had. No name to the victim, that seemed almost a given. It was extremely hard to identify someone without a face. Even if she had her hands, unless she had committed a crime, her fingerprints wouldn't be on file, and even then it would take days to match them. But that was not even up for debate. With only a few scars and birthmarks to go by, it was amazing how difficult it would be to identify a body.

What did he know? What did they, whoever *they* were, know? The murdered woman was a female, probably in her early twenties.

Her hair color was unknown, possibly brown. Tim had cringed at even thinking how they determined that. He hoped it was from an armpit, and tried to let it go at that.

He fought off a bit of gorge rise inside him.

Moving on, he thought. She had probably been pregnant, and had had an abortion. "These things were important," Tim thought to himself, "But I still don't want to know this. Jeez."

Death was likely caused by massive blood loss. "No kidding," was Tim's first dismissive response. "I could have told you that."

Her extremities were removed after death. "How do they know that?" That fact was somewhat more disturbing. "Someone did that to her after they killed her. Sheesh, sick." Why would someone do that? Only to hide the identity. But that only painted a more maniacal portrait of the killer.

Most people killed people they knew. Tim was aware of that. That poor girl here on the island that was killed by that boy, everyone knew who did it as soon as they heard. Why did this killer want to hide his victim's identity?

"That guy is long gone by now," was all Tim thought. He was trying to think about what he would do, like if he were a murderer. Then he felt a little sick again. He wasn't a murderer. He didn't have it in him. It was hard to kill a person, real hard, and you had to make that choice to do it. Someone made a choice to kill this girl and then dismember her and leave her to the ocean. She wasn't even from here, he realized, which meant the killer brought her down her to do this.

Or did it somewhere else and brought the body.

Tim crossed out the bulk of what he had written down and wrote up a short news clip for the station, saying that at the time there was no new information on the identity of the victim, and police were following all possible leads.

Then he got up to wash his hands, real well.

8

The Island Legacy Church met an old building that had been built back in the 1950s, and Reverend Brin Darrow was more than tired of being in it. The building wasn't the church. All the different religions said that, he knew, but in his case, it was more than some metaphysical bit of religious claptrap he fed to the congregation. Their current building was an old community center built by the parents of the locals, including some that currently attended his sermons. The new church that was being finished now was "new" in name only; they had taken an old church and stripped it down to the foundation and bare studs, then rebuilt it. There was something about the location that made it desirable. The Island Legacy Church would be moving to the new church soon. Not soon enough for Reverend Darrow.

The current church building had been built over thirty years ago, and not much had changed since then. His office was the same office that former pastors had used in years past when the building was a church and not just a community gathering place. He felt their presence every time he went in there. Like somehow they were looking at him. Which he hoped wasn't true. "Well, those cranky old farts probably got a show they never got at home," he thought to himself. He would be very happy when he got into the new church with the new office and his new private room, as well as a nice new parsonage that wasn't anywhere near the church but was near his secretary's church provided beachfront condominium.

He shook his head. "Later," he told himself, thinking about Darla and her dresses with the short hems, too short for church and the stuffy fat ladies that attended, but not too short for Darrow. Darla, all short dresses with the low cut neck, big round fake boobs which made up for her stupid nerd glasses and rat face snarl, who was always willing and easily manipulated, "No," Darrow corrected himself, "she is rewarded for her dutiful service."

Rewards needed to come, but later, like he told himself. He was alone in the old church, the old smelly church that he couldn't wait to get out of. And he needed to prepare for the Wednesday night sermon. Wednesdays didn't count like Sundays, at least he didn't think so, but it was another day to run the collection plate around, another day to stir up the church, and he was more than ready to stir the pot. With the recent murder, grisly and so sexual, he had fodder for weeks of Sundays, and Wednesdays, too.

He had notes, of course. He always got notes about how to approach the congregation, but he wouldn't need much. "Blame the radio, blame the music, blame the youth," all that was easy. The congregation was mostly older people, relatively successful, in the little villages, but they certainly had enough money to help fund the church. There were some younger members, a few teens forced to show up by their parents, mostly doughy boys with homemade haircuts who thought washing their camo hoods was dressing up for church. The boys would love it if he blamed the kids that didn't include them in their little groups. Especially the girls that didn't give the boys attention. Darrow made a note to include something like that in the sermon. He had watched the teen boys as they watched Darla every Sunday. Which helped because he knew all the little old ladies and the fat wives watched him when Darla came in. At least he didn't have his eyes on his secretary when he gave his sermon.

Darrow looked at his watch. He needed to get going. He consulted the notes provided to him. They seemed small in comparison to the wad of cash in worn bills that were piled in the same envelope. The envelope sat next to the deed to the old church, which had recently been transferred into his name personally. As soon as the congregation moved into the new church, he would sell the old one to a developer to be torn down and summer homes could be built on the land.

He may even buy one, just to rent. The parsonage would do him well as a personal home.

He occasionally wondered who it was that supplied the envelopes with the extra funds to keep the church going. He tried not to wonder too much, in case he would break the spell and the money would dry up. As long as he kept his sermons going, good brimstone stuffed full of hate for everyone except whoever was attending his church, the money would keep rolling in. Unless he had a serious change of faith, which wasn't going to happen, he was sure of that.

He wondered if Darla knew who it was that delivered the envelopes. She had to know what was in them. She put them on his desk. But she never said anything. Darrow was sure she must know, and was probably having sex with him. If it even was a man. "It has to be," thought Darrow. There's no way a woman could be this conniving.

Darla's involvement was a small price to pay, along with the bigger price of her condo on the beach. But as long as she was available to him, and kept her little rat mouth shut, and the money kept coming in, he didn't really care.

He hurried to finish his sermon. He needed to have dinner.

9

Steve had made it home just as the sun was rising over the Atlantic Ocean at 5:59 in the morning. He regularly kept track of the sunrise so he could, "hopefully," he always thought, get to bed and go to sleep while it was still dark. Especially here on the coast, the sun rose earlier and earlier as it approached solstice. He had made a note to himself to begin a longer two day work week on his shows now, so that he could get home earlier. At least in Asheville, the sun rose about ten minutes later, and was blocked by the mountains.

Here on Hatteras Island, the sun boiled up early out of a dark ocean. People, especially fishermen, rose with the sun to make their day begin. Steve's day would just be ending.

He would have to get prepared for some morning sun, realizing that he would never fully escape the morning rays filtering into his house, no matter how tree lined his property was.

He had gone to bed, hungry but tired, with Tim's words still in his head, "This had happened before." Exhaustion won out over his mind wandering, and Steve had fallen into a silent and deep sleep.

It seemed like he awoke immediately. Steve lay in his large, soft bed, looking over at the side table where a cheap digital clock hummed a red 4:00. He had slept nine hours, twisted up in his king sized mattress. He untwisted the blanket from his body as he had slept on his side, his knees pulled up to his chest, head crooked down off his pillow. He rolled over onto his back, looking up at the window with the blinds still closed over his headboard. Soft light, filtered first through the clawing branches and green waxy leaves of oak and yaupon, then stopped at the cheap roll up blinds over the window, found its way through the cracks, forcing the afternoon sun into the room. Steve could see the waving shadows as the afternoon land breeze began to blow across the sound.

He wouldn't need to get up just yet.

He laid in the bed, unwilling to stretch just yet, closing his eyes to the light.

A half an hour passed.

Steve awoke, again, to the same light filtered through the blinds. He had to get up now. His stomach grumbled for food.

His bare feet over the old wood floor of his house made soft padding sounds as he made his way to the kitchen. A long night, the exercise and stress of the evening before, had taxed him, making him extremely hungry. He was awake, alert immediately, hearing the sounds of life from the outside as he searched his refrigerator for food.

A steak called to him, red, air drying in a box, but he had no desire to go outside to grill with the bright lights of the afternoon. He resisted the call for the steak and made a pizza instead. He worked quietly, and let the sounds of the island whisper through the old house.

In the far off distance, the occasional truck would roar through Highway 12.

Pickup trucks would be heading home, coming from the beaches, with fishing poles embedded in racks over the front grills. Somewhere, a cooler would be locked down. It was filled with fish if the fisherman was lucky with his catch. It may be the remaining unfinished beer if the day had not gone as well. Though it was unlikely to have the latter if the former didn't happen.

Steve heard the old trucks roaring down the road, hurrying to get home. Somewhere along the drive, there would be other vehicles. A family or retired couple, somehow able to get to the beach before the tourist season kicks in, perhaps spending a quiet day in nearby Ocracoke. They had made the afternoon ferry so that they could get to Hatteras and farther north to find dinner. The man in the car drives slowly, looking for a sign to pop up through the brush proclaiming Fresh Seafood.

Behind him, the pickup truck tailgates relentlessly, the driver ready to be home. He knows where he's going.

The car driver and the pickup truck driver curse each other from their own vehicles, oblivious and silent to the hate filled language of the other, one to hurry up and get out of the way, the other to get off their ass.

Closer by to Steve, the world still spun. Steve sat on his porch now that the sun was down low enough not to be too bright. The sun finally started to touch the tree tips that lined the edge of the dusty road of Steve's house. They were a welcome barrier and border to the new development going up closer to the sound side waters. More were being built and occupied every day. Steve could barely make out a whole line being constructed on the sound. The rest of the area had been cleared and raised up to accept almost a hundred new homes. Wood was stacked two and three stories high, ready to be framed into walls, floors, ceilings, roofs, and finally houses.

The homes were being built with wood supplied by the very people that would soon occupy many homes there. A local lumber company, seeing the writing on the wall, decided it would be easier to have a mill on Hatteras Island to supply lumber in bulk for all the future houses that would go up in the next ten or twenty years. All of the Outer Banks was growing, and Hatteras would grow, too. Now, people came down from Manteo and Wanchese, with the promise of good paying jobs, both at the mill and a nearby seafood processing plant that was attached to the marina near where Steve worked. He had noticed the sign that welcomed the new employees, a big, happily smiling tuna fish, with the words "N Sea" promising fresh local fish, as well as shellfish, to consumers and restaurants up and down the east coast. It meant more work for the commercial fishermen, along with more jobs desperately needed for people ready to work.

The homes in the new development, named Coree Woods, a moniker inexplicable to Steve and even some locals, was bordered by the trees and wild vines that grew along a creek, cut long ago. It was for draining the low water that had allowed mosquitoes to breed by the millions, feasting upon any flesh and blood that they could get their greedy little straw mouths into. In one small section, a set of boards had been thrown unceremoniously to bridge the gap and allow the few kids that lived in the neighborhood to sneak across and onto the clay and shell street that fronted Steve's house. It let them from the homes to the nearby ice cream shop and other stores that were on the main road, without having to ride or walk on the busy Highway 12.

As afternoon mixed with evening, one person used the bridge to her advantage.

10

Jackie Wood walked her bike across the bouncing and unstable bridge, appearing out of the shade to hop back on and begin pedaling again. She rode by the nice old cottage that had recently been bought and moved into, spying the man who owned it sitting in the shade of the low front porch. She skidded to a stop and pranced off of her bike, leaning it against a tree.

Jackie walked up to the picket fence that bounded the house and without a care or pretense, she spoke up.

"Hi! You're Steve Brodie, aren't you?"

"Yeah," Steve smiled a white Cheshire cat grin from the shade and darkness as he sat on the porch eating his pizza and drinking a Coke. "Hi." Jackie saw him stare out at her, all white teeth and bright blue eyes. It was slightly haunting.

Steve saw a teenager, a local girl, not only by the direction from where she came, but just by the mannerisms and dress. In LA and the California beaches he would be used to the flash and overwhelming style that women and girls embraced. It was a see and be seen scene. The girls here embraced a simpler realism. She had just hopped off her bike, wearing a bikini and cut off jean shorts, not the racy short shorts that men ogled as a woman walked by, but just regular jeans that wore down and got cut. The only addition she had to her wardrobe were brown flip flops, as most people around here just went barefoot on the hot ground and sharp rocks.

"I'm Jackie, I live over there," she pointed vaguely in the direction of her house in the new development, "I guess we're neighbors, huh?"

To Steve, Jackie seemed like the kind of person who didn't slow down waiting for an answer. "You're the new DJ at the radio station, right? We all have been listening to you. Everyone at the school thinks you're great. It's cool to hear some rock music down here. About all we get to hear is our parent's country records.

"Well, except my parents. They like the Rolling Stones."

Jackie walked up to the picket fence that bounded the house. Steve had noticed that the local folks cherished their fences. They were a known measured distance, not described in feet or yards, but in a distance that would not allow anyone outside the fence to discern intimate features of those on the porch, while at the same time close enough that a conversation could easily be held without shouting.

Jackie had no notion of the boundary.

She opened the gate and walked up the steps to Steve's front porch.

Somehow, Steve didn't mind. The girl was young, a teenager, full of the brightness in the world without any of the experience to make her hard and bitter. She smiled a slice of sunshine with white teeth out of brown skin, tanned well before the summer sun would come to the island. Her brown hair had turned gold, racing its way to blonde, long and straight. Steve noticed the way she looked, no pretense, no hairspray, no wild makeup that teenage girls and boys liked now. Her eyebrows were still dark, narrowing to a long nose, but not too long, as if when she looked, she was lightly judging whoever she looked at, but she was pleased with what she saw. To Steve, she had a mix of sweet honesty and brutal sunlight, happy, but intolerant of foolishness, while cherishing nonsense. She was a strange person.

Steve looked at his own dress, making sure his body was covered, and not covered with crumbs. He was dressed as if the directions Jackie had received had somehow been twisted in a funhouse mirror. He wore long linen pants, just wrinkled enough to show he didn't care, and a thin white shirt. Instead of her straight golden hair, his was tousled and knotted in long rings to his shoulders. He had just gotten up, after all, and had not wanted visitors.

"Guests," he realized, even if Jackie had invited herself.

They had both found what had made them comfortable. Jackie was bright and open; Steve dressed to blend in.

"You're from Los Angeles, right? I've seen you on TV. You were on MTV, right?"

Steve stopped himself from name dropping the VJs he had known from the days on the west coast. Jackie probably wouldn't really care. She was just making conversation.

"I think we are the first people down here with cable that can watch it," she shared. Jackie wasn't waiting for an answer. "I like MTV, do you like it?"

Steve waited a moment to see if she really wanted an answer this time. Then, "Sure, there's a lot of creativity in those videos." This wasn't where he thought this conversation was going to go. "Though I do wonder if there are people who have to see a song in order to like it."

"I never thought of that," Jackie took the comment more deeply than it was meant. She thought for a second. "But it is nice to see how the songs are interpreted. I mean, look at Phil Collins, it isn't like he's a great looking guy, but he makes some cool videos. It makes me like the songs more."

"That's what it's all about," Steve agreed. He took a bite of his dinner.

"Is that pizza?" Jackie asked like she had never seen it before. Steve wondered if she had ever seen a homemade one around here.

"Yes," Steve answered through the bite of food in his mouth. He gave in and offered her a slice. "You want to try it?"

"Sure!" Easily amused, Steve thought. "What is this?" she looked at the slice with that strange and beautiful admiring judgement. Steve felt his usual standoffishness melt a bit. The kid wasn't simple, just honest, real.

"It's prosciutto. It's like ham." It was ham.

Jackie bit into the thin pizza, unlike the thick plain food she usually had here. "I only get Pizza Hut when we go up to Kill Devil Hills," she said as the food slushed in her mouth. "This is delicious. What's that?" she pointed at the strange triangle hidden under the melted cheese.

"Pineapple, it goes well with the prosciutto."

"You're right." Jackie finished the slice and gnawed at the thin piece of crust.

"You want a Coke?" he offered her a drink out of his cooler, "Or a Tahitian Treat?" The sublime and the exotic, probably, to this girl.

"I'll take a Coke." Jackie popped the can open and sipped. "Mmm," now running a minor high on burning carbonation and a waiting caffeine rush, Jackie got her courage up. "I'm going over to The Peach Tree to get some ice cream with my friends. You want to come over? They'd love to meet you. You're a celebrity here."

Steve jerked his thumb at a pile of collapsed boxes. "I still haven't finished even moving in, as you can see." He had as many waiting inside, a chore he didn't entirely relish. It wasn't the important stuff, just the mundane, the books, plates, pencil holders of life that you only missed when they weren't there, but never noticed when they were there. Every day was one or two less boxes inside.

"Okay, well, it was great to meet you! You should come over some time and see me. We have the blue house over there." Jackie, now buoyant on her sugar rush, skipped down the stairs and through the picket fence. With a push, she was off, pedaling in her flip flops, tearing across the shell lined road toward whatever adventure she saw in the next five minutes.

Steve watched her as she rode out into the still bright light of late afternoon, her figure shimmering to a haze in the sun. She had stirred up Steve's feelings. He wasn't attracted to her, still just a young girl, though he knew his near permanent youthful looks made him appealing to girls that age. As well as the celebrity that he carried with him. It's why many DJs changed their names, just to not have to deal with fandom in their private life.

But she knew where he lived. He didn't entirely see that as a bad thing. Maybe it would be nice to at least have a friend around here.

11
Friday, May 17ᵗʰ

"With little updated news on the murder, the Dare County Sheriff's Office has announced that it will no longer be holding regular press conferences, and will only release briefs when the State Bureau of Investigation or the state medical examiner has more information available. The victim's identity is still unknown, and the investigation is ongoing." Tim grimaced outwardly, since no one could see him, and took it back before speaking again. He didn't want that face showing up in his voice. He was still a pro jock first. "WZHX will continue to bring you any updated information on the case as we get it.

"Now the weather..." at least it was a better transition than just going to a commercial. The sponsors would kill him if he lead to their business after a murder news report. "Bad choice of words," Tim thought. At least he was able to keep the rest of his thoughts to himself.

Most of the island had responded with shock and concern over the murder. Tim had seen and heard the tributes, the worries, and the responses.

Including a rather poor response by one group.

The Island Legacy Church had found a whipping boy in the radio station. They had already complained about, well, everything else, Tim realized, and now they came after him.

"They're barely a church," Tim had complained to himself, keeping his thoughts silent as he worked the commercials through. "They mostly like to threaten to sue people." Tim had avoided them like the plague.

Now they were coming after him.

More specifically, they were coming after Steve Brodie, his star. They blamed the murder on Rock 'n Roll, spreading the word of sin to the locals, somehow. "It's like I'm living in the 1950s," he thought. "They're coming after Elvis."

Tim had seen this in the past, with protests at radio station and concerts about the sins and horrors of rock music. But he had never experienced it personally. Only now he was getting telephone calls harassing him for putting on rock music. "Yeah, like I'm only gonna play The Carpenters on here," he snorted as he spun a 45 onto his turntable, backing it up and priming the song for play. The commercials were coming out, and he needed to get his head back in the game, "I'm Chris Stone, and this… is Tom Petty and The Heartbreakers…" The melodic twang of Petty's new hit single, *Don't Come Around Here No More*, patted its way out the studio's speaker and into the airwaves across Hatteras Island. It seemed like an apropos song for the time, but for who?

"I don't need any shit from these people," Tim said derisively.

He had two more hours until Steve came in for his Friday night show at ten o'clock.

At least he had made the decision to turn off the phone. No requests, and no complaints, tonight.

Steve showed up at 9:30. "I was up and had nothing to do, man, so I'm coming in," he explained simply. The truth was, he was restless. He didn't get his run in, and hadn't been out on the beach in two nights since he had found the body of that girl. "You want me to take over?"

Tim waved him off. He enjoyed the show, the evening that was not really drive time, but quiet time, when people were more tuned in to the TV than the radio. He felt like he was talking to ten people who just wanted to listen to him. "Go ahead and get your list for your show," he handed Steve a copy of the Billboard Hot 100, with a check made in black marker over the songs he had played. Tim tried not to play the same song twice in a day, but when people want to hear Simple Minds, they want to hear that one song by Simple Minds right now, and that meant it got played more than once.

Steve was okay with that. Tonight, he was going mellow, with some deep cuts, no Solid Gold, but a lineup of what he called "the dark chill," songs to embrace the evening. The Doors would do for a start.

"Just so you know, we're still getting' more shit from those Island people. They are trying to blame you for that girl's death now. Saying this didn't happen before we started playing rock music. Like Johnny Cash never sang about death. Morons." Tim didn't suffer stupidity well, and Steve saw it. But Tim definitely knew his music.

"I saw Johnny at the Carter Fold once," Steve told him. "It was incredible, all intimate, beautiful singing. I guess that doesn't count for much here, does it?" he laughed off the implied threat. He had heard worse. "These people know Little Richard is black, right?"

Tim laughed, the first time all day, really. "Hang… comin' out," Tim plugged in a new set of commercials and set his watch. If he was distracted, he would miss the cue. "I dunno, I mean, …" he struggled to find the words, "some people are, you know, set in their ways, a little hardheaded, don't listen? But these folks, they are telling their kids not to listen, and to go after the kids that do. They are talking to sponsors. And they are starting to make threats."

"Threats?" Steve asked, "Like what kind of threats? You mean like violence?"

"They are," Tim was having a hard time with what he had already heard. He didn't want to upset his star and have him leave, but Steve had to know. And Tim realized he shouldn't mince words. "These people don't think they have to answer to anyone. They make the laws after they break them. They have been saying something bad might happen, like burning down buildings. But they say it like 'You don't want something bad to happen. Someone might take it into their own hands and burn down a store.' Shit like that. It's like mob goons on TV."

"Have they threatened you?"

"Me, no, not like that. I think even these morons know better than to burn down a historic site like the weather station." Tim stopped, put up his hand, and Steve got silent. "You're back, with me, Chris Stone, with back to back music, another twenty minute rock block," he grinned at the lingo to Steve, but the listeners ate it up, "with Prince and The Revolution," The spare beat of *Raspberry Beret* began to kick in before Tim turned the volume down and his mic off. He held up a blue and white cloudy album cover. "You listen to this yet?"

Steve wasn't a big fan of Prince, but he had just played the entire album a few days ago. "Yeah, man, that's stuff's awesome. That's an incredible album.

"You know, I met Prince back in LA once."

"What was he like?"

"Nothing like you think, he's a really nice guy, kind of shy, actually. A lot of that stuff he does is persona. He came over to my place when he found out I had a ping pong table in the garage."

"No way," Tim laughed. "Prince is into ping-pong?!"

"I shit you not," Steve looked Tim in the eye. "He's good, too.

"Now, before we get too distracted, tell me for real what's up with these people making threats. Are they making threats against you?"

"No…"

"Me?"

"Yeah," Tim hid his eyes. He wasn't going to bow down to a small group of nuts, but he didn't like to keep things from anyone. "Right now, they are just saying things like I should tell you what to play, or not play Rock 'n' Roll. As if…" They probably thought anything with a guitar was Rock 'n' Roll. "One of them left a message suggesting," telling, Tim didn't need to add, "that I let you go.

"Look, I don't want to do any of that. I know you just got here. And I'm going to back you. All the way. I'm not gonna take shit from these people, and no one else really likes them, either. It's just that you need to know. You don't know who all these people are. You're not out days, I get that, but just be on the lookout. I don't really know how you'll recognize them. Well," Tim had to think, "they almost all look like they know they are right, and they are wrong all the time. Kinda people who park in the handicapped spot and blame someone else for being crippled, that kind of person."

"Assholes," Steve said offhanded. He knew these people well.

"Yeah," Tim confirmed. "Assholes."

12
Tuesday, June 11th

The fear and insinuations had stumbled their way down to a low boil as May had past into June. For Steve, he had wondered just how things could go downhill from a brutal murder, and yet it felt slightly worse now than when the killing originally happened. There was still no resolution to the crime, and there seemed to be no break coming.

Those Legacy Church parishioners had kept up their fight against the radio station, but at least no more sponsors had left. Steve couldn't help but feel he was to blame, just because he became their preferred target. Tim had been supportive, and even wore the threats as a badge of honor.

"I think it's down to a slow burn," Tim nearly yelled over a raging jukebox. Tim, Steve, along with two other jocks sat at the local watering hole nearby the weather station. Steve had taken to calling the radio station by the old nickname, as he joined in with the other members of the crew. Along with Tim, Steve sat with Ellen Gaines, who did a talk show about the history of the island, and Isiah Farrow, who went by John Dunn, and did a beach music show every Sunday, and often worked the morning show to spell

Tim. The sun had finally gone down, and Tim had turned out the lights of the station, then headed to The Hatteras Moon, the nearby bar that had originally catered first to the charter captains and mates from the nearby marina. It now saw an uptick from the second shift getting off work from the new processing facility down the road.

The workers at the seafood plant and the charter crews had drawn an invisible line down the middle of the bar, in order to keep each group pure. The radio crew from WZHX were notably out of place, even as they huddled in a corner away from both sides.

"What?" asked Ellen, a bit too loud just as the song on the jukebox ended. She was slightly embarrassed, looked around, then hid her eyes.

"I said," continued Tim a little more quietly, "That I think it's at least gotten down to a slow burn. We haven't lost any more sponsors, and we haven't gotten too much in the way of problems from those clowns." Everyone at the table knew who he meant. The phone messages of burning down the station had slightly abated.

"I'm just surprised the sheriff didn't do anything more about it," Ellen was still worried. No one had come to her personally to complain about the station from the Island Legacy Church. Her label as a local historian gave her special credit among the locals.

"What's he gonna do?" Tim shrugged as he swigged his beer. He wiped off the wet foam and syrupy spit from his lip. He had taken too big a drink. "He said that one of his deputies is in the church. He spoke to him, and the deputy said it wasn't them. And that he wouldn't go against his church anyway even if it was. So you know it was them. He pretty much admitted it without saying it."

"I think the sheriff is hoping that this whole thing disappears," Steve said with the clarity of someone outside looking in. "If it never gets solved, he doesn't have to do anything. A girl goes out swimming…"

"Is that how you got your name? I always wanted to ask," Isiah spoke up, smiling now that he had the chance to change the subject.

"How'd you know it isn't my name?"

"Just a guess," Isiah smiled slyly. "And I guess I was right, huh?" Isiah knew that almost all jocks had a radio name and a real name to keep their private lives private.

"Can't pull anything over this guy!" Tim clinked his near empty bottle on Isiah's.

"Yeah," Steve answered finally. "Well, that's where I got Brodie, from Jaws." He had just quoted the mayor of Amity trying to justify the death of Chrissie Watkins after her mutilated body had been found on the beach. The mayor had tried to cover it up as a boating accident. "I had been working regionally, down in San Diego, and needed a name, and I had just seen Jaws at a theater."

"Where'd you get Steve? Is that one real?"

"Nope," Steve shrugged this one off. "It came from a guy I knew, Steve Crowe. I thought he had a cool name, and he was a nice guy. I just liked it."

"So, what's your real name?" Ellen asked.

Tim and Isiah got quiet, Tim softly clearing his throat. If Steve had wanted them to know his name, he would have told them.

"S'okay," Steve waved it off. Ellen wasn't really a jock, she didn't know the rules. "Steve Brodie is my name, actually. I changed it before I went national. You wouldn't believe me if I told you my real name, anyway."

Ellen, tempted and now a little tipsy, pushed her luck. "Try me."

Steve looked conspiratorially at Tim, then Isiah. He flipped his hair back, a golden curled mane over his slowly browning skin. He had fought being outside in the day, but the days were longer, and even his evening strolls had colored him, and cooked him a little. He wasn't used to the sun. But he looked like a dream date with a chiseled chin, a bit of Don Johnson stubble, and white on white teeth. Steve overemphasized his good looks with a preening motion. Ellen, middle aged, a mom, and not the least bit attractive to most men, felt herself go a little weak, as if the man had charmed her with his good looks. She was glad she was seated. She hadn't felt like that in twenty years.

Steve leaned in and whispered in sotto voce, "Morton… Frisch…"

Then he laughed, and the others laughed loudly at his joke. "It's such a beautiful name for a guy as handsome as me!"

"Alright, we better get going, we can't all we nighthawks like Morty here," Tim grinned. He noticed that this was the first time they all had been together in the last month, and probably the first time they all felt more comfortable, after all the shit they have been through. "My bill," he insisted.

Tim went over to pay the charge for the rounds of beer they had. It wasn't a major blow to the company wallet. Steve was the only one to drink three beers, and Ellen was a lightweight with only one. He paid with cash and then left an extra ten for the effort of the bartender hoisting the bottles out of the cooler. The bartender took the bill, nodded, and inclined his eyes slightly but gravely at a group of people nearby.

Two of the charter boat mates, both somewhat drunk, had eyed Tim as he approached, trying to judge if they could make the distance to him without stumbling.

Steve watched over his left shoulder, the back of his neck tingling with the sense of danger to Tim.

"Hey!" was all they got out before Steve appeared behind Tim. He had just popped out of the dark, like that, Tim thought.

Mate One opened his mouth to speak, as well as to put a fist up, but Steve already had the man's wrist in a grip. Steve had stepped on the guy's foot, pinning him to the ground, while twisting the mate's wrist into his own chest. The inebriated mate, young and thinking he was experienced, tried at first to force his way out of the grip.

"Hey!" echoed the other mate. "You're the ones causing all these problems with that radio station," he said it like he meant it was a sewage treatment plant. Mate One merely twisted himself, unable to speak as Steve stared at him while holding on in a grip that shot frozen pain into his arm, not letting up.

Steve reached across his own body to grab the unsuspecting Mate Two, twisting the collar of a soiled shirt. It didn't look like much in the way of control, but Steve had a hold of the drunk mate's throat, choking him as he closed off his throat, blood vessels, and nerves. The mate's eyes began to roll up in his head.

Mate One could only gnash his teeth. Somehow, he had been held in a prison with his arm locked too tight against his own elbow. The pain was so much his body wanted to pass out, but the hurt kept him awake.

"You two want to rethink your choices right now, don't you?"

The two stood immobile.

"Don't you?" the words were even more calm, as the bar had gotten a little quieter with more people noticing the scene. It didn't look like Steve was doing much to the two men, but they were helpless, frozen, and if they could speak, would have begged for release. Only Steve's words and a cold glare from his green on green eyes were felt by them.

One fairly nodded, his neck and jowls flabbing into a second chin as his face tried to pull away from his body and the tightening grip.

Steve merely looked at Two, who could only press his own chin into Steve's hand.

"Now, you're not going to do anything stupid like try to look tough after I let you go." It was a statement, not a question. Steve leaned in and whispered something very quietly to them.

Then he dropped his grip, and the two fell, lost in their new balance, the alcohol tipping the scales and their feet, as they fell backwards into the stools and floor.

"No problem here, is there?" Steve looked menacingly at the bartender. No one was calling the police at this bar. The bartender's look of fear said so.

The four jocks walked out, with three following a pace behind one.

13
Wednesday, June 12th

The beer had helped. It wasn't the alcohol, but the camaraderie. Tim had been joking about how Steve was the nightfly of the group, a little outside the rest of the small team that ran the radio station, as well as being a star, a celebrity, as opposed to the plump and pink usual that many DJs took on as their look. The evening and overnight jocks rarely got to hang out, go out for dinner, or anything else, and with Steve's strange sleeping schedule, it made interacting even more obscure.

But with the last of the weekday sunset hours set on the station, soon to be ending as Tim planned more nighttime hours, an evening gathering had been possible. Steve had been amiable, easily connecting with his peers, not standoffish, and he kept his name dropping to a minimum. Even though Ellen desperately wanted to hear every story about life in LA, and all the musicians Steve knew.

When they had left the night before, with the confrontation and Steve violently staring down the two drunks trying to start a fight, things had gotten a little colder. Tim had at least asked if Steve was okay to drive. Jokingly, Steve responded, "Oh, I'm fine.

I have three kidneys. It takes a lot to get me drunk." It was a lie, but the best lies have a bit of truth, Steve always reminded himself. The joke had taken the edge down, but maybe not off.

"Everything is hard," Steve reminded himself as he sat up late into that night.

He woke up the next afternoon, after a hard, dark sleep through the early morning gloom, into the warmth of the day. It was getting harder to sleep through the sunlight, and the house was a mix of dark and filtered light through the blinds. He would have to go out in it sometime, but hopefully he could wait it out until after the Solstice. At least the porch was in shade, and faced vaguely east, so that it was shadowed the rest of the day. He didn't like being cooped up behind the doors, being closed in a box.

He also had been skipping his evening runs. Ever since the girl was found, he had been avoiding the beach at night. He still couldn't shake the sense that more was going to happen, and his senses were always right.

Just sometimes his senses weren't always firing in the right direction.

Jackie pedaled up the road, through the hidden path in the trees, with purpose. Her purpose became clear as she stopped in front of Steve's house and leaned her bike against an old twisted live oak that provided shade for the home, one of many in a forest that stretched to the sound behind the cottage.

"Hey, Steve, honey," she had long ago become more comfortable with Steve than he was with her. He was still getting used to this generic sobriquet that it seemed everyone used. It was more of an addition or title, less a term of endearment, to be called 'honey'. He found himself uncomfortable with the term, but liked the attention and meaning behind it.

He still was not used to seeing this girl riding by, and now up to, his house in her bikini.

"No pizza?" It had become a bit of jest now. Jackie half expected to get fed when she showed up at Steve's porch. Steve drank a spring water from a green bottle. Not having another, and thinking that no teenager would want the sulfurous and bicarbonate tasting stuff, he shook his head no, and held out the bottle.

To his surprise, she took it and drank.

"You like this stuff?" she did her best not to spit over the porch.

"It's an acquired taste. What's up?"

"I enjoyed your show last Saturday. Me 'n a girlfriend of mine stayed up listening to you."

Steve noticed she said "you," not "it," referring to the show. "I'm glad you liked it. I wasn't sure if anyone would." He had done his late sounds, the post midnight music, on the incredible thrash and glam rock that he had enjoyed in his days, well, nights, on the west coast. He had a rather liberal collection of local band albums, the great proto sounds of hard rock, that were only barely coming out now in mainstream music.

"What was that one band? Y'know? With that song?" Jackie asked, the typical vagaries of a teen trying to compute a world that moves so fast. But Steve knew who she meant.

"Hollywood Rose, yeah, I just got that one. That's some great shit, uh, stuff."

"You can swear in front of me," Jackie giggled, "It's not like I haven't heard it before.

"Anyway, we were talking about your show. A lot of my friends really like this music you're playing. Some of the parents aren't happy with us staying up late, but, hey, screw them." Jackie threw her own minor oath in to help clutter the language barrier even further.

"Yeah, not everyone likes it," Steve sighed out the comment with a sip of water. The pain of the carbonation burned him like a self inflicted punishment for teaching the kids a bad word they already knew. "I'm still getting grief from some of the adults around here."

"Don't you give up on us!" Jackie poked her finger at him. "You're about all we got down here. We gotta pay extra for MTV, and all they play is Madonna."

"What's wrong with Madonna?"

"Nothing, it's just that now half the boys want us to dress like her." She spun around on her flip flops. "Can you see me dressed like that?" She pulled her sunglasses down her nose with a pout.

Steve cringed inwardly, while trying not to show anything outside. The girl wasn't even trying to be a tease, this just was who she was. He had seen the Madonna lookalikes, the Pat Benatars, all the trends of fashion pushed out onto Hollywood Boulevard down from the music stars to the hookers that came out at night. But none of them wore a bathing suit just as their around town clothes. What was common to Steve was complex to Jackie, and the opposite was probably just as true.

Steve kept his mouth shut. While he had no desire for Jackie, she was too young for him, he still had desires. It was a part of his life, with his good looks and charm, that he also suffered from feeling like he was perpetually 19 years old. And he couldn't turn off his looks. He had grown accustomed to the admiration and, for lack of a better word, lust from women and girls, but the familiarity had not helped much with self control.

"No," he said finally, "I guess not."

Jackie smiled, thinking he was imagining her dressed in Madonna's clothes, when she was exactly wrong on what his mind was picturing.

"You know, I never see you at the beach. You should come out, meet the other students from school. The cool ones, that is. Some of the boys are going surfing out by the light this afternoon. I'm going that way now. A bunch of my friends will be there. I know they would like to meet you. You should come, go swimming, work on your tan."

Steve gathered his shirt together. He hadn't noticed that it hung open and unbuttoned in the early warmth of June. Maybe Jackie was as used to shirtless guys as she was to walking around in a swimsuit, Steve thought. He usually got more than his share of admiration when he took his shirt off.

"I'm usually busy," he made up an excuse.

"You don't have a show tonight, you don't work on your other show, and you are obviously not busy. You should come, meet people, get out. This is why people are here, to go to the beach, go fishing, get drunk, go windsurfing like those Canadians do. We want you to come out. What, you afraid of getting sunburned, it's like 4 o'clock!"

Again, the simplicity of her myopia both pleased and puzzled Steve. Jackie and her kind had no more concern in life than what happens within the next few hours. And those concerns could change with the wind as the land breeze replaced a sea breeze around here.

"I haven't eaten breakfast yet," Steve started.

"Breakfast, ha!"

"I haven't eaten yet, I just woke up a little while ago," not really a lie, but a vague truth. "I'll tell you what, after, lunch, whatever, I'll try to come out."

"We'll be out by the jetties. Don't you stand me up. I'm going to tell everyone you're coming. You better not make me look bad." Jackie didn't seem like the kind of person who took a broken promise lightly, even one as pedestrian as this.

"Okay, okay, go away, let me get something to eat."

"How come you never let me come inside?"

"Because it's my house," Steve said simply but firmly. Jackie was taken aback by the frankness of the answer. "And I haven't cleaned up." This was a lie, but one that Jackie believed, and it worked.

"Alright," she gave in easily. "But you better come out today."

"After breakfast," Steve said, a reluctant promise.

But one he wanted to keep.

14

It was late enough in the evening that Steve felt comfortable being out. He had only been out at night and alone before today. Now he sat on a beach towel over the course sand and ocean washed shell fragments that made up the beach at the Cape Hatteras Lighthouse. He was still not used to the east coast shore. It was rolling and windblown, but also lumpy, with footprints everywhere. The sand was harsh, sharp, with bits of everything in it, well worn pebbles, broken shells, sharp microscopic shards of sand, broken into perfect cubes. The beach was cluttered with dry bristles of sea straw, broken reeds of spartina that washed from who knows where, along with the bits and pieces of humanity, where trash, burned wood from late night fires, and cigarette butts were strewn across the shore.

West coast beaches were so different. Wide, flat and smooth, where people could walk across the finer sand almost without leaving a mark. Here it was hard to distinguish whose footprint was whose among all the dents.

But the water got warm here, at least he had been told.

Steve watched as set after set of perfect, foaming waves rolled in from out to sea, and some local boys, along with a few older adults who had driven down from the northern part of the county, rode the curving tubes. He could tell the difference between the young, new riders, just happy to stay on the boards, and the older or more experienced surfers who twisted themselves as they milked every inch out of the churning surf.

"You want to try that?" Jackie plopped down gracelessly on Steve's towel. Wet and disheveled, she still made the look work for her. A yellow boogie board flopped next to her, still attached to her wrist.

"Not today."

"You really should try the boogie board. It's easy," she shook her hair free from her wet shoulders, splattering Steve with salt, but neither took notice of it. To Jackie, is was just the way things were, they had always been that way, wet hair, rolling waves, gritty sand stuck to her ankles, the beach was like that.

Steve ignored the spray of salt water, not wanting to make a big deal about it. He was wondering just why he felt the need to fit in with Jackie, and to a lesser extent, her friends. They were the ones who listened to his music, but there was something more to them.

"This is great, isn't it?" Jackie leaned on Steve, just for a moment. He had seen her do this to everyone now, and didn't take it as any personal intimate contact. Well, it probably was personal. She seemed to lead the group. Jackie was confident, self-assured, and a leader. She benefited from being right most of the time, and rarely, if ever, doing something that the others would criticize. She would have been called "righteous" if she had been in Beverly Hills, a term of great honor, Steve thought. "See what you have been missing? Everyone is glad you came out."

And she was right on that, too. Almost. All the girls were happy to flirt and giggle at him, talk about hearing the songs he played and stories he told. They had all heard of him, seen him that time on MTV, or knew him from some band appearance. The boys were a mixed bag. Most liked the music, some were really into it, and knew their bands. Steve was happy to talk music with several, tell them about the concerts, the clubs, what new sounds were going to be next, maybe. A couple were standoffish, not liking it when the girls paid him more attention than them as they surfed or stood trying to look cool holding their boards. Even those guys warmed up when he said that Hatteras had better waves.

"I mean," he had explained, "Huntington Beach, sure, it's got good waves, but they are not really as big, and its crowded there all the time. And the other spots, well, if you don't mind them crashing into a cliff, sure you can find big waves, but where is the fun in that? No, this is nice. Now, Hawaii…" and then he had to tell about his time in Hawaii, and he felt like he was letting more and more out. But it was comfortable being with the teenagers, most of them, who lived for the next hour, and would forget half of what happened today before they got home. The world may be small for the kids on Cape Hatteras, but it was a pearl in their oyster. They seemed incredibly happy right now. School was out, the weather was nice, the water was warm, and they had someone to play their music, not their parents', and so they were set until they got hungry.

"Yeah… this is great."

Jackie sighed, a long contented exhalation. "Don't you wish it could stay like this forever?" she asked, probably more a wish than looking for an answer. "Never get older, always stay right here. Right here on this spot, the sun just setting, everyone having fun, not a worry in the world.

"Seriously, if I could, I would wish never to grow old. I'd stay right here, and I don't think I could ever get bored with this." She sighed again, longer.

"Careful what you wish for." Steve half smiled, half smirked.

"What do you mean?" Jackie looked like she wanted to know this answer. Like she had wanted to ask Steve that question for a while.

"I'm just saying, sometimes you need a challenge, to move you, make things not so perfect. Then, well, I guess things get more perfect than they were. Do you want to stay a teenager forever?"

"No, it's not that, well…" she thought on it, "well, yeah, I guess I would. I get that we get to be more in control of our own lives, and yeah, we move away, go to college or get a job, but right now, here, this is my time, and everything is great. I don't want to change it. It will change, I know that. I'm just saying I don't want it to, I don't want to be the one who makes it change."

Jackie leaned her head on Steve's shoulder, then lifted it, leaving a wet splotch of ocean on his white shirt. "Thanks for coming out. Everyone was glad to meet you."

Steve pointed at a couple of nearby teen boys, not part of Jackie's larger group. "Not everyone," he could easily see they were not happy with Steve being here.

"Don't worry about those guys," she pffted at them. "We aren't part of that crowd. Those boys go with that weird church people thing." She almost stammered out the words. "Their parents say you're a bad influence."

Steve laughed a faintly maniacal cackle, "Oh, I am," he insisted.

"They blame you for that girl getting killed. They somehow think you had something to do with it."

Steve held back from reiterating that he did have something to do with it; he was the one that found her. That he didn't immediately tell everyone had been a cause for concern among some locals, including the folks from the Legacy Church and some other old timers.

"Funny how they still don't know who she was," Jackie commented.

Then she got up abruptly and wrapped a towel around her. "It's getting late, I think we're all gonna go home now." With that, the entire group followed her vague but direct instruction and began to gather up their beach detritus. "You want to come over for dinner? My dad really wants to meet you. I think he likes your music as much as we do."

Steve thought it a strange way to invite someone over to meet their parents, but to Jackie, everything just became exactly what she meant it to be, no subterfuge, no pretending. Just a chance to have dinner and meet a fan.

"You forget, I just had breakfast like two hours ago," Steve said as he, too, got up.

"Well, lunch then."

And to Jackie, it was decided.

15

"It's called cord grass, and it just dries up and gets lifted out during storms and floods."

Andy Wood held up a single rod of the many pieces that were ubiquitous to the shore. "Well," he half shrugged, half sighed, "this may not be really interesting to you," and he tried to laugh it off. Sometimes he got caught up in his work.

"No, really," Steve insisted, " I love this stuff. It's interesting. Look at all the things you get to know, being a marine biologist. That's like every person's dream job, going out on boats and ships, being out on the ocean like Jacques Cousteau…"

"Daddy named me after him," Jackie spoke up, trying to get back into the conversation.

Steve had come over with two bottles of wine, unsure of what to bring, so he grabbed a red and a white from his dwindling collection of California wines. He learned from his namesake's pal, Matt Hooper, to bring both, just in case. Unsure of how he would be received, he quickly got the feeling he was very welcome by Dr. And Mrs. Wood, who were both joyous and engaged the whole night. And Steve quickly took a liking to Andy, when he discovered he was a marine biologist. He was unsurprised when dinner consisted of pan fried fish, baked potatoes, and a rather tangy cole slaw.

"I make my own mayonnaise," explained Phyllis Wood.

Jackie rolled her eyes at the comment.

Now Steve and Andy stood looking out at the marsh from the Woods' back porch, drinking the last of the wine, watching the remains of the late sun already well below the horizon.

"They are going to build a hundred houses out here," Andy pointed. "All new homes, some affordable housing, all for people at the mill and lumber yard, and the processing center. Plus, they are all going to need people to work in the grocery stores, more restaurants, all the things that the village will need to support more population."

"How do the locals feel about it?" Steve had already heard the bitching and moaning about the beach houses going up on the shore for tourism.

"Most don't mind, actually," Andy was upbeat. "These are mostly locals anyway, well, from up in Manteo, Wanchese," he pointed in the direction of the northern towns of Dare County. "And these aren't rentals. They have to be owned and occupied. No part timers, no property owners coming down for a few weeks every summer. They are going to live and work here. We're going to finally get separate schools now." Cape Hatteras School had long served the needs of every student from four to eighteen. Soon there would be a separate high school.

"Not everyone is happy about it," chimed in Jackie as she came out to the deck. She tried to grab her father's wine glass, but he pulled it away. She then looked at Steve and he downed the last of his drink. "Tough luck. Who's not happy about it?"

"Those Island Legacy Church nuts," Jackie said offhand.

"Now, Jackie," started her father.

"Well… they are. Some of them have bought up the land near the old naval base out by the light and built rental homes all over the beach. Tore down some cool old places, too. They wanted this land for more cheap rental homes. Then they decided to create some little enclave and build their new church over there." She pointed toward a marshy outcropping. "No one else around here wanted it."

"Why not?" to Steve it looked like a prime waterfront piece of real estate.

"Come in, I'll show you."

Andy shrugged his shoulders. He gave the look of someone used to being bossed around by his daughter, because she usually ended up doing something really interesting. Then he motioned Steve to follow him in. "You think I know my stuff? This girl, she knows every legend on this island."

Inside, Jackie went straight to a shelf and pulled off a book. "Have you read this?" she handed the book to Steve.

Taffy of Torpedo Junction, read the title. It had a young girl, a horse, and a dog on the cover, looking out to sea. "No, I haven't had much time to read yet." The book looked like a children's novel.

"It's a great book. Don't be fooled by the cover, it's popular with all the locals. It's about a girl who discovers a Nazi plot to sabotage a military base here in Hatteras during the war. One of the stories hints about some soldiers coming ashore from a U-boat with enough dynamite to blow up the island.

"See, the funny thing is, the story may be true."

Jackie waited for an anticipated reaction. But her father knew the story, and Steve had no preconceived idea of what was supposed to happen, so they both just waited.

Jackie, disappointed, continued. "So, I found out that during the war, they were so worried about spies and saboteurs that everyone who showed up on the ferries were suspect. There was this German couple who came down, asking about Ocracoke and Hatteras, and when they left, they were arrested and taken away by the FBI or something.

"But here's the really strange part. A group of men came down here, saying they were from Manteo originally. They all spoke English without at bit of German accent, but everyone was wondering who they were. They said they came down to work on some of the military buildings, but these Hatteras people didn't believe them. See," she was really getting into the story now, excited, "they spoke English perfectly. But they said they were from like up in Rodanthe or Manteo or somethin'," she emphasized her accent now for effect. "But nobody down here talks without an Outer Banks accent. She called it," Jackie pointed to the book's author, Nell Wise Wechter, "their Elizabethan Brogue."

Steve had heard the accent well. Everyone had a form of it. Far from just the typical southern drawl of dropping their R's and G's at the ends of words, they made an 'oi' sound for 'i', and instead of a long O, it was a stretched out mix of vowels, almost an 'euw' sound.

"So, these fellers," she was really into it now, leading up to the climax, "the Hatteras fellers, they knew they weren't from around here. They figured out they were German spies or soldiers, meant to blow something up, or steal secrets. Somehow they found out for sure, because they took things into their own hands and went one night and killed them all."

Steve was slightly surprised at the bloody turn the story took. Andy just smiled and laughed, he had heard the punchline before, and obviously didn't entirely believe it.

"You laugh if you want, but there are people who will swear it happened," Jackie insisted, upset that her father would ruin a perfectly good bloody story.

"But what does that have to do with the land out there?" Steve asked, trying to get back to the point of the matter. Jackie could take a recipe for mashed potatoes and turn it into how Idaho became a state, he thought.

"Well, they couldn't just go to the Navy and say 'Hey, we just killt these ten Nazis. What do you want us to do with them?' So, legend has it that they buried the bodies out in the marsh over there, where the water would wash over them and the bodies never would be found.

"Some of these people don't want anyone building over that spot, see." She finished the tale with a note of finality.

"But the builders don't believe that stuff, or they don't care. That's over and done with long ago. There are no ghosts out on that point, and there probably never were. They are going to build a pier and boat dock out there. They even brought in the wood for it a couple days ago," Andy added his final note to the story as well.

"Is that what I smell?" Steve asked. "I thought it was diesel, but it must be creosote."

"You can smell that from here?" Jackie asked, taking in a big whiff.

"Well, not from here," Steve pointed to the floor of the living room where he stood. "But when I was outside, I smelled it."

The three of them looked through the living room, toward the front of the house, that looked out at the far away sound. The Woods' home was near the entrance of the development, with five other houses, but more houses had either been built or were in the process, along with piles of lumber for future homes. The five nearby, plus some of the newest homes, were occupied.

"Funny," Andy said, "I would have thought the sunset would have been down by now." It was getting late, after 9 p.m., and there should be nothing but the slimmest hint of purple light in the early summer sky being chased away by starry darkness and moonrise, but an orange glow came through the unseen windows of the front of the house, reflecting on the kitchen appliances and a hall mirror.

Just then, Phyllis came running into the room. "Andy, the houses, they're all on fire!"

16
Thursday, June 13[h]

Tim secretly hoped for a hurricane to report on. "This isn't why I got into this," he griped silently. He couldn't even risk saying the words aloud, to himself, with the mic off, while he was broadcasting. He had been asked to build a community radio station, something to broadcast local news, car wash fund raisers, school closings, events over at the community center, even bulletins on weather and when the island would be ordered to evacuate in case of a hurricane coming up from the tropics.

Not this.

"Buxton Fire Department has reported that the fire started in multiple places along the new construction. Only one of the five finished homes was occupied at the time. Unfortunately," Tim hated to go on, "one fatality was reported. Fifty five year old Marcus Dupree died of smoke inhalation after being trapped in the blaze. All five homes, along with wood for a pier, and lumber for another ten homes were lost in the fires. Buxton Fire reports that the fires were likely to be deliberately set in multiple locations at the same time, and that the investigation of the cause and culprits," 'culprits,' Tim snorted derisively in his own head, like they were kids stealing apples from a 1950s fruit stand, he would make sure to change that copy the next time he read it, "were still unknown and at large.

"In other news, the murder victim of May 15 found on the beach near the Hatteras Light has been identified as Linda Annette Patterson, of Virginia Beach. Patterson, 22 years old at the time of her death, was reported missing one week after her body was found on the beach. She was positively identified by a tattoo of a black lily on her inside ankle. Virginia Beach police are currently in search of Patterson's former boyfriend, Aaron Dail, a construction worker from Virginia Beach as well. He did not show up for work yesterday after Patterson's identity was released last night."

Just play the music, he told himself. Don't say anything, don't say anything, just play the music.

"And now, Fleetwood Mac, and *Secondhand News...*" just play the song.

He turned the mic off and left the booth. He needed just a moment.

In the front of the weather station, he didn't get a moment, but he got some welcome companionship. Ellen Gaines stood waiting for him.

"You alright?" she asked, a little taken aback by how ashen and tired Tim looked.

"No."

"What's wrong?"

Tim shook the copy, twisted but forgotten in his hand. Ellen couldn't read it from anywhere but inches away, but she knew just what it was. She felt the same way. "I don't want to talk about it," he said angrily.

"Okay. I hate to ask now. Can I borrow your car? Mine's not starting. I got Obie to come over and tow it to his shop, but I need to get home."

Tim lived near enough to walk or drive himself, and he could always call someone. He could just ask over the radio for someone to come get him. Or he could get Steve to drive him home, any of those options would work.

"Sure, go ahead, I'll walk home. I could use the exercise." And a little stress relief.

He tossed her the keys and headed back to the booth. The song would be over soon, and he hadn't loaded anything into the other turntable.

17

"Blame the radio," the note read.

Brin Darrow read the note haphazardly. He was distracted by the large amount of worn cash that flooded the envelope it came in. But he had to read it, in order to keep the envelopes like this coming in.

It continued, "Blame the music they play, and the people that play it. Discourage the congregation from listening, but then say how bad the music is. Make it a bad influence on the young. Anyone who listens to it is a sinner.

"Blame the fire on people being out late, staying up to listen to the devil's music, being led by the people that play it."

"Never mind that the fire started at around 9 pm and the radio station was off the air," thought the Reverend Darrow. Then he silenced himself. If there was a god paying him to say stuff like this, he might read Darrow's mind, and then where would he be.

"Hammer it home on them, that all who partake are filled with sin, and unworthy to be part of the community. Blame the people who are moving here, blame the people who let them in. Discourage neighborhood integration."

"That was it, huh?" thought Darrow. The person that died in the fire was black. Several families moving down were black, and there were hints of Hispanics, too. Just talk, idle rumors.

Darrow didn't need to bother with that. Most of his congregation was violently but silently racist as hell. But he would do what he was told.

This would be a good sermon, Darrow told himself as he wrote. He would be ready for next Sunday, ready to fleece the idiots with his words. He glanced at the wad of cash and folded the envelope up, then turned back to his writing.

18

Jackie had her own group of idiots to deal with. Summer usually meant a bit of freedom, but to be free of the morons from school on a small island was tough. Right now it was Tommy Gray and his toady pal Ray Ray Twine, "Ugh, his dad named him Ray twice, literally," she had said when she first heard it, "So stupid." The two had confronted her out at the beach by the lighthouse access and were getting too close to her. The fact that they were willing to do this in public made Jackie and her friends more than a little uncomfortable. Most of the time, while there were some students that tried to bully their way around the fringes of teenage society, they knew not to mess with Jackie. She was just too well liked, too popular. Anyone who spoke out against her risked serious ostracism from the entire teenage clique that existed across the villages.

But Tommy was big enough to cause problems, and he was outsized only by Ray Ray. Most of the other kids were afraid either one would use that size, considerable as it was, to do more than just push their way into any closed conversation.

"We know your boyfriend did it," Tommy insisted. "He's a killer. He cut her head off and left her there. He'll do the same thing to you."

"Yeah," Ray Ray was less engaged, torn between ogling Jackie and insulting her. "He probably drank her blood."

Jackie felt cornered. Even with her friends behind her, in the open parking lot, she felt a little alone. Those two could do some damage if they wanted. They looked a bit like they wanted to. Jackie wondered if they were drunk. It was noon, after all.

"You don't know what you're talking about," you fucking morons, she didn't say out loud. "Steve had nothing to do with her getting killed." She wasn't sure why she wanted to defend him, and why all of a sudden her words sounded hollow.

"*Steee-eeeve*," Tommy mocked her. "See, you know his name!" He tried to grab at her arm, but she pulled back. "I'll play you some music, come over to my place!"

"You mean your mom's?" Jackie knew she was pushing it. He could go from mocking to violent quickly, and standing out in public at the beach access didn't seem to matter to these two any more.

Jackie's friends grabbed her, pulling her behind them. "Leave them alone. They're just trying to get in with us," her friend Lauren glared at the two boys. "And it's not working well, is it?" Dumbasses, her look said to them.

"We don't want to be friends with you," Tommy almost cried. It came out more as a childish whimper than with any sincerity. "You're all in love with *Steee-eeve*, and he's going to kill you all!"

"Just go away!"

"You go away!" All this wasn't working the way Tommy and Ray Ray wanted. They didn't know how to talk with the girls, and only knew to bully the boys around them. And threatening Jackie hadn't been the icebreaker they thought it would.

"You got it, we'll do that," and Jackie began walking away, her back turned completely from the two. It was risky. She couldn't see them if they came up from behind her. Only good fortune in the form of the local Park Rangers driving up put any fear in the thick heads of Tommy and Ray Ray. They understood that the park narcs were armed, and would be happy to turn them over to the local police if they caused any active problems. The two stopped, put their hands crossed in front of them, and looked down. In any hopes of looking innocent, they looked guilty as hell.

It allowed Jackie and her group to walk to the beach, now unmolested by the two.

"Jerks," one girl said, only willing to halfway look over her shoulder.

"Assholes," Jackie corrected her.

"They're just hearing that shit from their parents," Acey Midgett spoke up. "That church they go to, they're blaming us listening to the X at night. And they really, really don't like Steve Brodie."

"They just have to have someone to hate," Jackie added. "Those people are nuts."

"Did you see they rebuilt that old church on the sound? They are going to turn it into a school, too."

"School for dumbasses," Jackie said, looking back over her shoulder as she sat down on a beach towel. Part of her wanted to go kick Tommy Gray in the nuts, but it probably wouldn't hurt him much. Just make him mad. At least they hadn't followed the rest of them out to the beach.

"Fuckin' fishheads," spat Acey.

"Still, what they're saying," chimed in a younger boy, John Bailey, "there are a lot of people saying it." He was only fifteen, included in the group, but still learning where his place was in it. Anyone would have told him he was at the bottom, lucky to be there, and should have kept his mouth shut, but at fifteen, he wanted to be in with the cool kids, and he wasn't going to be noticed if he was silent.

"First of all," said Lauren, "Shut up. Second, what are they saying?"

John had no idea how to answer. But now he had attention. "I'm just saying, I heard that them Legacy Church people are saying stuff like he killed that woman in some sort of Satanic ritual, and drank her blood. They are blaming it on the music he played."

"He's no vampire," Jackie defended.

"I'm not saying he is," John felt the group ganging up on him. "But they are saying it. And people notice. He only works nights, he never comes out to the beach in the day. He found the woman, he is not from here…"

"Let me guess, he doesn't eat garlic," Acey added, more than a hint of incredulity for effect.

"He never invites people in his house," joked another boy.

"No," corrected John, "It's 'he can't come in to *your* house unless he's invited.'"

"Great," Jackie said, "Now you're our expert vampire hunter. Gonna go after him with a cross and stick?" She jokingly made a cross sign with her fingers.

"No!" John answered, a little pedantic and sad. He didn't want to be the bad guy in this. He had just hoped to look smart in the eyes of the other kids, and it wasn't going well. "But, he doesn't go to church, either. Everyone here goes to church."

"He's from LA, no one goes to church there," Jackie said, but she didn't know if it was true. But then none of them knew it wasn't true, either. "And he sleeps during the day because he works nights. Sheesh."

The group decided to drop it, but Jackie began to have her own doubts. Steve had never invited her into his house, and he didn't like being out during the day. She had seen him out in daylight, but always in shade, or in the afternoon or evening. He never was out in the bright sun. Yet he had a slight tan.

She tried to remember if he had garlic on his pizza.

And then she remembered that she had invited him over to her house the night the fire started.

He had been there, in her home.

After the frightening confrontation with Tommy and Ray Ray, Jackie felt shook with the thoughts in her head.

It made her wonder. Who was this guy?

19
Sunday, June 16th

Sunday meant it was time to lean in on the parish, thought Reverend Darrow. He looked out over the pews, filled now with the willing, the hate filled, and the manipulated. All of them had a desire that brought them here, he thought, and he was going to give it to them.

In return, he got what he wanted.

Darrow looked out over the people there. One of them was his benefactor, they had to be. Not everyone was wealthy, he knew that. Some might have more money than they show, others spend more than they have.

He called a roll in his head. Cale and Louise Drey, they always sat near the front. Louise was fat and smiling, smiling and fat, always has a "bless your heart" on her lips for anyone who finally had enough of her. Everyone pretended to like her, because she could turn on anyone who slighted her in an instant. Her husband was a bit of a simple man, even fatter than her. They ran a drywall company. Hardly the ones who would have money to spare, but they also are the ones likely to spend everything they had to hurt someone. Not fire, though. Louise used her words, talked to people, made up stuff, hurt people that way, took away their livelihood, not their lives.

"They're also ugly," thought Darrow as he watched them sing. "They have a kid, God, I hate the thought of those two getting it on." He shook off the vision by staring at Darla, a vision in a shiny green dress, tight in the right places as far as he was concerned.

Darla was probably the reason the families, especially the men and sons, showed up. The women, the daughters, they came along. He wondered if the women felt the eyes of the men slipping out from behind the hymnals or opening during prayer to get a look at Darla from behind.

He had to shake that thought off, too. His robe may or may not hide an erection when he was in front of the congregation.

He looked around more. Two sea captains, charter skippers, and their broods, both with money enough to burn. Mike Gray, definitely successful, and also definitely ungodly racist. "Well, racist, at least," said Darrow to himself. He also abused his wife. Darrow could always tell by the way the wives acted. And Ronald Twine, a dimwitted and dull copy of Gray, with his own son a rather obtuse chip off the father's block. Either or both could be the donors, with the money they made. Likely, but they weren't that participatory in church. "Maybe that's why," thought Darrow, "they keep a low profile." He never considered it might be two people.

There was Bruce and, "What's her name? Claudia? Doughy? Biscuit?" he never remembered the wife's name. She was a strange mix of all weirdly unremarkable. Thin, but not really, soft, not fit, but not big, well, not Louise Drey big. Her husband Bruce worked for the county as a local parole agent, and he was well known as a dick that used the easily manipulated criminals. But they were criminals, so no one really cared. They had two kids, a son and daughter. He thought the son was retarded, and the daughter had gone from cute to Big Doughy Junior real quick. They were unremarkable except in their ability to be unlikable. They were always looking for another business to run. So maybe they had money. They always seemed to be buying something new, a new truck, and new boat.

Harrison Boarman. His father, Greg, had owned the marina, as well as several commercial fishing boats. He probably had other businesses as well off the island. The son, Harrison, was here now. He had come down from Virginia when his father had decided to retire. The kid, "kid, ha, he looked like he was thirty years old," thought Darrow, was the spitting image of the father. Fell in step in the business like he was born to it, which he probably was. He had only been down since May. That family had enough money to throw around the amount he had been getting without feeling a pinch. But the boy had only been there a month. He watched Darla, too. Who could blame him? But he was young, handsome, hard edged like his old man. Unmarried, though that wouldn't stop Darla anyway.

The hymn ended, and Darrow had to get his game face on. It was time to deliver the sermon. This would be a good one, full of judgement, hate, and wrath. And then a big punch to dig deep, again.

"We live in a time and place full of sin, and we, the people of this church, are the ones that stand in the path. We must remain pure," that was always a good one, purity, "to stop the sin where it stands. We must not let it spread.

"Look at your own hearts," this was the church's catchphrase now. His benefactor had insisted. They all had been given old silver mirrors, all seemed to be cut from the same sheet of glass. It was supposed to be a daily ritual, to look into it. Darrow had them planted at every home. It was a way to remind the church just what they were supposed to look like. Some idea that they see themselves as better. That they should be successful, and that they can see themselves as flourishing.

"Take your success, your money, your income, and make more. As it says in the book of Matthew, invest your money well, and deliver what is your own with interest. But the ones that do not, that hide their money, the wicked, the slothful, they will find what they have taken away, and given to those of us that are successful, and the poor will be cast away into darkness.

"So look away from the poor, the ones that struggle. They are not in the heart of God. God rewards the righteous with success, with luxury, with comfort, and in return, we, the children of this one and only God, reward him." One of the tenants of his church was that their faith shows through their wealth and power. The poor, and with that, anyone who generally couldn't succeed, was not devout. Wealth was a sign of their piety and godliness. And the best way to show wealth was to give as much as possible to the church.

Getting someone to give you a house, well, that was no way to get into heaven.

Buy them a condo, on the other hand…

"Now is the time to dig deep, brothers," he barely liked to include the women in the call, but they often controlled the wallets, "and sisters, to show the prosperity of the church. We are close to opening our new home, to restore the church to its glory of old, and to have a home for our sons and daughters," your sons and daughters, he thought. The "new" old church was almost complete, with an addition of a small set of school rooms, a home for a small, private, and expensive school.

And Darrow got his new parsonage.

Darrow watched as the collection plates went around. Louise Drey put a check in the plate. "Yeah, not her," he said to himself. Mike Gray pulled out a wad of cash, and peeled off some bills. Darrow tried his best not to leer at the money. He noticed that the father glared at his teenage son, who reluctantly pulled out his own wallet and put a bill on the plate. "That's a lot of cash," Darrow was envious, but also, he liked only working two days a week. Indoors, mostly.

The plate moved around, with more and more envelopes, green cash, the occasional tinkle of some kid giving a quarter in hopes of winning favor for a test the next week, Darrow guessed. "It's not gonna help, kid," he said only in his head.

The collection plates were returned, and Darrow held them aloft, a vanity of showing off how much they had. He always liked it when the plates felt heavy. He would lighten them by ten percent, later that afternoon.

20
Monday, June 17th

Monday nights were going to get more crowded. Steve sat with Tim, Ellen, and Isiah. Tim had been happy to add a kid to the evening spots to get him out of the booth on Mondays. He would need days off, and he also liked having some of the teens from Cape Hatteras School interested in radio. Tim had Steve to thank for that. With Steve's notoriety, suspicious good looks and popularity with the girls, all of a sudden, being a DJ was a thing. This night he left a new kid, Kelly Meyers, a promising baritone of a seventeen year old, at the helm after a week of training. Then he simply said play the Top 40, get the commercials in, do your promo, "It's Kelly Meyers, on WZHX, Hatteras, on the X!" and play a cool rock song on the punch in. Sign off at 11, and lock the doors behind you. He knew Kelly's parents well, so Tim figured he could trust the kid with the keys.

Which meant Tim could have a beer with his pro crew without a lot of worry. At least until they went to the weekly midnight sign off time next week. The sunset hours for the station during the week had ended now that the sun wasn't setting until after nine o'clock, and the kids were listening late into the evening now, into the morning on the weekends.

But tonight, Tim drank himself happy, with his second beer already downed, and a planned walk home. It was early, and he and his crew were really having a good time at the Hatteras Moon. It was a beneficial distraction.

"I tell ya," Tim's voice slipping into a mildly higher pitch already, "It's going to be a hot one." It was about all anyone could predict with regular success for the summer. No one knew what would happen this year with tourism, especially with the murder in May, and now the fires.

"You think this will be a quiet summer?" asked Steve. He was still unused to the wiles of the tourist trade. The summer dinks coming down in droves, already covered in zinc oxide and Hawaiian shirts, overweight, red faced, dads screaming at the kids, all he knew were the stereotypes he had seen from TV and movies.

"No," said Ellen, still nursing her first and only beer of the night, "Nothing slows the tourists down. Well, maybe shark attacks, but even that, maybe not. Power outages, that would do it."

"Hurricanes!" chimed in Isiah. "They get *pissssed* at storms, like we can control the weather, and somehow we make it happen to them.

"You ever been in a hurricane, Steve?" he asked.

"Once," it was a bit of a lie, he had been around more than one, but they were both long ago. "Once when I was a kid, we were," he had to think, "down in Florida, and one went through. It was kind of wild, but it didn't seem to bother me much." Another lie. "I think I didn't know what to expect, and I had been through winter storms and tornadoes, so this was just warm, windy rain. It wasn't until I came out the next day and saw all the palm fronds everywhere and the roads closed, and a couple of roofs gone, that I realized how bad it was.

"What are they like here?"

Tim spoke up, "'bout the same," he said, "except change palm fronds to pine needles. We get them all blown off the trees, all still green, and they cover the roads. When people drive out, they crush them and the whole place smells like pine sap. It's a little overwhelming, but also sort of pretty."

"Down here," added Ellen, the historian always, "It's sand, and water." Isiah nodded in agreement.

"The ocean comes up over the beach, through the dunes, you just wait," Isiah said, a warning reckoning for those who would doubt him. "It'll just wash right over the S-Turns up north."

"Then what do you do?" Steve was wondering how they could be so nonchalant about being cut off from the rest of the world.

"Nothing," Ellen tried to explain it to him. "We're just used to it. The dunes will be pushed over the road, or the roads will flood, and some people will still drive through it anyway. Then the water goes down and back out, and the DOT brings in bulldozers and pushes the dunes back, and the roads get opened, and we just keep on doing what we're doing.

"Been that way for over a hundred years," she insisted. "There's the old timers, they'll tell you, before the dunes were built…"

"Wait, the dunes were built?" Steve asked. He always thought they were natural.

"Yes, in the 1930s." Ellen was in her element now, telling her stories to a willing audience. "They thought that the island would wash away if the storms kept washing over the beach. So in the 1930s, during the Civilian Conservation Corps era, they hired everyone who could run a bulldozer or earthmover and made probably fifty miles of dunes, to stop the waves and save the islands."

"So I guess it worked?" Steve asked, prompting Ellen who was clearly enjoying this.

"Well, yes, and no," she said cryptically. "See, yeah, it stopped some of the waves, but before then, we would have the storms wash over the island, and deposit the softer, thin sand on this side, leaving the shells and beach sand on that side," she pointed east, toward the beach far away. "Some places got really good fine soil, and a lot of locals had prize gardens. We had people growing peach trees, vegetables, everything.

"But when the storms were stopped at the beach, the waves just pounded the dunes, and the sound side, well, it stopped growing. We don't get those big fans of silt anymore, so the island is shrinking from the west, as well as eroded from the east.

"Back in the days before the dunes, the locals would talk about how a hurricane would blow up, no radio back then, you know," she winked at Tim. "What would happen is that the storms would just blow the waves over, or if it came from the west, blow the sound in, and flood the houses. It looked like the homes were ships on the sea, and the hills were little islands covered with cows and deer. Then the wind would finally stop, and the water would just," she made a motion with her hand, "flow on out. The dunes weren't there to stop the waves, but the water had a place to go. It wasn't trapped.

"Now, it sticks around."

Ellen was in her element, joyous to tell a story. It was her true medium, her well polished skill that she did weekly on her radio show. She knew she was telling stories that the locals already knew, but they liked hearing them, over and over. It reassured them of the connection to the island and the culture they generally shared. "Yeah, it floods the roads and everything else. You have to wait for it to find its way out. And even then, it all just sorta pools up. It sits there for days. The ground becomes saturated and there's no place for it all to go.

"Then we get all the bugs, and it starts to smell. And you gotta wait like two weeks for the county to get their act together to come and haul off all the junk that floated up into your yard."

"You'll love it!" joked Isiah.

"Sounds wonderful," said Steve. "What have I gotten myself into?" he wondered in his head. "I think this calls for another beer."

"One's my limit," Ellen said. "Especially with me driving someone else's car. You sure you're okay with me keeping it another day? Mine should be finished tomorrow morning, but you know how Obie is. It should be done in the morning, he'll tell you by noon, and it's done at 2 o'clock." She shook her head. The mechanic worked on island time, understood by the locals, no matter how frustrating it was.

"No, it's fine," Tim answered back. "I can walk home from here anyway. I barely need it."

"Thanks!" Ellen smiled at the group, saving a sly and bright glance for Steve in particular. Her face said the words in her head that she couldn't bring to say out loud, even with a beer in her. "He's just gorgeous!"

Ellen walked out and the remaining three men ordered another round. It came about a minute later. They had just taken their first sips when a loud explosion was heard from just outside the bar.

Everyone sprang up to see what had happened. There, in the old gravel drive, littered with sea shells and fossilized stone, Tim's car was torn to shreds. Fire burned from the front and back, engulfing it. The paint and metal blistered, peeled, and bent.

Poor Ellen Gaines was barely visible in the driver's seat as her body was cooked to a cinder by the growing fire.

21
Tuesday, June 18th

"Who would want to do that to poor Ellen?" Jackie asked Lauren. The two were on a break, a lull in the business of selling ice cream and desserts to the tourists that were just starting to show up in Buxton. She had given in and gotten a job at the uniquely named Hatteras Waterfront Restaurant, a place that quite literally delivered what it promised in its title. It was in Hatteras, it was waterfront, technically, because it was just off the sound, and they sold food. Jackie was put in the freestanding ice cream and soda shop, The Ice Box. With its only slightly more creative name, it was still more fun than inside the restaurant with the hustle of getting food to tables and cleaning up. Everyone came out smelling like fried food.

Or cigarettes, Jackie thought.

Lauren responded with typical teen disdain. "I know," was all she said, but it was an agreement of something best left unspoken. They had no idea how to respond to the death of Ellen Gaines. Neither had really faced death before, and had no way to filter it through their experiences.

"I still think he did it," came a voice from the nearby dock.

Jackie and Lauren looked over from where they stood behind the ice cream stand, then they wished they hadn't. "No wonder I smelled cigarettes," Jackie thought.

A pimply busboy who was always covered with steam and sweat from running the dishwasher stood out on the dock with a few other employees. It was hard and dirty work, but not challenging. The kid, actually two years older than Jackie, was a vague graduate of high school that she didn't remember when she was only a sophomore. He was named Donnie, and that's about all she even bothered to know about him. Mainly because of his professed knowledge and skill at having absolutely the wrong ideas and opinions on everything. She had heard early on that because he thought he was being nice, he got to grab the girls' butts on a nightly basis. Jackie had at first made sure that she never turned her back to the guy, and when he had tried to grab at her friend Lauren, she had pushed him, hard, into the waiting dishes. The clinking and crashing pile of cheap thick china and drawn the ire of the manager, and Jackie had made it clear that Donnie was easily more replaceable than her and her friends that worked there. Donnie hadn't exactly gotten the message, but the manager did give him enough of a warning that he kept clear of Jackie, at least.

"What are you talking about, Donnie?" Lauren spoke before she could think, then added, "And, shut up."

Donnie didn't hear anything past his name. "That guy from the radio station, he killed that woman on the beach. *I* heard it was some satanic ritual he learned in California. He probably didn't get enough blood and had to kill again."

Donnie was insistent and self assured. He knew everyone in California was a devil worshipper because he heard it once.

While he tried to claim to be an expert on everything on the West Coast, Donnie could only claim to have left Dare County because he had been over to Ocracoke, which was part of mainland Hyde County. Other than that, the farthest he had been away from Buxton was either to a basketball game in Manteo High School, or offshore in the Gulf Stream. Geography was not his strong point.

Donnie bummed another cigarette off of the cook, much to the chef's chagrin. The cook threw his own butt to the ground and went inside. Jackie and Lauren decided to do the same.

"Just because you like him doesn't mean he won't do the same to you," said Donnie, alone now, in hopes of getting the last word. He was rewarded by standing by himself in the darkening sky.

Jackie and Lauren worked the evening until closing time. They quickly cleaned up and closed The Ice Box. Lauren took the money up to the restaurant in a bank bag while Jackie waited for her to drive her home. Jackie counted her tips, wondering how many days until she could afford a car.

"No one to come rescue you?" came a voice from the darkness. Jackie saw the cigarette light first before recognizing Donnie's voice.

Jackie wondered if her eye roll was severe enough to be heard. "Ugh," she thought. "Where's Lauren? I don't want to have to stand around with this guy."

Jackie was about to say something, thought better of it, pondered just shoving the guy again, when she saw that Donnie wasn't alone.

"She's waiting for *Stee-eeve...*" Jackie knew the voice, and the condescending tone. Donnie had friends. Tommy Gray had come to pay a visit. "Probably trying to get free food," Jackie thought. As he walked forward, he held a bag with a box in it. Jackie was not very surprised she was right. He and Donnie seemed like the kind of people who would steal leftovers.

"What are you... nevermind," she said. She knew what Tommy was doing there. "Just go away."

"Waiting for your *boyfriend*?" he continued to mock her.

"No. I guess you found yours." She nodded at Donnie.

"Hey," Donnie was fast to process the insult. Tommy made a dark face in the dark night. There wasn't much light to see if he was puzzled or mad. Only the light from the restaurant porch and the sign out at the street put much glow into the little picnic area where people normally ate their ice cream.

"Fuck you, bitch!" It was Tommy's go-to insult for girls who rejected him. He used it often. But now he had been insulted and called a faggot by a girl. It hurt more. He wasn't going to be the one who was hurt.

Tommy lunged at Jackie, trying to grab her arm. Smaller, faster, and ready for Tommy's reaction, she still knew she was in a bad place. Tommy was by far a bigger person, physically, and could hurt her bad. And right now, he seemed like he wanted to. Jackie looked toward the restaurant, hoping someone would come out, but no one did.

She darted toward the stairs, hoping to just get close, get into the light, away from the darkness where Tommy and Donnie could hide. Donnie had fully processed what was said, and he cut her off before she could get to the paved sidewalk. He grabbed at her arm, gripping it tightly as she tried to squirm away. He twisted her smaller wrist as his grip, wet and sweaty, slipped. Donnie only gripped harder.

"Ow, let go! You're hurting me!" When her friends played too rough, they always relented when they went too far. Donnie wasn't her friend. He only squeezed tighter.

"I'm not doing anything, you're the one twisting your own arm." Donnie fell into his full bully mode. He had her in his grip, and pulled her closer.

Tommy tried to grab her other arm. "We're not hurting you. We're just trying to be friendly. You're being a bitch. Be nice." He found his grip and pulled her closer to him.

Jackie felt her arms stretched. Her shoulder hurt where Donnie pulled at it. She already felt like he had done damage to her. And he wasn't stopping.

Jackie's legs were still free. They might expect her to kick at them. Jackie stomped on Tommy's foot instead, hard. She felt like something snapped inside.

The pain shot through Tommy's foot, up his leg, and into his head. She had broken his toe, or his foot. Dropping his grip, he tried to grab at his foot to rub the pain. "You stupid bitch, you broke my foot."

Jackie didn't care. With her hand free, she swung with all her might at Donnie, who still had a tight painful grip on her wrist. She smacked him open handed in the side of his pimply face. It felt awful to have to touch him, slimy, wet, puss filled. As much as she had a desire to scrub her hand clean, something in her realized this was not the usual teenager fight, where they regret it after it starts. This was for real.

Donnie was flung away from Jackie. His sweaty hand slipped off hers. Jackie felt him dig his fingers and nails into her hand, tearing at her flesh. But she was free for a moment.

A moment was all Tommy needed. He wanted to hit Jackie, hit her like he knew how. But she was only inches too far away. He reached out to get her, as she staggered away, grabbing at her hand. He jumped toward her and pushed her into the ground. If he could get her down on the ground, pinned in the rocks and sand, she couldn't get away, he thought.

Jackie fell, turning as she tumbled, into the gravel rocks and packed sand. She felt something tear. She only hoped it was her jeans, until she felt the warmth, and the pouring liquid from her knee. Jackie rolled over and saw that her pants had been torn open, with a huge wound on her knee and shin. It took a second, a heartbeat, for her to go from seeing the pain to feeling it. It looked terrible, and then it felt so much worse.

Tommy stared at his work, realizing what he had caused. He knew he had begun something, and now he wanted to keep it up. He raised his hand into a fist, but something in the back of his mind told him not to hit her, not to use his fist. He had seen how it was done, how to hit a woman, he knew it from what he had seen at home. What he had been taught. He opened his fist, just enough, just to fold over his fingers, just so it would do damage, not just hurt or sting.

But it wasn't a fist. He didn't hit her, his mind told him as he swung and punched Jackie across the side of her head, spinning her to the ground from the horrid cuff.

Jackie had tried to scoot back, while also trying to hold back the blood on her knee. Now she was turned sideways, laying on the dirt and gravel. Her head swam from Tommy hitting her across the face. It hurt, but more than that, it felt like she was disappearing into the darkness around her. She was losing the ability to focus, as if her mind couldn't believe what happened. She knew if she didn't get away from Tommy, he would only hurt her more. He would hit her. And hit her again. That's what they did. She knew what was coming. He would hit her until he broke her and then blame her for it and there was nothing she could do.

Jackie began to sweat, a cold ice of droplets from her head and back. It poured off of her, and she felt the cold shivers overcome her. She was going into shock. She felt like she was going to puke, which might be the only thing that would stop Tommy from touching her.

Her head swam as she felt her mind disappearing from itself. She knew it was bad, what was happening, and she tried to force her body to respond, but she was in a fugue. Her head clouded over. She felt herself rise up, but her legs weren't working. Somewhere in the clouds she saw Tommy leaning down, over her, close, pulling at her shirt, pulling her up by the collar, stretching it and twisting it. She felt the back of the collar tear at her neck, giving away from the stress of her own weight.

It was all she could do to hold on to his arm, using it to hold herself up, to stop him from tearing her shirt away.

Then she heard something, a vague banging. Shouting.

Lauren ran down the ramp toward the three of them, the two boys and their victim, shouting indistinctly.

Tommy let go and stood straight up, ready to fight another girl. He had now learned, "I can take on a girl and win," from the violent hit he placed on Jackie. "I can get away with it." Until the front door opened and Oak Meekins came out. A burly man, the owner of the restaurant, he had size on Tommy, and almost everyone else on the island. Tommy saw the big man coming, his fists clenched, ready to do damage, real damage, the kind that adults knew how to do. He was far more dangerous than Lauren or Jackie.

Tommy tried at first to speak up, "She started..." but Oak didn't slow down. Something in Tommy's head screamed over his bloodlust, "Run!" And Tommy ran to his pickup truck, abandoning donnie. He drove out, skidding in the dust, escaping into the night.

22
Wednesday, June 19ᵗʰ

"I'm alright."

It was an emphatic claim, and one expected by everyone, Jackie knew. She was the strong, positive one, the one who stood up to the bullies, the one no one would mess with.

Right up until now.

And she was shaken, no matter what her words said.

She knew, you hid these things. You didn't admit weakness or fear. That was akin to blame. She didn't want to be blamed for what happened to her. And if she was alright, then everyone would leave her alone.

But there was no one who thought she was alright.

Steve had come over in the evening, called by her father. "I don't know what to do," he had admitted. He knew what he wanted to do. He wanted to find the boy that had done this and kill him. It was a singular mind of parents when something happens to their child, especially a daughter. He couldn't say that, of course. He may have whispered it, in the quiet confines of his house, when he and Phyllis had held each other, scared, and relieved. Phyllis knew it could have been much, much worse.

"So, the sheriff already arrested the kid?" Steve asked. He was sullen, quiet, too, but with a snarl on his face that he tried to hide. He had looked at Jackie, who was bruised on the left side of her face, her neck still marked red, and with a big ugly gauze bandage wrapped over a big ugly swollen knee. She had it propped up, her bare foot dangling, small, tanned, a little white line from where her flip flops hid the sun from tanning her. Her toenails still were the de rigueur red. That would change as the days passed. She wouldn't be able to bend her leg to reach them to repaint her nails for some time.

Jackie tried to put on a brave face, but she was in pain. Tylenol did little to really cut the pain of her leg, and nothing broke the cold grip of shock, and the memory of what had happened. When she saw her father looking sad, she attempted to smile. When she saw Steve, and his own white toothed snarl, showing bared teeth, pointed canines seemingly sharp and ready to tear, she shivered again. She thought back to what Donnie had said to start all of this.

"Yes," answered Phyllis. "He's up in Manteo right now. The problem is, he'll still be able to get bail. The thought of having to go through all this again, and that *boy*," she said the word like only a mother could, with obvious hatefilled derision, "will still be able to walk around."

"They better put him under the jail," muttered Andy. His thin frame looked like a wire twisted taut. He needed to spring, to pop, just to get some release. Steve understood. He felt terrible for them, but he felt worse for Jackie.

She had opened up to him, been accepting, nice, just friendly, never expecting anything more that from him. She had shared the wonderful innocence of being seventeen, that perfect time, where nothing is important but everything is great. She was going to live forever, never grow old, spend every evening watching the sun set over her beach.

Now she had seen the first lessons of the real world. Bad things happen, sometimes really bad, horrible, awful, uncontrollable things that shake you. And they can't be taken back. And they can't be fixed. And they sometimes can't be punished. No matter what happened to him, she felt inside her heart, now cold, dark, afraid, that somehow Tommy would get away with this. He would blame her, he would go to jail, she hoped, maybe, and then he would get out and he would still see it as all her fault and none of his.

Jackie grimaced, this time the pain was greater in her head than her knee.

Steve saw her wipe away a tear that welled in her eye. He shivered, only inwardly. He hid the reaction from the outside world, but he felt her fear. The living room felt all plain and yellow, the lights of the evening glowing in an incandescent sandy amber. Decorative fish swam over driftwood, and a plant needed watering. It was all the usual decorations of a family that had made no steps yet to bond with their new home. It was so regular that the scent of Jackie's terror was almost overwhelming to Steve. It was the only thing he could notice in the room.

"Listen," he said to her, looking her in the eyes. He wanted to touch her, put his hand on her knee. People always wanted to touch a wound. It was a desire to hopefully soak out some of the pain, an imagined healing power that really only made things worse. Steve put his hands behind his back. There was nothing he could do to heal that wound any faster.

"You didn't do anything wrong," he went on. "Someone else did all this to you, and you reacted. What you are feeling, even if you don't want to tell us, or speak it or show it, know that's the part that *is* 'alright.' You don't have to be alright for us, for your parents. That's going to hurt." He pointed at her knee without touching it. "let it hurt. I mean," he tried to laugh, making Jackie smile a little as another tear welled up and spilled over, "still take your meds. You don't need to suffer or anything.

"But that's what I mean. Don't hide how you feel. Let your parents and friends help. You don't need to suffer by not talking about it. Don't keep it inside.

"I've seen this before," Steve felt himself slipping parts of his life into hers. He had to be careful. "It really helps to talk with someone. You discovered something. You feel like you can't trust people now. You're right, but in a way, it's not really that. Now you know, you *know*, that someone is a bad person. You can trust your feeling that he is just bad. But you can also find that you will trust others. Your parents, your friends, they all know this was hard on you, and they are happy you are, well," he hated to say it, but it was true, he knew all too well, "still here."

23

Tuesday, June 25th

Tommy Gray tried to mumble something under his breath, but he was afraid his father would hear it, even though his father was far away, inside the house. Tommy leaned over the engine bay of his old Ford pickup, with the hood open above him. He needed an excuse to be outside, and a place to hide. This was the best he was able to do.

It had been a week since he had assaulted Jackie. "Assaulted," he had snorted out the word, like he had done something wrong. In his mind he had just said to himself that he pushed someone who needed a beatin', but afterwards he had been warned, very well, to keep his mouth shut. He had been hauled up to Manteo in a sheriff's car after being pulled out of his house late that night. His father was mad as hell, but couldn't do anything. His mother cried, unbelieving that her sweet boy would ever hurt a girl. "She has to be lying," she said through shocked tears, "My boy wouldn't do anything like that. We're good Christian people. We raised him right." As he was being pulled out of his house, he proclaimed his innocence, thinking he could just yell his way out, "That stupid bitch started it! She's lyin'! I didn't touch her..." His father had grabbed him and told him, real firm, "Shut up. You don't say *anything* until I get there. Nothin', not a word, you got me? Or so help me…" And his father looked at the deputies that had his teenage son in handcuffs. They stared back, almost unsure as to how to respond. Sometimes, they just knew that a kid who misbehaved needed a parent to take care of the discipline, but in this case, the father seemed to be promising more than a whuppin' or taking away the car for a week. To his credit, Tommy's father let go of his grip on his son and said nothing else. He knew where the boundaries were, at least with witnesses present.

So Tommy had traveled in silence to the jail in Manteo. They had to keep him overnight in a holding room. The jailer and the deputy both had made it clear that if they put him in the regular overnight pen, and he was dumb enough to run his mouth about what he had done, he'd probably get the living shit beat out of him. And they didn't want to deal with the paperwork. So Tommy had stewed in a room by himself. He thought about letting them know just what he thought of those deputies. He would show them who really was in charge. But they had guns and he didn't. That's the way he saw it.

The next morning his father showed up at his bail hearing, and had sprung him as soon as a bondsman could post bail. They rode back in silence, because while Tommy wasn't afraid of those deputies who thought they were so tough, he knew not to say anything to his father. It was a long hour's ride.

The rest of the week had been uneventful. Tommy walked on eggshells around the house. His mother had crying fits that made his father stew. He didn't like it when his wife cried. All his father did was glare at Tommy every time she cried.

Tommy knew it wasn't his fault. His mother was just trying to make him feel bad. It was that stupid girl's fault. She crushed Tommy's foot, and hit Donnie in the face. She didn't even get charged.

But Tommy kept quiet. Sooner or later, things would be back to normal. At least until the trial.

It had been a week since all that. Since the crying and the arrest and the silence and the glaring. Tommy had hoped that today would be the back to normal day, the day he could finally leave the house. He was getting a little sick of his parents.

Then came the phone call.

"Yes," was all his father said. It was all that Tommy heard. He didn't pay attention to his father's calls too much. This one might be about him, though. Maybe his lawyer. They had found a lawyer in Raleigh to defend Tommy, and that had stewed his father even more. His mother had insisted they defend her baby. She had explained the defense clearly. "He's a good boy."

"Yes… I understand…" His father sounded resigned. It was a tone Tommy wasn't used to. Whenever his father dealt with Tommy, the father was in charge, the tone was Do As I Say Or Else, and the Or Else was not what Tommy wanted to get, again.

His father hung up the phone, turned and walked slowly over to Tommy. He didn't say anything. Tommy just stood there. Things were going better. He wasn't going to do anything to screw it up, like asking who it was on the phone or if it was about him.

It obviously was.

Tommy's father stood in front of him, simmering for only a second. Behind the hate was this mix of feelings in his eyes. Sadness, regret, that was there, but also resignation, like his whole body sighed in realization.

Then he raised his fist and hit Tommy in his left eye.

After Tommy had finally gotten up, which was after the yelling from his father and the crying from his mother, he found his way outside. He just muttered, "I'm gonna work on my truck." He didn't have the keys. His father had just made it clear he wasn't going anywhere the rest of the summer, except to jail, and then he wasn't coming back to this house.

So Tommy hid his black swollen eye under the hood of his truck and mumbled. He wouldn't dare say anything about his father hitting him. If he had to, he'd blame the black eye on someone in the jail. No one had seen him since he had come back. Getting beat up by another prisoner wasn't something to be proud of, but he'd figure out something, just in case. His friends would believe him at least.

So he mumbled in the darkening sky under the dark hood. It didn't matter. He just needed a dark place to hide so no one could see his tears. He couldn't even wipe them off. His left eye was almost swollen shut and hurt like hell.

"Stupid bitch," he mumbled. That made him feel better, a little. He said it again, louder this time, "Stupid bitch!" He knew who he was really talking about, though. There was no way he could blame Jackie for this. This was his father's fault. And whoever called.

His ears were ringing, his nose dripping, and his eyes blinded by tears and darkness, so he didn't see anyone coming. Not that he would have if Tommy still held all his faculties. A black shape moved through the trees. It was tall, and moved gracefully, more like a hunting animal, ready to kill out of instinct. It made no footfalls. It was completely silent. Even its breathing was silent, a wet slow pattern quieter than the soft summer breeze.

Tommy looked up, not into the trees, but at the house with its warm lights. Completely unwelcoming to him. Tommy knew he couldn't go in until the lights went off. His parents didn't want to see their shame in the house tonight. The lights from the house blinded him to anything in the darkness. Tommy wasn't looking for anything from the trees. He wasn't afraid of anything out there, only from inside the house.

He turned back to stare at the engine.

Something slammed into his back, pinning him to the grill, pushing his head down onto the big air filter. He felt pain, lots of it, from all over his body. A hand, or something, pushed down on his shoulder. He felt fingernails digging into him through his shirt. For an instant, he remembered digging into Jackie's arm the same way, only this felt like it was worse. It felt like razors, or claws. They were going inside him.

He tried to turn, to squirm out of the grip, but all that did was allow the long nails to dig deeper into his flesh. He felt his body begin to tear. "Ow, hey, you're hurting me!" He wondered how his father had gotten out there without Tommy noticing. But this felt nothing like his father's thick weighty body.

Something stuck its knee into Tommy's back. That was what pinned him to the truck. It was pointed, digging into his spine. Tommy remembered the time he had clipped a kid in football, injuring the boy's back. He felt his own back begin to stretch farther than it should.

Another hand, or something like a hand, snatched his hair and pushed his head down onto the engine. Tommy felt the breath of an animal. Something, definitely not human, had come up and attacked him. A bear maybe. He heard the heavy violent breathing just behind his neck. Claws dug into his shoulder and head, pulling at his scalp and skin.

He had to find a way to escape, or protect himself. He tried to arch his back, to make himself into a ball. That's what he heard you are supposed to do with bears.

The bony knee thing released. Then he felt it jam up hard into his spine. Whatever it was had kicked him, hard. Tommy's neck tried to spasm in the pain, but he couldn't move. His mouth opened onto the dusty air filter. He tasted the dirt and sand from the engine. The smell of oil and taste of grease began to mingle with other smells, especially urine where he wet himself. Tommy tried to fight off the urge to loose his bowels, with only limited success.

The bear was going to bite him in the neck, he knew it. He had to do something. This animal, bear, whatever it was would tear him apart if he didn't fight back. But he couldn't do anything to save himself.

For a moment, only a few heartbeats, it seemed like the thing stopped. Tommy was too frightened to try to jerk away. The nails were still dug inches into his shoulder and arm. He felt the head come closer to him, a warm musky breathing. Tommy tasted the hate.

Then it spoke.

"You like hurting girls." It said. "You like being a bully. Then you cry when it happens to you." The sound of the voice was soft, but like the hissing of a snake, with a weird accent, almost a quiet scream. It was terrifying. Tommy gave up trying to hold back his bowels as he felt himself shit is own pants. The voice was horrifying. "You blame her for what you did. We can't have that," the thing was insistent. "You need to learn a lesson."

Tommy wanted to beg that he knew what he had done, and that it was his fault. He wanted to blame his father, who taught him how to bully women, but he knew somewhere deep down that wasn't the answer this thing wanted. He discovered how right he was when it lifted his head up.

Then it slammed his head hard into the engine bay.

Tommy felt a lot of things break. Certainly a tooth came out. He might have felt a crack in his jaw or cheek. His face was definitely torn open, because when he lifted his head up, he felt a stream of blood, thick, hot, pouring down into the engine.

"I'm sorry!" it came out as whimper, and a garbled one at that, but he knew he had to do something or he would get his head crushed. One arm was free, but all he could do was flail it around harmlessly. He tried to push the body of the monster, the thing on him back. All he felt was bits of cloth and hair.

The thing didn't like that. It pushed him down again. Tommy felt the cut on his cheek get worse. "No, you need to *learn*." It said with a hiss of hate.

"You did it. Say it."

"I did it," it was all he could get out.

"No say it all. What did you do? Say it all."

Tommy flinched. It wasn't in his nature to admit his fault. The claws dug in deep. He felt blood begin to pour onto his arm where the wounds were. Muscles were ripping. This thing would tear his arm off if he didn't do what he was told.

"I hit her. I beat her up, okay? I did it." It was about the best he could do. Throughout his entire life, his mind had never taught him to admit he was wrong, especially when he knew he was wrong.

"You will learn," said the thing. "You won't ruin our life here. From now on, you admit what you did. If you ever blame her for anything, if you say those words again, I will be here to find you.

"Now, say who's fault it was. All of it."

Tommy heard something creak.

"Say it."

Tommy cried. He couldn't admit he was the person who did it. He couldn't.

The hood came down on his back. Inside, he screamed. The hood lifted up again, and came down again. The hinges creaked with each drop.

"Say it. Who's fault is all this. We already know. You have to say it to you.

"Or do you get the hood again?"

Tommy wasn't sure if he would survive the next few moments. He had to say it. His brain that was trying to protect its body and and his mind that was trying to defend the indefensible battled. Tommy knew he had to admit it.

"It's my fault. I'm the one who did all that to Jackie. I did it all. I hurt her, I hit her, I did it!"

"You will tell everyone that you did it. You'll never blame anyone else again. Or this gets finished. Do you understand?'

"Yes…" it came out only as a sob.

The thing let go.

Tommy slid down the front of his truck to the gravel drive. He didn't even care that the stones dug into his body. Anything was better than the death grip on him. His breathing was labored. He probably had broken ribs. Blood poured from his mouth and face. He felt his body begin to go cold, even though it was a warm night. Sweat ran down his forehead, mixing with blood. His back was drenched as it poured over him. He felt himself go dizzy. His head lolled as he gave in and let his body fall flat. He couldn't stop from passing out if he wanted to. And he didn't want to.

"Am I going to die?" he wondered. "I hope so."

The last thing he saw before he passed out was the darkness of the trees swaying in the night.

24
Wednesday, June 26th

Tim played a song. It was all he could do. "This is where I'm at now," he thought. He was too old to have to cope with what was going on in the villages. "First that poor girl on the beach," he thought. She was, what, 22 years old? Okay, not a girl, but a girl compared to Tim's age. "Then Ellen in my car. Then poor Jackie, she gets the shit beat out of her by two boys, *that's* just creepy as hell," he thought. Tim double checked to make sure his microphone was off. There was no one in the studio, no one else in the whole building, as Steve wasn't due for hours yet. "And now the boy that beat up Jackie, he gets attacked by a bear? C'mon…" Tim knew well and good that no bear attacked that kid Tommy. Even if nobody was saying anything, they were all saying it. Everyone knew his dad beat the hell out of that boy.

"No matter what the kid did," Tim thought, "No one deserves to have a father like that." It was such a weird thing to think. In the days after Jackie's attack, he had wanted to find the boy and beat the shit out of him with a big stick. The whole community wanted to get their hands on him.

And now, here he was defending him.

Tim shook the thoughts from his head. He was too old to go beating up kids, he thought. Then he realized that's why he thought what he thought. He was old enough to know better. An adult grows, takes the lumps of a lifetime, and comes out better for it. A dad is supposed to help raise a child, make them come out better. Tommy's dad didn't do that. "At all," Tim insisted to the empty DJ booth. He said it out loud just so he could tell it to himself. He was right, and he was reminding himself that he was right. If he had a kid, and the kid had done something that horrendous, he still would have tried his best to protect his own son. A dad beating up a son because the son beat up a girl explained a lot.

He wondered where beating the dad to a pulp fell on the spectrum of crummy behavior.

"Still, the kid got what's coming to him."

Tim couldn't report on any of this on the radio. He had no evidence, there were no reports to quote, even though everyone knew it had happened. He couldn't go on the air and say anything.

But it just felt so weird how these things were suddenly happening on the island. There had to be a reason.

25
Friday, June 28ᵗʰ

Steve had made his phone call. He realized he needed to two nights ago, the night he came home angry, sweaty, shirtless from a late night run. He had worked off his anger over what had happened to Jackie with what worked best for him. He let loose his inner anger, that frustration, on a long, fast, physically draining run. He had learned the roads and paths where he could run without being seen. If anyone saw him running at full speed, a marathon pace, these Hatteras people would have freaked. They were a strange, superstitious people, distrusting in the outside world. He felt his anger flare again. There was no time for a run tonight. A cold shower, then off to work.

Music hath charms that soothe the savage beast.

He often said the quote in his head. He knew that it meant something to him. His show would be a decidedly mellower sound this night. He needed something to calm the rage he felt.

He wouldn't get it.

When he got to the station, Tim had something to show him. "So, those Legacy people are up to something again," he started on about the church and their petition of hate. Tim refused to even call them the Island Legacy Church. They did nothing for the island, though the group certainly was isolating, and their beliefs had nothing to do with any church Tim had ever been in. "Hell, I think even the Satanists wouldn't be as awful as these people," he had once said.

"What's up now?" Steve fairly groaned out the question.

"Okay, I don't know what to start with first," Tim picked up a newspaper. Better ease him into it, he thought. "So, these Legacy as… uh, weirdoes, took this ad out in the local fishwrapper," The Inlet was a simple magazine style paper, just a few pages, black and white, with a one color banner. It was mostly for local businesses to advertise and have a list of a few events in the towns listed. There was usually a picture of a big fish caught or a student getting an award. In this one there was a big ad announcing the Island Legacy Church was reopening the old church building, with a call to the righteous, and the righteous only, to come. "Be free from sin!" it exhorted, "Come receive God's reward NOW!"

"Subtle, aren't they?"Steve mocked them.

"Yeah," Tim snorted back. "And look here," he pointed to an icon in one corner. Steve stared at the small circle with a slash through it. "Is that a guitar?!" He almost laughed at the absurdity of it. "So, the Legacy Church has declared war on Rock 'n' Roll, huh? Ask the ghost of Elvis how that turned out."

"That's not the worse of it," Tim waved Steve over to the desk, as he checked his watch. He had a minute, maybe a bit more. "Listen to this." Tim played a message on the answering service.

"We know who you are, and what you do. Rock music is a sin against God, and you will burn for it! Repent and leave! Or face the wrath of an angry God!"

Steve looked at Tim, who waved him back toward the DJ booth. They both went in, with the song soon coming out. Tim simply switched tables and played another song in, then they got up and left again. Tim closed the door. For some reason, he felt better away from the microphone for once.

"I don't know what these nuts are up to, I tell ya that for free." Tim didn't seem worried. He seemed mad. "But I can't really do much about it. I really think they had something to do with Ellen's death. I think they were after me." He hated to say it out loud. It meant he was partly responsible. If he hadn't loaned her the car, maybe she would still be alive.

But then, he wouldn't.

Steve said nothing. It was a lot to hear. He didn't want to believe that a group of people would be so cruel as to blow a person up, but then, he had seen a lot of cruelty, a lot worse than that.

He couldn't talk with Tim about all that. Not now. Probably not ever. Tim didn't seem ready for all that stuff. Instead he just commented.

"Subtle."

Tim nodded, and added a word of his own.

"Assholes."

26
Friday, July 12th

It had been two weeks since the phone message that Tim had played for Steve. It was unfortunately only the first of many. After a week, when every evening the phone would ring and a new message was left, all the same version of the first, Tim simply unplugged the phone and turned off the answering machine. He wasn't sure if he should even mention that he no longer had a phone at the station. It would only encourage the Legacy people that they were getting under his skin.

But Steve was tired of the harassment. He and Tim had tried to talk with the sheriff. Sheriff Midgette had contacted the church, and Pastor Darrow had made a point not only to deny any involvement, but to also overtly suggest that any hint of impropriety without proof would be reported to his lawyers. When Midgette talked with his deputy that attended the church, he was met with a sullen mix of silence and defiant commentary. He had come back to the station saying that until something happened, there was little he could do.

Tim was crestfallen. He didn't like how his station, meant to be a lighthouse to the community, now was a target from a small portion, full of hate. Isiah Farrow had stayed on, but Tim could tell he was a little reluctant to be there later in the day. Tim had let the high school kid, Kelly Meyers, go. Kelley had been pretty defiant. He liked the attention he got at school, and was really getting into the job. Kelly hoped to get a regular time slot as a jock in the future. But Tim had talked privately with Kelly's parents. They just couldn't take the worry that something would happen to their son. Tim had agreed. He said that once things calmed down, Kelly could come back.

"If things ever got back to normal around here," he had said to himself much later.

But Steve Brodie couldn't stand how these people were bullying and hurting so many others. Poor Jackie was just the evidence photo. Behind the scenes, kids were being told to turn off the radio at home, especially when some family members came over. Sponsors were still being pressured, and Steve had noticed how the radio was turned down in stores when he was out on his nights off. There was so much more going on behind the scenes, and he knew it.

He felt it.

What concerned him the most was how, even though all the calls had said different versions of things, "stop playing your music," "repent and leave," "You are going to Hell," a personal favorite of Steve's, one message was always there, right at the beginning.

"We know who you are."

He had no idea what it meant, but it bothered him. No one there knew him. They knew Steve Brodie, the star DJ, the voice, the name, but no one knew him. He made sure of that. There were very few people in the whole country who ever did know him, and most of those were dead. His history belonged almost entirely to him, alone.

Yet he kept feeling like there was more to everything, this sense of control, demand, lies, and hate. So much hate.

He was going to find out just what these people at this Island Legacy Church knew about him.

He just had to wait until dark.

27

The old community building that The Island Legacy Church had been using as their church was on its last days. It had been bought and paid for long ago. Reverend Darrow didn't bother to pursue any provenance to the building and land. The "Legacy" in Island Legacy Church started with him, as far as he was concerned. He had acquired the deed to the community building personally from the church non-profit account about a year ago, once the intent to rebuild the historic church on the sound side started in earnest. As soon as the "new" church opened there, he was going to put the "old" one up for sale to the highest bidder. Several locals put up a fight on that. They complained that their fathers and grandfathers helped build it, and that it should go back to the community. Reverend Darrow used that idea in one of his sermons.

"If you *want* something, it must be earned. It cannot be given to you. You do not just ask for a blessing from heaven; God doesn't give those out freely to the weak and poor. He saves his blessings for those who earn them."

Privately, he had been even more blunt. "If you want it, buy it. I don't care where the money comes from. I can't just give it away.

"That's Communism."

Boy, those folks didn't like being called Commies.

The rebuilt church looked great. It was almost ready for his first sermon, and Darrow had planned a doozy. He was going to get his parishioners so riled up that they would do anything for him, and give anything to him that he asked. And the rest of the island would show up, just to hear what he said.

Darrow had noticed a slight uptick in numbers. The bulletin counts were going up by ten a week. And the collection plate was getting a little more filled.

"They are afraid to be left out," he said to himself. "Gotta get on God's good graces." He laughed at that thought.

Darrow stood in the empty nave of the church. It was all white walls and brown pews, with comfy red plush cushions. The best money could buy. Already the air conditioning was cranked down to a chilly temperature. It was a few days til Sunday, but that was just the way Darrow liked it.

Hanging from the ceiling, dangling over his head, was the giant mirrored cross. It was unlike the usual wooden simple crosses, or the fake gold brass standards that most churches had, "Like them Methodists," Darrow chuckled. It was one of the items that was insisted to be in the church. It looked old, with a faded mirror and broken mercury black veins crackling through it. It was obviously a reminder of the mirrors given to parishioners. As if to continually be a reminder of how they were better than everyone. "Look at me!" Darrow huffed, "I'm at *church*!" That made everything they did the rest of the week okay.

Outside, the summer evening just began to burn down. No expenses spared out there, either. No gravel and shell parking lot. There was a well lined blacktop, with lots of lined spaces. There was the de riguer basketball hoop at one end. Darrow had put in a bit of the concrete surface himself a month ago. All churches had to have a basketball court, he knew. At least this one still had a net on the rim. The kids would tear it down from hanging on it in due time. They would pretend they could dunk like real players, like the blacks, Darrow thought. Most of them couldn't get a foot off the ground. He should have lowered the rim for them.

And all around the lot and the church it was perfectly landscaped. Boxwood hedges, a few twisted oaks still left around the parking lot. They always looked good. A yaupon grew by the sign. We had to have one of those, for the old timers, Darrow knew. And all across the edge of the property, as well as along the church, even in a mix with some hydrangeas, were scads of tall blue buttercups.

His benefactor had insisted. It had cost a small fortune to bring them in, already grown, and then water them in so that they would take root and flourish. He had no idea why these flowers in particular. Actinum, they were called. Some knew them as Monkshood. It was a pretty flower. He had made a note to remind the parishioners not to pick the flowers, as they could make them sick.

"Maybe he just likes blue," Darrow thought. Who cares? He pictured the congregation, crowded in the church, shoving money into the collection plates as he stirred them up to a fever pitch that Sunday morning. Blessing them all, blessing the money.

Then, when they were all gone, he would lock the doors and throw the money and coins and checks all over the floor. Then, he would have Darla, sweet, sexy Darla in her too tight dress, with the cold air conditioning blowing very, very cold, take off all her clothes and stand in the middle of it naked for him.

That would be the right way to christen this place.

Then he would be in his god's good graces.

Darrow left the church and locked the doors. It was getting late.

28

Jackie was alone in her house all day. It didn't help her mood to have her mind wander with no other distractions besides her thoughts. Everyone, everyone that mattered to a teenage girl that is, which pretty much meant anyone in her high school that was about her age, was talking about how Tommy got the shit beaten out of him. Some of Tommy's friends had spoken to other friends, a very small branch of the coconut telegraph for teenagers on the island, and had told some version of his story. Something attacked him. It may have seen like a bear, but it was a person, and it wasn't his father. It was something monstrous, scary, scary enough to keep Tommy from coming out of his house.

Jackie was glad to know that, for once, now, Tommy, the shit for brains punk that had beat her up and down, and had ripped her knee open, was the one trapped inside. Jackie couldn't do much; she couldn't really go to the beach, much less swim, and she couldn't ride her bike, but her knee had healed to a dull and very ugly puss filled scab that usually stopped splitting open every time she bent it. Her bruises had healed enough that a bit of makeup covered what was left. She could walk around the neighborhood without jumping at every noise and surprise behind her back.

But she was alone. Her friends had come to see her, but only when their parents told them to. Most of the time, she was with her parents. But tonight, they left her alone. Her father was out of town, and her mother had gone to Virginia for an overnight. "You have to leave me alone at some time," she had said, the bitter whine of a teen emphasizing that she didn't want to be treated like a little kid.

But now her voice in her head kept being the only one talking to her.

She kept hearing all the noise, all the garbage that had been said, all the lies about Steve, how he had killed that girl. How he was some monster...

A monster... The words and descriptions came back in her head. He only goes out at night, he killed that woman and drank her blood, all the weird maniacal ideas that came out of some dumb fifteen year old boy, but said enough, it preyed on her dreams and thoughts. "What if he had done all that?" she wondered. "What if he really was a vampire?"

It was a stupid thought. Vampires weren't real. She knew that.

Even though the grandparents of most of the kids around here were superstitious as hell. They believed in ghosts, phantom fiddle players, witches, demon bulls, sea monsters, everything but what science showed them, it seemed. Down in Ocracoke they thought skeletons climbed out of graves and the dead walked the streets.

She realized she didn't really know much about Steve Brodie, except what he had told her, and what she had seen on MTV. He really did only go out when it got dark. "At least, only at twilight," she realized. She had never seen him in the full light of day. "And he never invites me in to his house," she thought to herself. "That's a vampire thing?" She couldn't remember if it was that vampires don't invite people in their houses or they can't come into your house without an invitation.

Then she remembered she invited him over for dinner.

Jackie began wondering just who Steve Brodie really was. She couldn't ride her bike, only walk, but his house wasn't far. It was getting dark already. She turned on her radio, already tuned to

WZHX, and immediately Steve Brodie's recognizable voice came over the air, with a lead in to a song by Aerosmith.

"Those church people are gonna have a fit with that!" Jackie said. She didn't necessarily care about the song. She had just heard Steve's voice on the radio. She knew he was at the station, twenty minutes away. And not at his home.

This would be her opportunity to see who was Steve Brodie.

29

Steve sat, still and quiet, hidden in the night behind a copse of trees and a twisted yaupon bush. The darkness that enveloped him was a double edged sword. People were afraid of the dark, especially right now, with monstrous boogiemen and bloodthirsty killers on the prowl all over Hatteras. People were locking their doors at night, traveling in groups even just out to their cars. They didn't like things in the dark.

The lateness of the hour meant most people were in bed, or at least home, by now. He had waited until after midnight to leave the radio station, to return back up to Buxton, near his home. Now he was alone, in the dark, the syrupy inky blackness of the shadows of trees, even darker than the night. The good part of the darkness was that no one would see him.

The bad part was that if someone saw him, they would know he was up to no good. No one was out prowling around the island in the middle of the night, in the dark. No one but the killers and monsters all the islanders feared. It made him extra cautious, moving silently now that he was in the woods.

His destination was the rebuilt church that the Island Legacy group had built. They were causing too many problems in the community. Everyone knew they were speaking out against the radio station, and Steve in particular. But he kept feeling like they had something more to do with that poor woman's death on the beach. And he knew they were stirring up people like Tommy Gray to commit violence. There had been more men beating on women, threatening some women owned shops, and a lot more threats toward the new employees at the fishery. The new housing development had slowed considerably, and Steve, along with everyone else, noticed a distinct lack of color in the few people moving in. Most of the black families that had planned on purchasing a house had backed out. The houses and wood that had burned off near the sound still sat there, charred to ash, waiting to be removed. The only people happy about all this seemed to be the Island Legacy members, who seemed delighted to have run out the families.

No one admitted to anything, of course. They knew well enough not to say a word, neither perpetrator nor victim. Most of the islanders were afraid of retribution. The wives and girlfriends had long learned from their abusers to shut up and not make more problems. That was the way the abusers liked it. It kept them in power, and kept their victims quiet and fearful. Steve pictured a poor wife, long suffering, continually cleaning that one spot on a counter, too fearful to move around the house until her husband left.

It was easier, for everyone, to just keep quiet. Just keep quiet and no one gets hurt. "That's what they always said in the bank robbery movies," Steve said to himself. "Right up until they start killing someone."

What was the other line? "No one go be a hero." That was it. Now Steve was sneaking through the woods at night to go break into a church. He worried how much of a problem this might cause, especially if he got caught. He didn't feel like a hero. "At least I have one way out of it," he sighed, knowing one thing he could do, that no one, definitely not these Legacy nuts, would suspect.

He crept through the trees, following the road to the church on the sound side. As he turned along the bend in the street, he saw lights, just a little glow. It wasn't coming from the church, but more like the parking lot. Steve was curious first, but not worried, not yet. If someone was there this late at night, just like he had thought before, they were up to nothing good. He would take his time.

He moved deeper into the woods, trying to keep as far from the church as possible, without losing sight of the lights. They were a strange mix of soft warmth, almost a dying fire, but they didn't move nor flicker. The lights were stationary, whatever they were.

Steve finally made it around to the far south side of the church. He could see what the lights were now. A truck, some sort of off-road vehicle, idled right in front of the doors of the church. Its headlights were off, but the parking lights gave off an amber and red glow from the front and back. The dome light, yellow and hazed on the inside, lit up the empty front seats. Even from where he was, Steve could tell the engine was still running.

He also recognized the vehicle. The big light on the top gave it away. It was the sheriff's Blazer, the same one Steve rode in to bring back Linda Patterson's headless body.

Steve got closer. If anyone was there, especially the sheriff, he wanted to know what they were doing. The Blazer certainly was conspicuous and not a good vehicle for clandestine meetings. "Where's the sheriff?" he wondered.

His body tingled a little. It was a strange and somewhat unpleasant feeling. It was not something he was used to, but he simply marked it up to a strange rush of adrenaline late at night. It was unusual for him, though. He felt his body stretch a little, as if his bones were growing, and he felt his gorge rise. It was only a small bit of nausea, but again, not normal for him, even in this situation.

He put aside his feelings, and moved forward. He needed to see what was going on, and that meant getting closer. The church was dark, its doors closed, and no lights on inside. He had not bothered to look closely at the Blazer since first seeing it was empty.

Steve parted through the tall plants that bordered the parking lot. He felt his body begin to itch now. At the same moment, he saw a shape by the running truck. As he moved, the lights from the car changed the shadows they cast, and he could see a large black lump on the ground by the open driver's door. It was obviously a person, definitely overweight, and not moving as it lay flat on the parking lot.

Steve lurched forward, suddenly panting. He realized first one thing. Poor Sheriff Midgette was probably dead on the ground there. No one else looked like the big man. His body was still and splayed by his car. Steve had to get closer just in case. He noticed that there was no strange scent of death, no feeling of a deceased body nearby, even though Sheriff Midgette was not moving. When he went to smell, all he got was a clogging feeling of cloying sickly sweetness that made him cough. He moved without thought or concern now, his brain starting to fog. As he got near the truck, he could see that Sheriff Midgette was definitely dead. His throat was cut almost in half, with blood poured out over his stretched and stuffed uniform.

Then Steve realized one other thing. He looked around, wondering who would have done this, and if they were still around. He saw no one. The church was as quiet and dark as a sepulcher. No one was there. But he could finally make out the yard and parking lot to see the way he had walked in. He saw the tall green plants with the blue flowering cups all along the edge of the property, dark blue, almost black, but just different enough in the amber glow. He didn't need the headlights to see what they were.

Steve realized, just as he felt himself begin to fall into cold sweats and dry heaves, that someone at the church knew his secret.

30

Jackie had snuck out of her house under the cover of darkness. It wasn't like this was the first time. She had, on occasion, met her friends at the beach at night, but this was the first time she had been out since her attack. Her parents had been understanding of her wanderlust, but had made it clear, with the increase in violence not only to her, but to her assailant, and the general edge of anger and hatred that seemed to permeate the island made them very uncomfortable with her going out, even with her friends.

But this time she wasn't going to the beach where other people would be. If she was successful in her clandestine exploits, no one would see her or know she had even left.

Jackie kept well to the shadows on her short trip. She had seen the occasional light far away, through the trees to the west, and could hear the soft steady drone of trucks just off to the east on Highway 12. But no car had come down the dusty oyster shell road where Steve's house sat, tucked away under the trees, darker still than the rest of the night. The trees gave the place an eerie shade, as if there was a second darkness, a cloak draped over the top branches, that stopped even the sparkle of stars from filtering through.

There was no Jeep parked in the yard; Jackie knew there wouldn't be. Steve was locked in a small box playing music for at least another two hours, and wouldn't be home any time soon. Plenty of time to snoop.

She still had the words of the kids from school in her head. She didn't know why she let them live there, but there they were. He's a vampire, he never comes out during the day. He killed that girl and drank her blood.

She was in love with him.

That one still stung.

She wasn't in love with Steve Brodie. Yes, he was good looking, charming, and she liked him, and maybe she thought about him when he wasn't around. But she wasn't in love.

"Am I?"

It wasn't something to wonder about. She didn't fall in love with every cute boy that showed up on her beach.

Yet he certainly was in her head.

No, he wasn't a vampire. But he had charmed her, that was for sure.

She just needed to know. She needed to know something.

"I'm not breaking in," she told herself. The window had never been locked. When Steve's house had been empty, the front window had lost its lock, and could just be slid up so Jackie could climb inside the front room, as long as there wasn't a screen in it. Most of the time there hadn't been a screen. But most of the time, she had no reason to climb into an empty old house. She had done it in the past just because she could.

Now, she felt like she had to.

Jackie stood in the tiny front room, looking around. "What am I looking for? A coffin?" she didn't know what she would find.

It was too dark to see anything. Jackie discovered that when she barked her shin on a low table. Her flashlight would be a risk, but a calculated one. She would see any car coming up the road long before it got there. She could easily turn her light off.

She shone the light around the little room. It looked into both a tiny kitchen and a tiny dining room, with a few clean plates in the former, and a small table and two chairs in the latter. The house was remarkably tidy. No empty beer cans, no dirty plate, no bag of chips. The floor looked swept and clean.

"Vampires are neat freaks, right?" she asked herself. She only knew they drank blood, slept in coffins during the day, and could change into bats. "And had fangs." Steve didn't have fangs. Well, not really. He did have white and pointed canines. She knew that smile intimately.

She walked through the dining room toward Steve's bedroom. "No coffin here," she noted out loud, just to tell all the others who were listening. She never believed he was a vampire. Not a bit.

The bedroom looked nice, with a well made bed, a soft, fluffy and worn comforter. The room smelled of sweetness and wood, Steve's cologne. Another scent she easily recognized.

On the wall, she saw a deep frame. It held a large knife in a sheath and a small medal. She shone her light onto it. The knife was unremarkable. It looked like a large camping knife, or more likely an old Army knife. Jackie only assumed that because the medal was a Purple Heart. There was no name attached, but she assumed it belonged to Steve's father. He had never said anything about serving in the military. And the knife was certainly old.

As she left the bedroom, she saw a sharp twinkling from the windowsill across the room. There was a cheap wicker bowl on the sill, and it held a small wealth of glass bottles. All were tiny, strange containers, almost like perfume bottles, which held various liquids of different colors. They were different shapes and designs. One was sharply faceted with a pointed top and a wide, flat bottom that contained a small amount of brown liquid. Another was a worn blue bottle, looking something like what she might find washed up on the shore. It was simply corked, but then sealed with a hardened wad of red wax. None of them were labeled. Most of the little vials were noticeable in that the liquid was sealed inside. There was no way to unscrew or uncork any except the blue bottle. Whatever was in there was going to stay unless the vials were broken open.

She set the bottles down and looked about. Shining the flashlight across the house, she had seen everything. There was nothing amiss, nothing to even define Steve. Not only were there no souvenirs or posters of Blackbeard, there were no pictures of anyone, no family, no vanity shots of him with Bruce Springsteen or Prince. On one wall was a collection of records, all stacked in straight lines. A table had a streamlined and fancy stereo with a turntable. His desk had nothing but a pen and yellow pad, with nothing on it. The only decor were a couple sand dollars and starfish, along with two big whelks on each side of a fireplace that was obviously unused in the summer heat. Above the mantle were sketches of ducks, a male and female, facing each other, from four feet away. The duck motif was a requirement of any old beach house on the Outer Banks, Jackie thought. Every old home had those. They had been there before Steve moved in.

"Well, might as well see where he cleans his fangs," Jackie quipped to herself. She headed to the bathroom, not knowing what she expected to find. Acne cream? Striped toothpaste? A box of condoms? What was his secret? He seemed to have nothing. Maybe he really was nothing more than a good looking DJ. "Not that that's a bad thing," She thought to herself.

The bathroom was no different than anywhere else in the house. Except that the bath towel was askew, and a washcloth was still wet as it dangled over the sink to dry. "He took a shower before work," Jackie said unnecessarily. It was obvious. She tried very hard to prove to everyone else in the room that she wasn't even slightly thinking about him getting out of a hot shower. She didn't do a good job, and she was the only one there.

But there just seemed to be something… off.

There was something wrong in the bathroom, but she couldn't figure it out. It was cleaner than hers, cleaner than her parents', even. Steve had an older razor on the sink, along with a badger brush and mug. Her father used a disposable Gillette and shaving gel from a can. But that wasn't it. Steve just had a different razor, is all.

Then she realized. How did he shave?

There was no mirror on the wall.

Her confusion slowly began to make connections, when she saw the lights shine into the house.

Steve had come back home.

31

"Who are you?"

It was a better question than, "What are you doing here?"

Thomas Fredericks had entered the little cottage with a key left for him under the front mat. "These must be trusting people," he had thought. He had never been to Hatteras before. He had only been to North Carolina once, and that was to Asheville, where it was cold and crisp, but steep, sharp, not like Ohio and Pennsylvania. Here in Hatteras it was still hot, and soft, and thick even in the middle of the night in the summer heat.

When he came in and turned on the light from a switch by the door, he had found a girl laying on the floor, until that moment, in the dark, with a wrapped welt on her knee that looked like it was getting more painful by the moment.

She was young, a teenager, obviously. Not robbing the place, not with that beat up knee. At least, not a smart move with that bad a wound. She likely banged an already wounded leg on something in the dark and had fallen over. She was obviously in pain, as he could see tears welling in her eyes as she clutched at her knee while rolling on the floor. She had been trying to leave when he pulled up.

So he knew, mostly, what she was doing here.

Who she was, that was a different matter.

She certainly was too young for Steve to be seeing as a girlfriend, unless he had significantly changed his preferences in the past few years. Which was unlikely.

So, he asked, "Who are you?"

"Who are *you*?!"

Insolent, but brave, Thomas thought. He respected that, especially with her on the floor, injured, in someone else's home.

"I'm Thomas Fredericks. I'm Steve Brodie's" he tried not to pause as he had to think of just where he was in time, "uncle." A lie. He could be closer to a cousin, but at his age, an obvious 65 years old, with whitening hair still cut short from his time in the Army, he didn't look like Steve's cousin, so uncle it was. "Now," he continued, "who are you?"

It had taken a few moments, but Jackie relaxed just enough to let Thomas help her to the sofa. He immediately went to the kitchen and got a bag of frozen corn, which he put on Jackie's knee very gently. Thomas looked through a cabinet near the refrigerator for some Tylenol, wondering the whole time if Steve even kept the stuff in his house. "Other people get headaches, Steve," Thomas had once said to Steve, long ago.

He listened as Jackie explained she was a friend of Steve's. "I thought he might be home. He's a night owl, and I was out. I can't sleep, with my knee, you know..." she trailed off. Thomas pointedly did not look at her. He knew she was lying, but his stare would give away that he knew in a heartbeat, and he didn't want to scare the girl any more than she already was. She certainly didn't let herself in with the key, since the door was locked, and wasn't waiting for Steve, since the lights were out. But he wasn't going to call her on it. The last thing he needed was a panicky teenage girl trying to call the police at midnight, and all the explaining and attention it would draw.

"So..." Thomas sighed, "Steve's not here, huh? I was supposed to meet him tonight. You know where he is?"

"Probably at the radio station," Jackie answered, too quickly. If she knew he was at the station, she knew he wasn't home.

"Well, he said he would be out tonight, but to meet him here." Thomas tried to let her confession pass. "Do you know when he will be back?" He had no idea if he could trust the girl, how much she knew.

"I have no idea."

He could tell the girl felt like she was digging herself deeper and deeper. She tried to rise up, but her knee must have throbbed, and she winced as she sat back down.

The last thing he could do, Thomas knew, was to offer to help. "Be careful, that looks painful. Did you ride a bike over?" Even that seemed like a risk, an invasion, something where the girl would give up information. Thomas began to really want to be somewhere else. "Never mind. Look, he said something about going to a church. Do you know where that is? Some church he was attending?" Attending wasn't the right word, Thomas knew. Steve had not "attended" a church in years, though he had been to several different ones in his life. Again, not something to get into now. He needed to find Steve and get away from this girl.

"He has been having problems with this group from the Island Legacy Church. They just rebuilt an old church on the other side of the woods from my house." She pointed, half-heartedly, down the road and beyond, into the darkness where her house was.

"Can you tell me how to get there?"

The girl was quiet for a moment. Then…

"I can show you."

32

"Wait here."

Up until then, the strange old man had been rather kind, even fatherly, to Jackie. She just wasn't sure who he really was. Not Steve's uncle, that was for certain. Well, not entirely for certain. But they didn't look alike, and this guy looked old for an uncle.

But then, most southerners referred to any old man that was a friend of the family but not related to them as an uncle. It was a term of endearment down in Ocracoke. He seemed kind, shy almost, and wouldn't look her in the eye while he had cared for her knee.

That had been stupid, banging her knee in the table like that. She didn't know if she would have been able to get out the back door or not. And then it would have led to the long walkway to the sound, where she would have to jump over the railing, into the dark woods, while wearing flipflops and shorts, with all those branches and yucca plants and…

The man got out of his big Wagoneer. It was funny for Jackie how the big truck was clean, without the squeaks and rattles of the old Ford pickups that most people drove around here, and definitely without the scent of salt, fish, and bait. And beer.

She wasn't entirely paying attention to her world, as it had made some significant changes in the past few moments to distract her. When the old man got out and ran over to the sheriff's truck caught in his headlights, she still was reeling from both the ache in her knee, and how this guy somehow showed up with a key to Steve's house at midnight and knew all about him, including that he might be here at the "new" old church. Her mind was fuzzy, distracted, right up until he stood up carrying Steve's body from behind the sheriff's truck.

Jackie struggled and fought with the car door, unsure of how to open it. She realized she was locked in with a flash of panic. Then she pulled the door lock and tried to get out.

She banged her knee, "*again*?" she said in her head as she cursed softly and hopped on her good leg.

Once again, the old man called out, this time more forcefully, "Stay there!" as he carried Steve back to his waiting truck.

"Open the door," he commanded, and Jackie did so.

"Is he alright?" she was afraid to ask, "Is he alive?" because, really, he looked very bad. Something rather horrid had dripped down his shirt, and Jackie got the faint whiff of vomit which made her gag.

"He's alive, he just looks like he might have," Thomas grunted as he straightened Steve's body into the back seat, continuing, "maybe swallowed something that made him sick." Jackie didn't know what to make of that. She saw the man stop as he stood up, looking out over the glare of his headlights. He reached in and turned on the high beams for a moment. Jackie followed his gaze to the end of the lot, past the old Blazer, and at the line of blue flowers surrounding the property.

Then he simply said, "In," and Jackie did what she was told.

It was a bouncy ride no matter how careful the man drove, but at least every time he hit a pothole or bump, Steve grunted in pain. At least it meant he was still alive for now. "Do we need to get to a hospital? We might be able to go to the Coast Guard station, or get an ambulance."

"No." it was a simple and decisive word. "We just need to get him to his home, and away from here." There was an obvious tone of fear in the man's voice.

The rest of the drive continued in relative silence, with Jackie only saying, "turn here," in case the man missed the road to Steve's house in the dark. She was worried. Steve was sick, maybe dying, as far as she could tell, and she was out after midnight with a strange man in his car going back to a house she had only just broken into. "Not *broken* in," she reminded herself.

But by the time they got back to Steve's home, he was conscious enough to put his arm over the man's shoulder. Jackie huffed her way to his other side, even while he still reeked of vomit. She didn't bother asking him what happened, yet. The two were able to get Steve inside and to his sofa.

Jackie's knee throbbed with pain. She sat down across from Steve, who seemed to focus on her.

"Jackie?" he stammered. "What are you doing here?"

"I found her here," the old man said. "She says she's a friend of yours. Kind of late to be out meeting friends." It was a tone that was somewhat judgemental of Steve, but somewhat accusing to Jackie. Even though he spoke to Steve, he seemed to be saying it to her. Jackie realized that none of her story was going to hold up, so she said nothing yet.

"I bet that was a bit of a surprise," he handed Steve a glass of water, who sipped it, then spit it back out. He took the glass and went to get another. "Maybe you want a bucket," he suggested.

"Just let me get to the sink," Steve said. "I gotta get this taste out of my mouth."

"Then you can tell me why you were snooping around that place with all that monkshood growing around it."

"I didn't see it in the dark," Steve replied. "I haven't seen that in years."

They were both talking in some secret code to Jackie. She didn't know what Steve was doing out by the old church, what monkshood was, why he was sick, and who the heck this old man was that knew so much about Steve.

"And what were you doing here?!" Steve seemed to regain some strength. He was sipping at water, keeping it down this time. The old man, Jackie still didn't remember his name, was helping Steve take off his shirt so that the sick didn't get caught in his hair and on his face. She couldn't help but notice that, even though he had been near death a few moments ago, Steve was fit, thin but muscular, with a tight narrow waist and chiseled abdomen. It was an involuntary reflex as her heart fluttered a moment. Then she remembered what she was looking for. Steve, the vampire, who set women's hearts afire before killing them and drinking their blood.

"I was…" she needed to come clean. "Look, I'm sorry," she almost started to cry. It would have been easy, with her knee hurting so bad, and she was tired, and afraid. She held back a tear while another fell with a sniffle. "That stupid John Bailey, and Tommy," she winced again, remembering how Tommy had beat her, throwing her to the ground. "They got to me. John was saying you were a vampire, that you killed that girl…" she trailed off. It sounded stupid now that she said it. Her eyes welled with tears now.

She didn't notice the look Steve and the other man shared.

"I just don't know anything about you!" she almost screamed it as an accusation, but her heart was no longer in it. She saw just how crazy she seemed.

"So you thought you'd find my coffin in here?" Steve almost held back a slight chuckle at the idea. "It's okay, Jackie." He walked over to her and knelt next to her, the same way he had when he first had talked with her while her knee was swollen and throbbing after the attack. He still didn't touch her. She didn't need that, not now. Steve shifted a little, just to put himself to her right, so that she was facing the front door.

"I'm not a vampire. I didn't kill that woman. I just had the bad luck to find her. We don't get to choose what happens to us, sometimes. Just like it wasn't your fault what Tommy did to you. Don't worry, you're not in trouble.

"As a matter of fact, you may need to get home now. And I really need to get back to the radio station. I have a feeling people will be looking for me, and I need to be there."

"That's right, I heard you on the radio, tonight."

"It's the wonders of audio tape, kid. But seriously, you need to go. No coffin, no vampire stuff."

Then Jackie remembered something through the haze of the night.

"Why don't you have any mirrors in your bathroom then?"

Steve was quiet for a moment. He looked at his friend, his uncle, who was expressionless. Whatever secret it was between the two, Jackie thought, the man kept it like a stone.

"Sometimes," Steve said slowly, with a sigh, "we don't always like what we see in our reflection."

Analepsis I

May 22nd, 1945
St. Georgen an der Gusen, Austria

"Hey, Frisch!"

Corporal Morton Frisch came at a run. He had been running since he first made it into Europe, running, fighting, and ducking, all the way to Austria. The war had been over for two weeks. Adolph had eaten a bullet, "Why couldn't he have done that a year ago?" was the gripe by every man that came ashore anywhere across France, and the Germans had surrendered a week later.

It was just that no one had told the fucking Nazis that kept on fighting.

"Captain," Cpl. Frisch didn't salute. They weren't at war, but it was still an active battle site. It was always active, something Captain Fredericks had burned into his troops. Don't salute, don't identify any officers to the enemy.

"Look at this, Frisch," he said as he handed the corporal a knife. "Made in Ohio. You might as well have this. Some other officer would just try to take it."

Frisch looked at the knife. It was, well, beautiful was an extreme word for a killing device, but the knife was much more ornate than his worn out trench knife. A black handle of ebony, with white wood, or maybe ivory, inlay, and a shiny aluminum guard. The blade was obviously sharp, about 8 inches long, a strange mix of delicate and industrial. It was so smooth as to show

167

no blemish. The blade looked too thin to stand up to damage, but also had a central ridge, a diamond shaped spine, that reinforced the blade into the handle. Running through the blade was a useless but beautiful piece of wood with a silver inlay. It was a deceptively delicate weapon, one that would enter the enemy and kill with ease.

The grip had none of the wooden discs and leather. It was all dark wood, smooth, but easy to grip. This handle ended with a unique cap, a pointed pommel of silver that ended at a point. It looked as if it could be brought down on the back of even the hardest Nazi's skull and crush it to useless shards.

An army marched on its stomach, yes, but it also marched on its supplies, and war took a toll on boots, watches, and knives as much as food and men. Frisch took the knife and attached it to his belt. "I know where this place is," he said, looking at the knife's manufacturer. "Dover is over in the eastern part of the state. I bet my ma wants one of their knives."

"Just don't cook with it, boy," said Captain Fredericks.

Not that they had any plans on cooking, or killing. Even though both Fredericks, Frisch, and the rest of his squad and larger platoon certainly had it on their minds. Frisch had been pulled out of his battalion halfway to Berlin when enough people realized he spoke German, a side effect of growing up in a family of Prussian descent in midwest Ohio. That and the fact that he seemed especially skilled at killing the enemy meant he was placed in a platoon that was going into central Germany at the end of the war to seek out any specialized warfare operations. They would be normally commanded by a sergeant, but an officer needed to be assigned to make higher pay scale decisions. Fredericks got his own rank upgrade, from a lieutenant to captain, and Frisch got moved to corporal. Both liked the slight pay increase, but would have been happier moving west rather than east.

Especially where they were right now.

"As if Bergkristall wasn't bad enough," Fredericks had said. They were in St. Georgen an der Gusen, in Austria of all places. The platoon had been sent there, with some vague orders known to

Fredericks, but kept from the others. Frisch knew a little more. He had to know what words to look for on any documents he was to translate. He had learned two of them very well. *Strahlung* and *nuklear*. Radiation and nuclear.

They had already found the underground facility at St. Georgen, as well as the usual detritus of the Nazi Pyrrhic defeat. The facility had been manned by slave labor, and thousands died. Frisch's platoon had been sent ahead to secure the area, and secure the plans from the nearby factories, especially the one that built the infamous Messerschmitt Me 262, the mysterious jet plane that flew with no propeller. The Allies had made it especially clear to protect the engineers as well as any planes left at the factory.

Now they were preparing for a trek into the Austrian woodlands. Frisch had found a location on a map, listed as a laboratory, but they all knew what it really was. Just like St. Georgen, just like Bergkirstall. The Nazis used slave labor, POWs, Jews, Poles, anyone they captured that could either be used or used up. Those that couldn't be forced into work through their technical skills were used for manual labor, until they got sick or died. The dead were the lucky ones. The sick were experimented on, tortured, and the Nazis only saw joy in their torment.

Frisch knew what they would find.

Two hours later, two deuce and a half trucks unloaded 40 grim men a mile from the wooded land that held a small building. "Sergeant Kline," Fredericks instructed a soft skinned, dark eyed man who's delicate features belied a quiet fierceness, "keep ten men here in reserve, approach from the north, to this side," he indicated with his arm to stay to the left of the road, "and wait until signaled to approach. If we take on fire, assault any front defenses to free up an area for us to escape." With that, Fredericks lead thirty men into the woods to investigate a mysterious and hidden building.

It wouldn't take long for Fredericks and his platoon to see the building was, or at least looked, deserted. "Look at that fencing," a private pointed out. "Why do they need all that?" The fence was a tall wire fence, with barbed wire across the top and bottom. "Look at the gate. It's like a tunnel." The gate opened to a short path to an enclosed lot, which held no vehicles. The drive was surrounded by the same fencing. "Like they are trying to keep people in. There's no threat from an attack here in Austria."

"Shut up, Jenkins, and go climb that tower." Even at the end of the war, opening your mouth meant you volunteered. There were several towers, but they appeared unmanned.

Jenkins got up the tower and called out, "No one up here. Left these 42s, still armed." He opened the action of an MG42 machine gun and took out the belt of bullets.

"There's…" another private began to speak up, then shut up before he was volunteered to go inside first.

But there was no need to be concerned. The building was empty. It seemed devoid of not only people, but documents as well. "Where did they go?" asked Fredericks. "Damn. Jenkins, go out and have Sergeant Kline come to the fence and set up a perimeter."

Cpl. Frisch looked for any documents, but the few boxes and files were all empty. The only thing to read was a red *Verboten* sign on a solid, very German looking door. No need to translate it. "Careful opening that," Fredericks said. It didn't have to be an order; everyone knew not to charge into the darkness.

The door led to a much more foreboding area, poorly lit, with nothing but a few shelves and an empty table. "An operating room?" Frisch commented. It looked like nothing else, but not much like that, either.

"I wouldn't be surprised," said Fredericks gravely. "Anything on those shelves?"

"Nothin'."

"Alright, let's keep looking. There's a turn down the hall. Let's make sure there is no one else in here.

"Then get the hell outta this godforsaken place."

The farther in Frisch got, the danker the building felt. By the end of the war, most soldiers had developed a sixth sense, goosebumps of impending doom, and Frisch was feeling colder than usual.

"You hear that?" Something scurried lightly in the dark, a soft click on the smooth floor. Frisch already had his pistol drawn, and stalked slowly down the hall. If anything so much as whispered, his M1911 would do dirty work. The .45 would not only stop any Nazi taking the turn, but put him back six feet, and then six feet under, if anyone was willing to dig them a grave. The Nazis sure didn't bother with them, so why should Frisch.

But when the thing came skittering around a corner, a black and hairy monster, on all fours as it bounded and bounced across the walls toward the soldiers, within a heartbeat Frisch and the three men behind him knew nothing was going to stop this thing in its tracks.

Frisch got two shots off, both hitting in the center of mass, but the shots did nothing to slow it down. It merely snarled as it approached.

Frisch tried to think as he reacted, but "They left a guard dog to attack anyone who came here," was too long even for the thoughts to flow through his brain, much less say them.

The giant beast was too big to be a dog, but it was obviously a canine. The wild twisted black hair, the long snout, and the wide, long, white teeth were all distinctive of the animal. But this was a grotesque twist on the creature. It was bigger than Frisch, bigger even than the tall Fredericks. Frisch, even after putting two bullets into its chest, stood no chance against the monster. It leapt from ten feet away and landed fully on the standing Frisch. He fell to the floor as he put up his arm in reflex. The beast bit heavily into his right arm, and Frisch's pistol fell from his grip. Frisch screamed in both pain and terror.

The other men now moved forward. One soldier tried to level his M1 to take aim at the giant beast, but the small confines of the hallway, the men trying to move around, to get close or stay away, made it impossible for him to bring the rifle to bear. Fredericks drew his own .45 and began to unload in the creature's chest. He was afraid to shoot into the animal's head, being so close to Frisch.

But none of the bullets seemed to affect the monster. It was still locked in a death grip on Frisch's arm, while long claws from its paws scraped at his prone body. Frisch felt one rear leg scrape down his abdomen, then down across his groin, and then the delayed but utterly painful feel as his testicles went numb, then began send a dull electrical shock up to his head. Frisch felt his eyes roll back uncontrollably.

He had to get the animal off of him, but the jaws only seemed to dig in deeper with every shot. He reached down with his free left hand, which had been unsuccessful in pushing off the heavy beast. He grabbed at his new knife, still sheathed, and felt it slip naturally into his hand. The pommel felt smooth, well weighted in his hand. It was a flashing moment, just a blink of the eye, a calm in a bloody maelstrom for Frisch. The knife flashed as he stabbed at the beast's jaw. He tried to jam the blade into the animal's mouth. A few teeth ground at the metal, but the creature's mouth did not budge. Frisch, desperate, felt the weight lift off him only a fraction. Fredericks had come around and was trying to pull the thing off of him. It gave Frisch mere inches, but it was enough. He spun his knife around, turning the pommel toward the creature. He smashed the short pointed end, a bone crushing point, dull but solid, into the beast's skull. He felt a slight release, and pounded in again.

This time he felt the bone break. Again he brought down the crusher of his pommel on the animal. By now the skull was broken, and he was getting to the softer, more delicate material, including the beast's brain. A third strike split the skull open, and Frisch felt something splatter onto his face.

With that, the animal slumped. It was still alive, still dug in, but the fight was going out. It pulled, and tried to tear, but all it did was shake its now mortally damaged brains in its mortally damaged head. Frisch gave one last bash, as he, too, was losing strength quickly.

With a last breath, the beast sighed, and his jaw went slack. Frisch plunged his knife blade into the animal's jaws again, and pried the teeth from his torn and and wounded skin. The large canines had sunk in so deep that Fredericks had to pry the jaws apart and break them to get them out of Frisch's arm.

As they dragged Frisch from the dark hall, up into the main part of the building, Fredericks gave the order, "Seal that door!" to the big metal portal with the bright red *Verboten* sign.

"Get a truck up here, now!" Fredericks bandaged Frisch's arm, but it seemed as if the blood just kept pouring through the gauze as it wrapped.

"What the hell was that thing?!"

33

"Someone knows who I am," said Steve. "No," he began to answer the question before Thomas asked it, "I haven't told anyone." Steve could see Thomas' mouth open wordlessly, and continued, "Not Jackie. She doesn't know.

"I have no idea where she got that crazy vampire shit, but she definitely doesn't know about my past." Steve wondered if he let anything slip. He had told lies so casually, mixed so well with the truth, that he didn't bother to check himself anymore. It came naturally. "But someone knows. Someone at that church. And I'm sure they will come looking for me, soon enough. Just make sure you get me back to the station."

Steve sat back and panted. The ride in Thomas' big Jeep was more comfortable than his Wrangler, but his body felt twisted and pulled. He was still recovering from the wave of nausea that hit him from the monkshood. Most people would get sick if they ate any of it. It could kill if enough was ingested. It would create a massive bout of nausea, then blood pressure would lower, and the heart would exhaust itself, and a person would die. It was a preferred method of poison from long ago, hundreds of years ago.

But monkshood affected Steve differently. The nausea hit, so did the resultant weakness, but all he had to do was get it on him, or breathe in enough of the pollen, and he would be incredibly, violently ill. He never knew if enough would kill him, but he felt like it would if he gave it a chance. That would be a rather horrible and tragic way to die. It was one of many ways that he didn't want to face. He knew that from experience.

"Is this why you called?" asked Thomas.

"Well…" Steve sighed, still weak. "Not *this*, specifically. I mean, I knew something was going on, but it just got pushed, way too far. And I took some of it out on someone. He had it coming, but, well, I just needed someone with a clearer view." Steve took a deep breath, coughed, and let out a little gasp. He was still weak, and even talking tasked him.

"Are you going to be alright?" Thomas knew more of Steve's peculiarities, as well as his strengths, than anyone else. He had been there from the beginnings, the studies, the prodded needles, the testing, the psychological damage and recovery. The relapse and recovery, again. The question was meant both for what had just happened, and more.

"Yes, I think so," Steve sighed as he sank into the seat of the big Wagoneer. "I'm just a little beat from throwing up." He tried drinking some more water, but he felt full and still a little weak and queasy. "As long as I'm sitting." Steve grunted. "My Jeep is over there," he pointed to a place he had hidden his truck, about ten minutes away from the church.

"You okay to drive?"

"Yeah…"

"You want me to wait with you? At the station?"

"Yeah, it might be good to have someone to back up my alibi. I just hope they aren't already waiting for me there. Whoever did this will need time to make things happen, but they will start happening fast."

The two men got to the old weather station, where Steve unlocked the door and let them in. He found his long playing reel to reel show playing unabated, right in the middle of a song. "Just hang out here. I gotta get to a place where I can take over." He looked over a clipboard to see where the tape was at. He was coming to a station break soon, and it would be a good place to stop the tape and go live.

"This is WZHX, Hatteras, on the X, with Steve Brodie LateNight," came the deep singsong patter of Tim Watkins, a prerecorded intro on a prerecorded tape. Steve immediately cut off the reel to reel and jumped in. "*I am* Steve Brodie," he smiled at the joke, "and lets turn down the late night lights with The Doors, and Riders On The Storm." He started the platter and quickly turned off his mic. "Okay, help me move this tape out of here. Just take it off, put it in that box, and put it on top of those in the recording studio," he poked a finger through a glass window at the room next door. "I gotta get some records. Someone is going to come looking for me, and I don't want any questions. They won't know what to look for, but I do, and I'm not giving them anything."

The two men moved with efficiency. Even though Thomas knew little about Steve's job in the mechanical sense, he figured out how to turn off the tape machine completely, in case he somehow turned it on and it played over the air, then he simply pried off the two tapes with a small bit of the ribbon between them. He put them in a box and slipped the lid loosely over them. They didn't fit, but at least they weren't falling all over the place. He set it carefully on the top of another stack of tapes, next to a carousel of large cassettes.

Steve was on the other side of the recording studio, which doubled as a library. He held a clipboard of the songs for the night, and quickly matched up the albums with the list, double checking against a stack of records. He carried the pile into the booth and set them down, filing half of them in his used shelf.

With that, they waited.

Steve almost began to wonder if anyone would show up. "Maybe they are waiting for me at the house," he said, half jokingly. The time gave the two a moment to talk. They still had worry on their minds, but tried to remain calm. As if calm was a possibility.

"What happened to that police officer?"

"That was the sheriff," Steve said. "It looked like his throat was torn open. Damn. I mean, Sheriff Midgette might have seemed like a typical southern good ol' boy sheriff, but he really was a nice man. He didn't deserve that. Whoever did this, they just did it to make it look like it was a…" he shrugged inwardly. He didn't need to finish the sentence. Thomas knew what he was going to say.

"Who are we dealing with that kills that indiscriminately? His death seems so thoughtless." Thomas shook his head. He was jumping into the middle of things. While it was part of what he did, even since his younger days in battle, he never would say he was used to it. It was a terrible thing to be thrown into the middle of a tragedy and be expected to make sense of things, and then find a solution.

"I have this feeling," Steve answered, "that we are in an unholy land." It was a cryptic message, but one that he and Thomas knew intimately. They used the term when they had entered Germany so long ago, and saw what they saw. It meant they were past the point where people had care or empathy. They moved into a place where life was less than valueless, it was forfeit, and forfeit easily. It was easier to hurt and kill than it was to not. They had seen that world move from compassion, to dispassion, to psychopathy, and finally into sociopathic sadism. Killing and hurting for the sake of doing so, that's what they had seen.

That's more and more what Steve was seeing now. Linda Patterson, Ellen Gaines… Jackie… Steve paused at the thought of her being beaten by that boy. And now Sheriff Midgette. Too many deaths and damage on this little island.

"What the hell did I step in?" he said to Thomas.

A banging came from far outside. "I guess we're gonna find out," answered Thomas.

34

early morning Saturday, July 13th

"So, you were here all night?"

Deputy Doug Brindley seemed more than a little out of his element. He was told to expect to find Steve Brodie alone at the station. No one mentioned anyone else being there. Steve was this good looking fit guy, but the man with him, old, but tall, grizzled, short hair cut like a marine, this man did not look like someone to mess with.

But Brindley had the gun, and the badge, and his orders. Well, some form of order, at least. But his orders didn't tell him what to do when he found two men at the radio station when he came to the door, banging to get attention. He was only supposed to be there bring Steve Brodie in "for questioning." The tall old man was a surprise there, and when he came in and asked Steve where he had been, Steve explained that his show started at ten o'clock, and he had been there since nine thirty. "You can check with Tim Watkins, he was here when I came in. He's probably in bed now, but you can check in the morning."

"So," Deputy Brindley tried to puzzle out what was going on, "you were here all night?"

"Yes. Why?"

"Someone said they saw you," he went on. He had no real answer for the simple question, now that Brindley wasn't getting the right answer.

"Someone saw me?! Here?!" He motioned around the windowless room. It was a room, in a room, in a building, in the dark in the middle of the night. "Who could see me here? They heard me, sure, all the night owls hear me. But see me, nope."

"Why was someone looking for Steve?" Thomas asked. He wondered what the younger deputy knew. He was going to find out.

"Well, someone just saw someone who matched his description."

"Was there a crime committed?"

"Y..eesss," Brindley didn't know what to say. Everyone would know soon enough. People were coming from Manteo. Someone was recovering the body. He was expected to investigate it.

"What happened?" Thomas asked.

"Yeah, what happened? What'd I do?" It took all he had in his still weakened state not to sound too smarmy in the face of this deputy. Brindley was looking away, shuffling his feet, like he didn't want to be there already. Steve didn't want to seem too cavalier; he knew the answer already, and murder wasn't something to laugh about. Someone *had* killed the sheriff. They had made it look like a wild animal, but it was still murder, not an attack.

Brindley saw no escape. "Sheriff Midgette was killed tonight." Steve didn't have to act shocked. He was tired, weak, still feeling sick, and sad about the loss of the man, as well as concerned about his own role in the murder. Someone had killed the sheriff to send a message and set Steve up. Just finding the body like that… Steve sighed, "No… What happened? The sheriff was a good man."

"I don't know. It looks like an animal attack."

Steve began to piece together more and more of what had happened. Sheriff Midgette was killed where he was found. He wasn't taken to the church and killed there. And he certainly wasn't attacked by an animal. "All that blood, all there," Steve saw it in his mind. He had seen worse. And he had seen worse recently, he realized. His look of sadness and shock fooled the deputy into thinking Steve was traumatized by the sheriff's death. Which he was.

"Then why are you looking for Steve?" Thomas asked again.

"Well, someone thought they saw his Jeep."

That was a giveaway for Steve. He had not driven his Jeep to the church. He had parked it and run there. He purposefully didn't take his Jeep since it would be easily noticed and recognized.

It was a set-up. A set-up where someone knew his secret.

"Well, it certainly wasn't Steve." Thomas spoke with confident authority, which he had. Even though he knew the truth, all of it, he also knew Steve didn't kill that man, and he also knew there was more going on, and it looked like the deputy was involved, or at least an unwitting accomplice. "But if there's anything I can do to help," he stood up from leaning against the counter where a record still spun silently, and reached into his back pocket.

The deputy tensed.

"Easy there, I'm just getting my wallet." Thomas pulled out a small leather wallet, which he opened for the deputy. In it was an I.D. and a large badge with the letters FBI emblazoned on a shield. "I'm Special Agent Thomas Fredericks."

"You from the Bureau?!" Deputy Brindley stood with his mouth open. "Are you down here investigating this already?"

"This guy," Thomas and Steve both thought similar thoughts at the same time. Thomas answered. "No, I've been down for a while now. I'm a friend of Steve's mom, from up north," it wasn't entirely a lie, "I just came down to do some fishing."

Deputy Brindley was taken aback by someone from the FBI in close quarters. He quickly decided to back off and find another way to deal with this. He definitely wasn't taking Steve into custody now, not with the weight of the Bureau showing up. He hoped he hadn't screwed everything up, whatever was going on.

"Sorry I bothered you. I was just following up a lead. No, I don't think the FBI is needed here."

Thomas decided to jump in, scaring the deputy more. "Well, I'm sure the State Bureau will show up in the morning. If they need anything, they will contact us, but those guys, well, they don't mess around. They'll find who did this, and fast."

With that, Deputy Brindley beat a hasty retreat. He needed to get out of there before he made more of a mess.

"The state police?" That was the last thing he needed.

35

Saturday, July 13ᵗʰ

Steve woke up on his sofa. He had given his bed to Thomas. "You're getting too old to sleep on a couch," Steve had joked to the big man. "And you probably won't fit anyway."

Thomas had harrumphed in contempt at the comment. "You're not a young man anymore, either," he had said with a dry chuckle. Steve was still perpetually nineteen years old, and had the soldier's ability to sleep anywhere at any time. He wouldn't wake up with aches and pains, not normally. At sixty five, Thomas couldn't make the same claim.

Thomas was already up. Awakening at daylight was normal to him. He had slept fitfully in the strange bed after dealing with the news of the night before. He had been up and out for most of the day, while Steve slept his usual day away. Now, at 2:00, he finally arose. The sun tried to burn its way through the shades of the windows, through the thick summer leaf canopy outside, onto Steve's eyes. He squinted and rubbed them. Bright light wasn't painful, but he was not used to being up during the day. "Once a nightcrawler, always a nightcrawler," Thomas had once commented.

"No wonder I'm awake," Steve said, "What's that smell?"

"Fried shrimp, probably," Thomas held up a bag. "Fries. Cole slaw. What's this stuff?" He held up a cup of green cooked leaves of some sort.

"Collards," Steve said. "They're good."

"And this?" a larger cup of strange breaded circles, its odor about as pungent, a little more off-putting.

"Okra, don't eat that."

"Don't worry."

Thomas took a bite of the shrimp. "It's not walleye, but it's not bad," Thomas said.

Steve stretched and yawned, closing his eyes to the light. "It's too early to deal with this… shit!"

"What … oh… shit…"

The syncopated sound of feet pounded up the steps. The inconsistent beat, as if someone skipped as they walked, gave away who was approaching. Steve had heard the footsteps moments before Thomas did. But they both knew who it was. Then the banging started.

"It's definitely too early for this shit," Steve groaned.

"She knows we're here, you can't just let her stay out there," Thomas answered.

"Yeah," came a yell from outside, "I know you are in there! Let me in!"

Steve opened the door to an irate Jackie Wood. "Come on in, Jackie."

"Alright, spill it! What is going on with you two? You are no way his uncle. And you," she pointed at Steve, "you know more about all this than you are letting on. Talk. What have you gotten us all into?"

Steve sighed. There was no way to explain it all to Jackie. What was he going to do, tell her he was secretly a werewolf? She wouldn't believe that. She had just thought he was a vampire last night, but she was not going to believe he was some strange wolf beast. He knew she wouldn't believe, no matter what.

No one ever did.

Steve looked at Thomas.

"Don't you look at him, look at me!" Jackie fairly screamed. She stood almost on one leg, favoring her wounded knee. "Whatever it is, I want to know who you are, and what you did."

Steve got up and walked around Jackie toward his bedroom. "Alright Jackie, you deserve to know." He walked over to the framed knife and a little medal.

Jackie made an involuntary gasp as he reached for the knife. She took a step backwards, towards the door, looking at Thomas as she did so. But the old man made no move to stop her. He stood still, a shrimp still dangling in his hand, forgotten.

Then Steve took the frame down and reached behind it. An old photo was stuck on the back of the box. He carried the frame over to his table and pulled the picture off the back.

"See that?" he pointed at the photo, showing it to Jackie. "That's me."

The photo showed a group of twelve men, all armed, dressed in military garb. A few held old M1 Garand rifles, others casually rested Thompson submachine guns over their shoulders. It was a classic pose, all smiling, but grim, dirty, worn from time. Barely visible behind them was a vague but huge castle. The third man in the row in the picture looked very similar to Steve, but without the long hair. The man in the picture, more a boy or teenager, grinned at the camera, his long pointed jawline and thin button nose making him instantly recognizable. "And that's him," Steve pointed at a tall man, in his twenties, standing at the end. He looked like a young version of Thomas Fredericks.

"That's Hohensalzburg Fortress in the background, that big castle. It's on the border of Germany and Austria."

"But this looks like it was taken in World War II..." Jackie stared at the photo, puzzled. She was not able to fathom the reality of what the image meant.

"It was," Steve said simply.

"That's impossible," Jackie said firmly. There was no doubt in her mind. This was utter fantasy. She knew when people were lying to her, and there was no way that any of this was true. "You posed for this, set it up."

"Yes," Steve agreed. "Yes, we posed for it, forty years ago. We were happy, well, as happy as we could be. We had just left Germany and entered Austria. This was after the war was over, technically. It was our assignment to secure and free any prisoners or technical buildings from the Nazis. There were still lots of them around, still wanting to fight us.

"All the things you learn about the war in school, none of that describes what it was actually like. The Nazis were monsters, horrific beyond measure." Steve looked at Jackie's knee, still swollen and wrapped. He wanted to tell her, he always wanted to tell someone just to get them to understand just how bad it was, what he had seen. "Just imagine," he thought, "what that boy did to you, but constantly, for a month, all over, without stopping. Until you beg for death. And then they know they have you. That's when they stop, just enough to bring you back to life, so they can do it all again, inside and out. The torture, it's unimaginable, but they still create something worse than the day before. They make your parents or your kids watch. And then they only kill you when they make a mistake, and go too far, or when you no longer respond. Then your body is left to rot, or, when the bodies got to be too many, they are burned to ash and thrown in a big waste pile. The names are forgotten, there is no grave, no place for others to say goodbye, because there are no others left. No one to mourn you, because they are all dead, too, dying the same way. Their bodies wasted away, beaten to leather and bone, or just shot. And the numbers are unimaginable. By the thousands, hundreds of thousands, millions. It did seem impossible, but the Nazis did it. And I saw it all, at the end."

But he couldn't say it to her. It was too much. She wouldn't understand. Kids saw monsters as creatures of the dark, imaginary, only a maybe in their minds. Jackie and all the kids on this island, even the older adults who had seen war on their coast firsthand, they had no idea. It was just too much, especially for a seventeen year old girl.

"We were there, at the end," Steve said simply. It would be a lie, but the better lies had an element of truth. "The Nazis were trying to find ways to fight a guerrilla war, after Hitler killed himself. Some refused to surrender. They were trying to find a way to create real super soldiers. We found a laboratory in Austria. It was about a week after this photo was taken. I was exposed to a serum that was an experiment to stop or slow aging, which was meant to keep their SS soldiers strong and young. I almost died from it, but then Captain Fredericks here got me to a hospital, and they were able to revive me.

"I know it's hard to believe. Have you ever heard of people that age prematurely, get old, wrinkled, lose their hair, go bald?"

"Yes," Jackie had grown quiet. She could see the story that Steve was holding back in his head. There was more to it, but she could see it was traumatic, even if she didn't yet believe him. There was no way he fought in World War II.

"This is just the opposite," he shrugged and tried to smile, a strange mix of apologetic and yet hungry, at the grim and scared Jackie. "I don't grow old. I'm stuck as that kid." He pointed at the picture. "Look at me, Jackie," he did everything he could not to touch her, to do the stupid thing and touch her chin to lift it to see him. He knew that wouldn't help, not now. It was a benefit of his age. "You have seen me on TV. I worked on radio for, what, ten years now. Have I aged any? Do I even look like I'm twenty, let alone thirty five? I look like a teenager.

"I know it seems impossible, but it's true."

Jackie looked at Steve, unable to keep his gaze. She didn't believe him, even with all the evidence in front of her. She wouldn't believe it until she saw a man age backwards, from some strange Nazi injection. She looked over at Thomas, who merely nodded as he agreed with Steve.

"Look, I'm not a vampire. I'm not a killer," Steve knew that wasn't true. He had killed in the war, and done it well. He even relished it some. He had killed monsters. He had, on occasion, killed or caused the death of men, just soldiers wearing a different uniform, but all that was a discussion for a different time. "I just want you to be sure of that. There are bad things happening here, and it seems like a lot of it is happening around me, and you," he glanced at her knee, "but we, I, didn't cause it."

Steve stood up and walked to the window, opening the shade. The sunlight was still filtered, but it was a strong summer sky, and the sun burned through the leaves, hitting Steve full in the face. "See?"

He walked over to his table, to a small wooden bowl full of the usual detritus of a life collecting things. Others had the same bowl in their own houses, full of shells, sea glass, an old pocketknife, change. Steve rooted through it, pulling out a thin black leather string. On the end dangled a tiny cross. He held it up to his face. "See? It doesn't effect me in the least."

"Do you wear that?" Jackie asked, trying to find some way to argue with Steve, and his utterly impossible story.

"No," Steve said, trying to sound casual. "It's Tibetan silver. They don't know to taint the metal with a little bit of nickel, so it's much more pure." He held it out to her by the string, offering her to hold it. "It turns my skin green. I have a weird allergy to it, that's all." That was not a lie, but a rather large understatement.

"Okay," Jackie stood up, trying to take over and regain some sense of composure. She felt cornered, and guilty. She had broken in to Steve's house and then found him almost dead at a church where the sheriff had been killed, torn at the throat. If she thought about it, she realized that Steve probably wouldn't have murdered the sheriff and then passed out and nearly died himself. But she didn't know what was going on, and she didn't like being powerless. "*If* this is true, and yes, I get it, you're not a vampire, that was silly, then…" she didn't know where to go. "Wait… why do you not have any mirrors in this house? What did you mean when you said you didn't like what you saw?"

Steve couldn't help but pause. Jackie, for a heartbeat, wondered if she had caught him. And then wondered if she was getting out of the house alive. But Steve merely sighed.

"Sometimes… sometimes people don't like… what they see in their reflection."

Jackie was confused by Steve's comment. He was young, good looking, successful, popular, everything that anyone would ever want to me. Her puzzlement showed on her face.

Steve knew the look. He had seen that same look, time and time again, in all the previous iterations of his lives. How could he explain it to a girl who hadn't lived one life yet? Who had sat with him on the beach, wishing for this very existence, to freeze time as a teenager, never grow old, never get sick and die?

"You," he started to say, "You wouldn't understand. You're too young," and he heard the words in his head as a teenager. He knew the contempt that those words would cause. He started again.

"You have only lived your life once, Jackie. You still have a lot of life ahead of you. Time to grow and change. You get to make mistakes, have some regret, and then to grow past it, to make a life that will be part of your future. It's not locked in. Your life, in your eyes, is limitless. You could get married and have kids," Steve almost choked on those words, but went on, "or you could not. You could choose to live life traveling, visiting places, seeing the world, growing old alone, but happy. And when you make either choice, you might wonder what would happen if you went another way. But you get to grow through that life.

"Okay," Steve found himself almost confessing now, "How about this? You've been a ten year old, right?"

"Yeah…"

"And it was fun to be a kid. But you're not a little kid anymore. You are a teen, and about to make a move into a much bigger world. It's exciting, a little scary, but thrilling. Go to college, get off the island.

"Now, if you had the choice, would you prefer to go back to being ten again? To live with your parents, have them cut your food, behave and feel like a ten year old?"

"Well, no…"

"I didn't get that option. I'm forever a nineteen year old boy. Even though I'm older. And I never got to be a teenage kid. When I was sixteen every boy was taken out of school once a week, taught to march, and given a rifle to learn to shoot. We knew, we just *knew*, when we turned eighteen we would be given a uniform and a rifle and either thrown onto a beach in Europe, or sent to Japan. And we were all going to die.

"And that's what happened. At eighteen, thousands of kids my age went ashore in France and barely made it to the beach before dying. They never got to be a kid, never a teen, and never a man. I was lucky. They pulled me aside because I could speak German and I was a little better at fighting than anyone else. Lucky," he smirked at the irony of the word, thinking of what it meant for him.

"I never got to be a sixteen year old boy, because it was always planned that I would be a soldier. And now, I'm forever a nineteen year old, and I never get to be a teen, because I'm old, and I never get to be old, because I'm forever, this," and he pointed at his face, a perfect summer beach boy, cute, fit, dreamlike in every girl's eyes, but never allowed to have been that boy when he was a teenager. Because he died and came back to life a monster.

That was something he wasn't about to explain to Jackie. He had come to terms with his life. Mostly. But it was still difficult to look in a mirror and see his face.

Jackie still had doubts. There was no way this was true. But at the same time, she always knew when someone was telling the truth. Steve believed the story he told, and Jackie could see whatever it was had hurt him bad.

"Look, kid," Thomas spoke up for the first time, "this is going to seem like too much for you because it is. I've been there for Steve here," he nodded softly, his voice and demeanor changing to kindly, fatherly. "We had to do this before. And it's difficult.

Sometimes impossible to believe until you watch him over the years. And maybe that's what it will take for you. We just hope you can understand part of it. This is something personal. Please don't spread this around. I'm not about to tell you to keep a secret from your parents," he stated this gravely, "I have been a parent, and I know you shouldn't keep things from your family. And if you want, we can meet with them and explain it to them, too. But it will cause problems. People will come after Steve, wanting to examine him, and he went through all that long ago. It was my fault for not protecting him then, and I don't want that to happen again."

Steve said nothing. That, too, had been discussed long ago. Steve never saw Thomas as the cause of his curse. If anything, it was the Nazis, long dead now. Or the scientists who wanted to see if they could make another one of him.

"Look, just keep this close to you for now," Steve asked, his voice soft and a little pleading. "I'm not a bad person," that was, not... a lie... Steve wondered if that was true. "If it's too much for you... I'll leave, okay? But right now, there is something more going on here, and I really think it has something to do with me. I don't want anything else to happen here."

The room fell into a cold awkward silence. The walls left like they were slowly closing in on the three people inside the small cottage. Steve, who had at one time felt the comfortable closeness of Jackie's youthful honesty and exuberance, now only felt like he had broken her trust. He had spent so much of his life dealing with his affliction, and he knew it was always best to keep it to himself. Now he had opened up, and to a girl. Jackie was a girl close to his age, but also so much younger. It was hard for her to understand, for exactly the reasons he spelled out. He was still a kid, like her, but not, not at all. And he was a man, old, with the experiences of life, good and bad, even though they didn't show through. "All my scars are on the inside," he thought. It was the same thought he made every time he saw his reflection, made thousands of times over.

Jackie got up, feeling enclosed and backed to the door, unsure, uncomfortable, and a little afraid. Thomas only looked on with a fatherly concern, more for Steve, but also for Jackie. He felt the hurt she had. He was a parent, and a grandfather, and he hated that Jackie had to feel this way. Steve looked even worse. He had to share a secret he obviously disliked, and didn't want to share.

"It's okay, Jackie," Thomas made sure she knew they weren't going to stop her. "Go ahead. Go home. Do what you need to do. We can take care of this." He wanted to add, "Just be careful," but his idea of a warning that there would be others out in the world that might come after her would sound like a threat, so he let it linger in his throat as he silently choked on the dangerous words.

Jackie left, limping down the steps to a hot and dusty road, as Steve and Thomas watched silently.

"Now," Steve said quietly as he looked through the blinds, "things are only going to get worse."

36
Monday, July 15th

Harrison Boarman suffered fools poorly. He missed the time when people followed his orders without question. But he knew he had to wait to resume his desire for power, control, authority. And one thing he had was time. He had an eternity.

The dumb sheriff's deputy had fouled up, but Boarman almost expected that. The young man was only a dupe, *ein Trottel*. "No," he told himself, "a fool. English. American. A sucker. A dupe."

But getting the FBI involved would only complicate things. He didn't need anyone looking closer at him. Not yet. But the *werwolf* was a different kind of threat. He sensed the presence soon after the man had shown up, but Boarman had no idea just who it was. In times past, the pricolici, the old Romanian cursed beasts, had long hunted his people. They were nearly unstoppable, and had an insatiable appetite. They killed indiscriminately, but seemed to take delight in hunting in the Austrian forests and castles of his homeland. They searched out the powerful to kill, the most dangerous threats to them, anyone who could organize and force the monsters out of their hiding places. The pricolici, the *werwolf*, they sowed chaos, and delighted in it.

It was no wonder the Nazis had tried to create them as a way to fight the Allies after the surrender.

But the Nazis had no idea what they were dealing with.

Boarman only shook his head slightly to remove the thought. It was a distraction to what he had to do, a delightful, sanguine distraction. Terrifying and wonderful, better than what he had done in the recent months.

He just had to deal with that idiot Darrow.

Boarman stood on the back deck of the church, facing the setting sun over the sound. The air was electric; he could feel the magic in the coming night, seeping out of the land. It was wonderfully wicked, almost painful, a delightful burn as the sun boiled down to an ember in the western water.

Boarman sensed the other man's presence even before he heard him, or felt his plodding trods on the walkway behind the church. "The 'church'," he thought. This was no temple to any god, except the worship of money. And Darrow was no man of god, that Boarman knew. It was curious how little Boarman could tolerate of religion, especially Christianity, and yet Darrow was truly intolerable, an irritant that Boarman hated as much as suffered.

Darrow walked up the wooden planks. He had been called by his benefactor, and he had come, like a lap dog, desperate for a reward. But the dog had to work for his treat. Darrow slobbered at the thought of more money, but would worry about any duty, any actual job he must do to earn it. It was easy to be an ass, to speak when told and say what he was told to say. Dirty work was different.

Boarman had never, in a long time, been afraid of dirty work.

Darrow came up behind Boarman, recognizing him as he turned. "You?!" Darrow almost gasped, then saw the look of disdain on Boarman's face. This was not the way to prostrate yourself to your master. Darrow removed the stupid, stunned look, and stared down at his feet. "I'm, I'm sorry, I didn't know," was all he could stammer out.

"Of course not," answered Boarman, "and we will keep it that way. No one will know. It is time for you to serve your master, Darrow, to serve your god."

"I am always willing to do the Lord's wor…"

Boarman brushed his testimony off. "Oh please, spare me," he spat, "We both know the only god you worship is the gold I provide, and don't try to pretend otherwise to me. There is no reason to lie to another liar. Just shut up and do as I say."

Darrow didn't like being called out like that. He had pretended to be a good steward to Christianity so much that he had almost begun to believe it. The fact that everything he had done was an anathema to living a Christ-like life shouldn't really matter. He had almost started believing that he really was a person of faith.

Boarman gestured behind Darrow, and Darrow turned to see Darla walking toward the two men. If there was anyone or anything that disproved Darrow's belief in his own faith, she would be it. Darla, sexy, stupid Darla, always willing, as long as there was a wad of cash involved, of course, dumb rat faced Darla, walked up slowly, deliberately. "She walks like a man," Darrow only half noticed. There was no strut, none of her wiggle that he liked and asked for. She merely plodded, one foot in front of her at a time, clunking along in the receding sunset. She seemed incredibly plain looking to Darrow, and he could not quite figure out why.

"Your secretary has agreed to help us with something," Boarman said. Darrow remembered thinking that Darla might be sleeping with whoever provided his money. He hoped this wasn't going to be some kind of threesome thing. Darrow just wasn't into that stuff. He didn't like sharing.

Boarman saw the thoughts on Darrow's face. "Simpleton," he thought in his head, but said nothing. "There was so much more to life than temporary gratification." Boarman merely moved Darla to him by pulling her arm. "I need Darla's help, and then I will need your help. You will do exactly as I say."

Darrow didn't like being pushed around, and his mouth parted to protest, while his mind and his wallet tried to fight against him saying anything stupid. He didn't have a moment to get his brain to fight out the indecision.

Boarman opened his mouth, too, and sunk his teeth into Darla's neck.

Darrow was stunned, unbelieving at first. He could only think of it as something sexual, even though he had seen, in a flash, the vicious bite into her flesh. It was nothing like the dumb controlling pain he had inflicted on her. There was tearing, damage.

And blood.

So much blood.

Darla slumped into Boarman's arms. He lifted his head back, mouth covered in crimson as blood dripped down his chin.

"Oh my God!" cried Darrow. He found his body frozen, his feet locked to the cheap wooden deck.

"Your god is not here," Boarman said, droplets of blood coming off his lips.

Darrow watched in horror as Boarman carried Darla's limp body over his shoulder. He lifted her easily, a strength belying his size. Boarman moved her over the rail, and carried her to a low raised mound in the earth. The long boardwalk from the church out to the soundside deck, meant to be a walkway for sunset weddings, had purposefully avoided the big lump of earth. The plans had been made in advance, noting that the raised land of small rolling tufts was to not be touched. Until now, Darrow had barely noticed them.

All of this began to stir something in Darrow's memories. He thought he remembered doing something like this with Boarman's father, Greg Boarman. Something about the basketball court. Back in May…

Darla was unceremoniously dumped in the middle of the little undulations. She looked pale, lifeless, even the blood that flowed from her looked dark and sickening. The sun had set, letting a slim waning sliver of a moon shed its white light on the scene. Darrow watched as Darla's life leaked out into the soil.

Darrow awoke with a start. He felt like he had passed out, but was still standing, as Boarman shook him roughly. Boarman struck at the pastor, calling his name through the fog. The blows were powerful, overtly strong, as if Boarman had gained strength. "Do you hear me?!" he demanded. "Get rid of the body," he said. "This time, make it so that no one finds it." And he walked off, silently, into the night.

Darrow looked at poor Darla, stupid Darla who got involved in the wrong people. Now dead Darla. Darrow moved with a listless uncaring conviction as he picked up her body, as if he had nothing else to do, but needed to complete a disagreeable task just to be done. Like taking out the trash on a rainy night.

He lifter her body into his arms, noting how significantly lighter it was. "This all seems familiar," his mind said from deep within the cobwebs that cluttered his thoughts. As he carried the body away, he thought he saw the mounds moving.

Analepsis II

Hatteras
June, 1942

The twelve men that showed up in Hatteras all said they were sent down from Manteo and Rodanthe to Buxton to help with civilian work on the military bases there. They were all manual laborers, meant to help build barracks and offices for the Navy and Coast Guard. They just needed places to sleep, was all they asked.

Arthur Midgette was immediately suspicious. Everyone was. It was wartime, and anyone whom they didn't recognize was deserving of suspicion. They had already heard of the German couple who took the ferry to Ocracoke, and had been taking pictures and asking about what went on down there, near the Naval base. Hatteras folks were a close knit lot, distrusting of anyone that they didn't recognize. Arthur discussed the issue at the docks down in Hatteras Harbor.

"Oi dewn't knewww..." he spoke with his hard Hatteras brogue. "Dese boiys dewn't seem roight. Oi dewn't recognoise them, ner their names neither."

A few locals were more intrigued by the offer of help. As soon as the bombs had fallen on Pearl Harbor, almost all of the young, able bodied men had either cast their lot with the Coast Guard, a desirable post and about the only opportunity for many to leave the island, or had been culled up and drafted to go fight in the Pacific, a world away. Another old timer, Luke Farrow, all of 44 years, spoke up, "Well, we ought to see what them boiys ken do, at least. It ain't loike we got lotsa help around here."

And he was right. While the young local men had all left, another group, even larger, had shown up. The Coast Guard had filled the old life saving stations with men from the interior of the country, hayseeds from Texas to Kansas, many of whom had never seen the ocean before. And they all had to be fed and bunked down, and kept away from the Kinnakeet girls, and they were all completely useless at doing anything except wandering the beach looking for Germans and shooting at anything that moved.

All that were left of the menfolk were mostly older fishing boat captains, a few sailors who went out on small dories or shad boats to catch blue crabs or mullet. Life on the island was hard, and short, so the men were hardened to those facts. Young available men who wanted to help were in short supply.

But everyone knew that loose lips sink ships, and to be quiet and wary of any strangers. And these men certainly were strange. It was just that no one could figure out *why* they seemed so strange. Luke suggested they get all of the men out and see what they could do for the island.

It would be Greg Boarman who would speak up against the idea. "You are missing the point," he explained. The locals all recognized the man immediately as he spoke. Boarman had been the captain of a regional steamer coming out of Savannah when it had been torpedoed. He had miraculously survived on a life boat and had floated to shore, waterlogged and nearly frozen on a cold March morning. He was easy to notice, before he was even seen. The sailor spoke with a decidedly European accent. He claimed to be Balkan, via a roundabout path through Greece, Italy, Tunis, and Spain, before ending up on a steamship from South America heading to New York. All the other captains knew was that he had been able to quickly move his wealth to more profitable work, though the US government was severely limiting that at the moment. Most boats were not allowed to go fishing, and many were being used for patrols. The locals begrudgingly accepted him, mostly because he was driftwood that washed in, and he stuck around. He wasn't harmful in any way.

He just talked funny, with his vague European accent.

Which is what he pointed out to the others.

"You are missing the point," he said. "Listen to yourselves."

"We are," said Arthur, "we're talkin' abaot it naow."

"No," Boarman shook his head. "Listen to you… Listen to the way you talk." Boarman himself still occasionally dropped z's and v's into his language, "Listen to *ze vay* you talk."

"Yer one to complain," said Luke.

"No," Boarman shook his head. "Peasants," he thought but did not say. "You talk like you are from here. I talk like I am from the Mediterrenean, because I am."

"So?"

"These boys that came here. They don't sound like Nazis, do they?"

"No," agreed most of the men. "But they wouldn't want to, would they, if they were spoies," countered Arthur. "They speak perfect English."

"That is my point," said Boarman. "If they are supposed to be from here… they would sound like you.

"They wouldn't speak *perfect English*." Boarman emphasized the words in a decidedly American accent.

The other men were silent for a moment, then another. It was a realization that they took in hard. All made the realization that these boys, men, were, possibly, probably, not what they seem. And what was there to do about that?

Boarman walked away from the group. He knew without a doubt that those men were Nazi spies or fifth columnists. He could smell them from a mile away. The evil was too hard to hide.

Now to see what these men would do about it, and how he could influence it to his benefit.

It would take only two days, and little prompting from Boarman, to make a decision. Arthur Midgette had even suggested it first. "If we let them boiys get away, they will be takin' secrets with them," he said gravely. The men had been wandering the town, trying to get to the coast guard base, offering to help, but only for military services. None wanted to do any personal labor, or fishing on the sound. It was almost a dead giveaway that the men were not sent from Manteo as they had claimed.

"Whoy not just call the G-men in?" suggested Farrow.

"We have no proof," responded Midgette, and the other captains agreed. That German couple down in Ocracoke had simply gone back on the ferry two days later. No one knew what had happened to them. It was as if the federal government didn't care about spies on the little islands of the Outer Banks.

Boarman saw this as an opportunity. "Give me a day," he told the locals. "Let me work something out, I will get them out of the boarding house for a day, and one of you go search it."

So, they waited.

True to his word, Boarman was able to get every man out of the boarding rooms for an entire day. He simply hired them to build a lookout shack in nearby Avon, near the new high school. It gave the others plenty of time to search. Boarman explained to them, "Check inside the beds. People always think they will hide something under a mattress, but no one ever looks inside the box springs, or inside the mattress. Check those spots." He already knew what they would find. "I saw a lot of these people when I was in Italy and Czechoslovakia. They may not have anything incriminating, but they have something personal. It is difficult to leave a past life behind."

And right where Boarman said it would be, one of the men found a soiled and stained sailor's cap. The stitched eagle and German writing certainly gave a clue to its history, but the swastika clutched in the eagle's talons was a dead giveaway that it came from the Nazi Kriegsmarine.

It didn't take the men long to decide what to do with the twelve Nazi spies. Boarman made only one suggestion. "Use a knife," he said. "People will hear the gunshots."

The men were lured out in the middle of the night and all killed, their throats slit and bled out into the marsh waters by the sound. The sickening smell of warm blood was easily masked by the odorous stench of stagnant water mixed with rotting grass. Arthur Midgette wanted to throw the bodies in the sound, "Let the crabs have a feast," he suggested. Boarman put an end to that quickly. He had other plans. "Those bodies will float before the crabs eat them up. And you don't want the graves detail finding these men. Bury them in the marsh. Wrap them up and bury them."

And so twelve bodies were thrown into twelve shallow graves in the dark of night. The men of Hatteras figured that the worms would eat them the same as the crabs.

One man knew better.

When Arthur Midgette tried to bury the incriminating officer's cap with the dead Nazis, Boarman took it from the corpse it sat upon.

He wasn't about to let one of these idiot islanders bury his captain's hat.

37
Wednesday, July 17th

Steve felt the hair on the back of his neck stand up. It was a stereotype, a common cliché or trope, he knew, especially with his hirsute malediction. He had noted it two days before, or to be more precise, two nights before. It seemed to be happening at night now, he thought.

At first he hoped it was just a reaction to the general malaise of what had happened over the past several days, but he knew better. He sat in his chair, squeaking softly in the otherwise empty radio station. It was two o'clock at night, and nothing good should be stirring at 2 a.m.

Steve felt more sensitive at night. Even now, with a new moon, he still itched more, felt more uncomfortable, when things were happening in the middle of night. A full moon would make it a little worse, just because he thought it should. He had long ago adjusted to his rather uncomfortable condition. But full moons for some reason, perhaps a chosen integration to run with the pack, so to speak, left him a little more uninhibited. He generally could handle alcohol well, but at full moons... Well, it just wasn't so much fun to get the dog drunk at those times.

But now, alone, he knew that there was something more than just generalized threats. Something was happening. It had been going on, getting worse, over the past two nights, and Steve knew it. He didn't know what it was. But something was coming.

He found a break in his recordings and made a call back to his house. Thomas was probably asleep; he had none of Steve's nocturnal habits. At sixty five, he had also lost his long held ability to wake up when called upon, used repeatedly in World War II and perfected, he would say, when he had a baby son long ago. Steve felt a little bad about waking the man, but desperate times…

"Hey, Cap," Steve said to a groggy Thomas. "Listen, I don't know for sure, but, something's up."

"How bad?" was all Thomas asked. "Are we on the other side of the map?"

"I don't know," was all Steve could say. "But it's starting to feel… close."

"Asheville?"

"Yeah," Steve answered, "Asheville.

"Listen, I don't know what's coming, but it feels like that. Like Asheville. Not as big, but bad. More dangerous. I'm going to find a stopping point and come home. But look, I think that maybe you should go over to Jackie's house. If this is someone targeting me, they may come after her first." Invariably, the bullies prey upon the weakest first. And Jackie was a weak point for Steve.

Steve gave Thomas directions to Jackie's house, then hung up the phone. He was almost finished with his recording of his show. "Just a few minutes," it was all he needed. Steve rewound his tape and quickly boxed up the finished product. Time was nebulous right now, a mix of the late night of the day before and the early morning of tomorrow. He wished he could just finish his show tomorrow, but the pickup was only hours away.

"As long as there is a tomorrow," he thought. It was a grave and serious thought that came to him. In all his days, he felt like there wasn't a tomorrow, just another today, the same day as the day before. The same age, the same face. "Or the same night,"

Steve joked ruefully as he stepped out into the heated darkness. He had been a nightcrawler for so long that he normally enjoyed the inky black. But this time it hid something. Or some things. They were far away from here, right now, but whatever it was, there were many of them, and they were getting closer. Not physically, but something was crawling deeper and deeper into his mind. There were monsters out there, looking for him.

Steve thought of the word Thomas had used. "The other side of the map." It was an old term, not used anymore. They used it back when his platoon was in Austria, on the wrong side of enemy lines. He hadn't heard the term in decades, but the feeling was the same. Steve flashed back to seeing what the Nazis had done, long ago. This had that same feel, the same smell.

It was a long, hot, and uncomfortable drive back to his home in Buxton. The night air was humid, sticky, salty from a southwest wind. At every turn, Steve imagined demons in the shadows behind the rolling yaupon bushes and Loblolly Pines.

The hair on the back of his neck stopped standing up.

It started to grow.

38

Thomas drove to the Woods' home, but realized he couldn't just stop out front and sit in his car and stare out the window. Not only would it be obvious to any threat, but if anyone saw him, he would have to answer questions that he definitely didn't have responses to.

The M1911A1 semi-automatic pistol loosely sitting in its holster would be even harder to explain.

Thomas placed the weapon on his belt and left the car by the side of the road. He planned to walk in the darkness to a better place to observe the house and the land around it.

The housing development had stopped work after the fire. Ostensibly due to waiting on insurance, there was still the feeling that it was no longer wanted by a certain crowd on the island. It meant that there were still several houses standing empty, and right now, at 2:30 a.m., all the homes were pitch black. There was no moon to give a glow to the night. The moon would have been a double edged sword. A full moon meant more light to see in the open roads and treeless lots, but also would create shadows to hide in. Now, in the dark, where there was structure, the shadows were dark as death itself. Thomas found his way through the back yard of an unfinished home that faced the Woods' house. It was going to be a long and uncomfortable night, he told himself as he rubbed his sweaty and salt rimed neck. The local mosquitoes had already sniffed him out, and were trying to find a bare spot to tap his bloodlines.

Thomas looked through the trees to his right. Somewhere over there, through those trees, Steve's house stood, but it was too far to see any lights or even notice if Steve drove up. He was too smart for that, Thomas knew. Steve would do the same thing Thomas did. Park his Jeep and walk up, moving slowly, so that he wasn't seen. Thomas wouldn't know if anything was happening there until he went there himself.

And Steve could handle anything that was thrown at him.

"Asheville," Thomas shivered at the thought.

He had settled in, trying to get comfortable in the covered parking spot. The concrete pad kept him out of the sand and scrub brush, but offered little comfort. "At least the bugs won't be crawling up my legs," Thomas thought as he shook his head slightly to keep the mosquitoes at bay. Any movement, even swatting at one of the little bloodsuckers, could give him away. But being still made him sore and restless. It was a cliché, he knew, but at 65 he was getting too old for this.

So was his bladder.

About an hour into the stakeout, he found that he could no longer hold it. Nor could he do what he did forty years ago when he was in combat, simply aim it down his trouser and piss down his leg. The tall posts that held up the house seemed as good a target as anything, so he unzipped his pants and relieved himself against one of the pilings. He wondered if anything could hear him. "They have about two minutes," Thomas thought, knowing how long it seemed to take to get it all out of him now.

He looked around in the dark.

That's when he saw the first movement.

"Of course," he said in his head. He had an agonizing wait to finish. With a shake, he zipped up and reached for his weapon.

39

Steve approached his house with a tingling apprehension. He knew that the world he was in was turning wrong, and fast. He felt his body respond, a mix of choice and involuntary reactions. It was the worst of all the feelings. When he would change, when it just happened, it was almost a relief, like a tightness being removed, his back being cracked by wonderfully strong hands to let out the tension. When he made it happen, there was a strange mix of cold and hot, both losing sensations and a feel of hot blood pouring through him, knowing he was going to be free, a wonderful animal feel of an upcoming fight. A bloodletting.

When he had to encourage the change as it happened, when it was too slow or just not enough, it hurt. His bones ached and his blood stung as his body both resisted and acquiesced. He needed to get inside before it happened, but he had little time. Steve had to both move slow to not be noticed, but fast enough that he wasn't curled up in a ball as his shirt and pants cut into his too rapidly changing body. His toes already hurt with every step.

He told his body to stop, and it listened. It didn't like it, it didn't completely obey, but it listened. Steve made his way through the twisted oak trees of the small maritime forest that stood in his back yard to get to the back door. The tall trees and towering branches offered a semblance of protection in the dark, the same as they shaded the bright sun of middday.

"I just have to get inside, get my clothes off, and..." Steve was telling himself his mantra. It was a marking of time and place. He used it when he ran, or in cases like this. He just needed one marker, something to reach, a doable goal. In this case, he just needed to get inside his house for only a moment. If he felt safe for a moment, he could undress, and get a weapon.

Not that he wasn't a weapon already.

Steve could smell them now. They were close, or at least close enough. He worried about Jackie, her family, and Thomas. The things, he knew what they were by feel and by smell, were much closer to Jackie's home than his. It would all be happening soon. He felt inside his pants pocket for his keys. His jeans were getting tighter by the moment as he struggled with the key ring. "I should have kept them in my hand," he chastised himself. He hadn't wanted the keys to jingle on his fingers. Now he fumbled with the keys as his fingers began to lose feeling and his nails grew. It took two tries to get the key in the lock. Steve began to feel things on the back of his neck. "Too soon," he tried to convince himself.

The door opened with a shudder as the old wood rubbed the jam. But Steve was in. He kicked at his shoes, pulling them off with his toe to opposite heel. The simple relief made him feel better, slightly calmer. Next his jeans were unbuttoned and he pulled at the legs, turning them inside out without care. His shirt came off last as he simply twisted it off over his head. Even in the dark, he could feel his body changing, a strange soft blanket of hair forming on his arms, back, and shoulders. Only a modicum of decency made him leave his long boxer briefs on. His hips twisted as he felt the muscles in his thighs and buttocks twitch. Steve flinched as he felt the sockets in his joints turn slightly, then pop with delightful relief.

He strode into his bedroom, leaving the lights off. Stars tried to twinkle through the trees, as the curtains washed out the subtle colors of nighttime. Steve was able to find and reach his framed display of his combat knife in the dark. It had been a specially made weapon, given to him because it had been made in Ohio, his home state. The long blade glinted in the darkness.

It was unique in design, as were all its brothers and sisters. Made in Dover, Ohio by cutlery maker Earnest Warther, it looked nothing like the typical Government Issue knives and bayonets used across the armed forces of World War II. The handle was black ebony, a popular hard wood used by Warther, different from the leather and wood bound handles of the Ka-Bar fighting knife. But the blade was nothing short of a work of art.

Long and thin, but with a diamond shaped spine to reinforce its strength, this knife also had a decorative strip of the ebony wood and a long line of silver to the curved pointed tip. It shone in the darkc like a thin string of a midnight lightning bolt from deadly tip to the handle.

It was familiar in Steve's trembling and growing hand.

His body relaxed. He let the change come, the stretch to his cheeks, his nose, his face. Everything went dark, then his world brightened again. Through the house he could feel and see to the outside.

And smell. The scents were delicious. Salt, earth, leaves, odors carried on the summer winds. The smell of still and pungent brackish water, the rotting marsh grasses and weeds. And the smell of rotting death, the breath of a corpse that somehow could still exhale, all surrounded him. He moved silently, a dark shape in a dark world, leaving the back door open, uncaring about the inside of the house now. He was as much a beast as he was a human now.

Steve's ears perked at a sharp sound, then another. A gunshot, quickly repeated, came from not far off, but not close. Somewhere beyond the trees. He knew the sound, but was not shocked by it. It meant prey was near, possibly wounded.

Easier to hunt.

Easier to kill.

Steve stood on padded paws and leapt ferally from his back porch to the roof of his house, landing silently on the low sloping roof. He knew they were coming now, and delighted in the anticipation.

40

The dark shapes moved surprisingly fast. Either that or Thomas was not moving as fast as he used to. Thomas decided it must be the former, because he certainly couldn't be getting as old as he felt right now, at 2:30 in the morning, as he ran toward the steps to the Wood home. Of course it had to be on stilts. His knees felt every step of the wooden stairs.

At least he didn't trip going up in the dark.

By the time he had gotten to the raised porch of the new home, one of the shapes was beating down the door. Glass from the window tinkled both in and out, falling on linoleum and wood. Whatever it was, it didn't try to get in the door by using the doorknob. It just continued to bang on the door, trying to break down the frame.

Thomas didn't have the same animal killing desire as Steve. No matter what the man/thing was doing, Thomas couldn't just gun the thing down by shooting it in the back. "Stop!" he commanded. He didn't know any more to say.

He *really* didn't know what to say when the thing turned to his voice.

The darkness should have helped hide its looks, but all the night did was make it more horrifying. Whoever this had been, it wasn't that man anymore. The face drooped, eyes sunken in and black, staring but without recognition. The body was emaciated with stretched skin, strangely tightened and wrinkled at the same time, a shriveled and rotting cooked animal that has been left to decompose. Bony fingers that were black and torn reached out to the sound of Thomas' command. What it was going to do did not include stopping. It turned, stumbled, then lurched at Thomas.

Thomas, his pistol already raised, fired, once, then again, a habit evolved from decades of practice. He saw the first bullet impact near the center of mass, tearing a dry and dusty hole through the thing's chest and pass through easily, too easily. He adjusted his stance, turning to his left so that the second shot would not pass into the darkened house. He tried not to rush, to place his shot, but the thing was moving, fast, too fast, too scary, too dangerous... The second bullet ripped through the lower jaw and neck of the thing, easily tearing the dried skin and rotted bone. Black teeth disappeared into the darkness as the head turned, too far for any normal human.

The second shot had slowed the thing, but not stopped him. It staggered, its head loose where bits of the tendons of the neck had been torn from the shoulder. But the bullets did not stop it from coming forward.

So conscious of the horrendous beast in front of him, Thomas barely registered the quick footsteps that came from behind, until it was too late. He felt the bony hand of another creature grab at his shoulder, then a rotting smell as the thing wrapped sinuous arms around him. Thomas turned his head only in time to see the other thing at his neck, a bony skull covered in stretched and desiccated skin like a demonic mummy. Its mouth opened as it sank black and broken teeth into Thomas's shoulder.

41

Steve heard the gunfire, first a group of two shots, then four in quick succession, then two more. Then silence. His mind cleared. Deep in his depths, his human mind took in the sounds, knowing that his friend, someone he knew, was dealing with a danger, a not close not far danger. The words and thoughts flowed through him, uncaring, unconcerned, free to pass. He was now focused but relaxed, a surreal joy of the hunt coming on him. A chance to jump, to pounce, to tear and kill. To kill, the joy to rip and tear, the feeling of victory.

Steve fought his mind back from his animal instincts. He couldn't let it get too far. He had long ago learned to control the beast within him. But he also knew when to let it go. This would be one of those times. Somewhere nearby Thomas was taking care of his threat. But for Steve the threat was bigger, and getting nearer by the second.

He knew what they were, knew by the scent and by his experience. Someone had called forth the dead, revenants, ghostly zombies, hunters and slaves of a master. Thoughtless, mindless, they only lived because someone had brought them to life after a death that had preserved them. They would be horrible, horrid, unrelenting.

And it would be a delight to tear and rip and kill and…

Steve saw the first one in a glint of starlight between the trees. In a heartbeat, more moved. They came from the sound side, up the shore, through the darkness of the trees. Steve felt a growl deep within that he forced himself into silence.

One creature found its way to the long wooden walkway that led to the house from the sound. The rest of them didn't bother. They just stumbled through the trees and broken scrub brush, the yaupon and waxy bushes that were a tangled labyrinth to get to Steve's home. They didn't care if they were poked or scratched by the growing yucca or briar bushes. They were unfeeling, single minded physical ghosts tasked with one charge, to find and kill Steve in his home. To perform the command of their master who brought them back to life.

Steve waited, measuring the distance. His haunches twitched, ready to jump. At twenty feet away, the first revenant was easily within range of his leap, but the human in him forced Steve to wait. Closer targets, more grouped together, more force applied, the soldier still commanded the animal in him.

Another revenant made its way onto the wooden path. It almost pushed the first one out of the way as the single minded task drove them all closer and closer. Neither cared about being pushed nor did they fight among each other for prominence. There was no pride, no manliness, no chest thumping to be first.

Just two of the several revenants were on the deck, but they were as good a target as any. Steve let his instincts lead him, and leapt.

It was only an indistinct shape that the revenants saw. Something black and silent, like a cape of night, blowing off the roof. They made no motion of recognition until the two revenants fell in a heap.

Steve felt it happening as if his mind was a second behind his body. His jaw opened and took in the closer of the two at the neck.

It snapped in his wide mouth, his long canine teeth crunching through the dried flesh and brittle bone. The taste was horrid, a mix of dust and rot, but his jaws hung on, closing, harder, harder, bones breaking and shattering as his wolf-like head with a long narrow snout, shook at the neck of the revenant until it broke and came apart. The head fell and rolled only once before stopping on the wooden walkway.

The other revenant fell with the first. Steve's long paw, no longer just a hand, with dark, heavy claws, had pounded into the revenant's upper chest, breaking the sternum and ribs with its impact. His fingers and claws sunk into the dried skin through tattered clothes. The revenant's chest broke, its bones torn from the body as it flopped to the wood walkway. Steve lifted himself from the first revenant by crushing the second, then ripping the ribs from its chest.

Even without a ribcage, the revenant tried to reach for the hairy and muscled arm that pinned it down. The newly opened hole in its body allowed Steve to reach through, past the useless lungs and unbeating heart to the thing's spine. A giant paw grabbed at the remains of the revenant, while his other hand stabbed his knife awkwardly at the bundle of nerves, muscle, and bone, and pulled.

The body tore open on the wooden deck, from its back through the front. A gory paw, covered in thick black blood, syrupy and useless in the long dead revenant, came out with the spinal discs. Its abdomen opened, spilling out a stomach, spleen, pancreas, and finally shriveled intestines as Steve split the body to its crotch.

The thing's neck tried to hang on, but was no match to the force of the beast pulling at the revenant's spine. Its neck opened on a long ago made gash from when the man's throat was slit by a local captain. Then the flesh began to fold, crinkle, crease, and finally, give way with a horrendous tear. The head, lifeless before and now more so, with its blackened eye sockets, rolled back as if looking up into the moonlit sky. It showed no signs of pain as it gave up its last moment of the undead life that it had.

Steve simply dropped the severed bones onto the torn, unmoving body.

The rest of the revenants began to swarm the porch. Dark, cadaverous, and skeletal, they crept onto the deck like attacking insects. Steve swung a long muscular arm, knife outstretched, to slash at the dark face of an approaching creature. Its skin ripped off in Steve's hand, but the demon kept coming, along with its brothers.

It took only moments, a shiver of time, the beasts belying their deathly look with an uncanny speed. They pulled at Steve's fur covered arms to keep him from grabbing them. Three of the revenants pinned his right arm with the long silver and black blade in his hand. Steve lashed out with powerful jaws to tear at the tense dry flesh of the revenants. Even as his teeth dug into the shoulder of one creature, who showed no pain from the attack, another dug bony fingers and black teeth into Steve's arm. He felt a strange diseased fire burn into his muscles. His arm flexed involuntarily, pulling another revenant closer to him.

Steve bit at the head of one of the demons, tearing at the face of the closest revenant. It struggled and pulled, which only allowed Steve's giant teeth to rip, tear, then rend. Its face tore, and then the bones cracked open. Brains spilled out, and the creature finally lost its death grip on Steve.

The others were unmoved by the loss. They would continue to fight Steve until they all finished, either destroyed by their prey, or they had killed the predator. Seven still fought against one. No matter the supernatural strength of Steve's wolfen curse, the numbers were great against him. One after another, they pulled, crushed, and bit, into his arms and neck, through the course hair that tried to protect him from the attacks.

Steve felt the anger and fear arise within him. It was the most vicious of his animal instincts, something injected in him from so long ago, as his body gave over fully to the cursed animal, the beast within him. His legs grew, his body stretched. No longer Steve Brodie, just the wolf inside, his feral blood coursed through his rapidly growing body. Muscles ached from the stress of change as much as from the torment of the revenants. In a final push, his lungs released with a wild growl that would terrify any person that heard it.

The revenants were no longer people, and had no idea what it meant for them.

Steve's hands grew long and flat. The knife clattered dully to the wood deck. With his arms held and the revenants trying to pin their adversary down, Steve, now the *pricolici*, the werewolf, was free only with his long hind legs. He used one with massive effect. Raising a horrid giant foot, its claws black and deep, it reached all the way up to the chest of one of the revenants and raked down. The entire body was torn off the front of the revenant. Gore rushed out in a flood of entrails, spilling on the deck.

Released from one more of his persecutors, the pricolici was now freed of one of many weights. It raised the foot again, still entangled in the offal of the last of its victims. This time it kicked away, with such force as to drive off an attacking revenant. The demon's teeth were latched into wolf flesh and hair, only to tear away from its meal as its body flew off, landing with a cracking thud against the wall of the old beach house. It collapsed with a crushed skull and snapped neck. The revenant's old bones were unable to withstand such a withering blow from the giant pricolici.

Five more revenants remained, and they did their worst as they were unconcerned that their numbers dwindled. Three worked at the right arm of the giant wolf, two struggled to contain the now free left. The pricolici beast bent and twitched, shaking in an attempt to free itself. The revenants pounded and pulled, trying to crack open ribs to get to a beating heart that none of the revenants had.

The pricolici began to rage. It swatted at the head of one more revenant in its course paw. The demon fell with a giant hairy hand on its head. The pricolici squeezed and pressed until the skull broke. In the claws, brain and bone spread like a bloody macabre dough. The head was twisted and pulled off, letting the body flop before kicking the remains away. Now the towering pricolici rose to stand over the shorter revenants while one more lost his undead life as his neck was squeezed to a snap in the pricolici's closing elbow joint.

The wolf's right arm was searing now. It was torn from the rotted teeth of the revenants, scratched and flayed by the bones protruding from long dead fingers. Fur may have hidden the wounds to the body, but the bruises were there, from ribs being pounded in hopes of getting them to break, to rend, open the heart up to spill blood, to pump it out to make the dark backyard wilderness a sticky and hot abattoir.

But with a freed arm and strength still in its legs, the pricolici now was in power. It pulled the three remaining revenants off, peeling them from its body like the unwanted parasites they were. They were tossed, one after the other, over the railings or into the trees. They struggled, the remains of their bodies broken and dysfunctional. Legs and arms were snapped, which did not allow them to crawl or stand to face their threat. They would pull themselves toward their enemy with a finger if that was all they had, but they stood no chance against the giant beast before them.

The pricolici was hurt as well. Instincts kicked in, and for a moment the beast stopped, a soft whine on its snout, as it tried to lick its right arm where it was torn open from the attack. Something deep within, the human side, was repulsed by the taste of dried and dead hands that had probed and torn at his body. Blood and gore flicked off a long tongue, lapping outward to get the awful flavor out of the pricolici's mouth.

The three revenants were still alive, and they had no concerns of pain, taste, or damage. They were tasked with one driven goal, to destroy their enemy. They had been tasked by their master, who had awoken them with his dark and ancient words. They were hell bent, obsessed, single minded, and driven toward one target. The three had no communication with each other, no plans, no tactic to allow one to attack while the others waited.

Two revenants rolled onto the deck, their arms and elbows broken or shoulders snapped, and stood to attack the pricolici. The third, with a damaged leg and knee, pulled itself up onto the wooden walkway and dragged its body along the rough planks as splinters and shards jammed into its flesh.

The first two attacked again, simultaneously. Not from any coordination, but merely because they arrived at the same moment. They leapt at the pricolici, hoping to bring it down and tear at it. Their fumbling bodies, thin and dry, and mindless brains knew no better option. They reached for the long arms and grabbed, as the pricolici shook at them to get them off.

The pricolici found purchase on the remnants of clothes on the revenants. It raked its claws into their shirts and skin and bone beneath, then raised the two high off the wooden deck. With the pricolici's great height, the two undead bodies were lifted twelve feet in the air. Then they were brought down with a shattering crash, breaking through the wooden walkway. One was split in two at the back of its chest as the body hit a solid joist. The pricolici lifted it again, its insides spilling out in a detestable mess of odor and offal as forty year dead guts, intestines, stomach, colon, all stretched from the split between the chest and the hips. Once more it was brought down, this time cracking its head on the same open joist, spilling out the remains of its barely functioning brain.

The other revenant fared no better. It had been broken across its body, arms, legs, hips, ribs, all shattered and speared through the rotting flesh. It lay in an even unnatural pose for an undead demon with its arms and legs bent horribly backwards as it was splayed across the broken wood. Only its jaw still worked as it tried in vain to snap at the pricolici's hand.

Almost as if an act of generosity, the pricolici placed its large course paw over the face of the revenant. Then it gripped the head and twisted, pulled, and squeezed until the face collapsed into a black porridge of blood and bone and brain.

So concentrated on the two revenants who had been able to attack it, running on instinct, the pricolici had none of Steve's calculating mind available. It had simply not seen nor felt the last revenant, broken and crawling, behind it. It seemed like nothing of a threat.

Until it picked up the knife and plunged it into the pricolici's lowest rib.

The wolf made a desperate howl of pain as the long blade cut in, scraping the bone and burning inside it. As it jerked away from the attack, the revenant's weak grip, kneeling on one leg, held on only for a moment, but a moment long enough for the wound to tear. The pricolici, aware, reacting, trying to find the human part, saw the knife, the wound, and pulled it out awkwardly with a spurt of blood, black in the starlit night.

A wound like that could injure or kill a man, if it hit right. It would normally have done little to a creature as strong as a pricolici. But the thin silver decoration on the blade burned like a sliver of fire. It was a poison to the stab, made double as it was pulled out.

The pricolici saw the offending revenant, barely able to move. In the moment, the pricolici was more animal, and the revenant was, if it could be, something somewhat human. If there was anything of Steve Brodie in the pricolici at the moment, he would have recognized a smile of delight from the demon revenant that had stabbed him. A Nazi smile, knowing that even though he was broken, dead once and soon dead twice, at least he had inflicted a little pain on his adversary.

The pricolici wiped the smile away with a giant stomp from its clawed foot. It tore the face off the skull, ripped the skin, then bone, from the chest. Ribs snapped as the chest unzipped, exposing a useless and black heart. The bloated and empty guts of the once Nazi spy poured out, ripped open past the hips, its tiny and useless genitals flung away from its body.

The last revenant was split in half, from head to hips. Fighting the pain in its side, the pricolici struck again, ripping harder, crushing the bones of the spine. Then, it finally applied the killing stroke, a wide and powerful swipe to the remains of the head, separating it from the shoulders in a splatter or gore that shot across the trees in the night.

Panting and suffering, bleeding and unable to lick its wound in its side, the pricolici collapsed on the deck, surrounded by the remains of ten revenants, decaying in a silver light. With the immediate threat gone, something would happen. It must, as it always had. The change back would come, but slowly, almost as if the pricolici fought against it. In a last gasp, rasping lungs filled and it let out a soft wail of pain, but also a calling to anything else listening.

This was still its land.

This pricolici still ruled its dominion.

42

Thomas leaned against the outside wall of the Woods' house. He held his shoulder in his opposite hand, trying to staunch the blood flow from an open wound. He had stopped the first revenant from breaking down the door to the house, but had not been able to stop the second one from attacking him from behind.

It had pulled him backwards, away from the falling first revenant, tearing and biting into his shoulder. Thomas felt the crush of a relentless attack, black teeth digging into his flesh through his shirt, before tearing the shoulder open.

Thomas had seen stars, going nearly blind from pain. The back porch light came on at the same time. The Wood family was awake from the breaking window and resultant pistol fire. Thomas had responded as well as he could; he crossed his body with his arm, shoving his service pistol under his armpit and into the mass of the biting revenant. Then he fired repeatedly, four shots, until the thing fell off. Turning to the heap of broken revenant, he delivered a coup de grâce shot into the thing's skull.

He was already weakening. The pain from his shoulder was worse than it should have been, and he felt the shock coming on, a cold sweat that began to pour down his head and back. The other revenant was twisted, broken at the neck, but still tried to turn to attack Thomas. With a shaking hand, Thomas took the time to aim, and blew the thing's head into dust with a single shot.

He then staggered to the door before falling in a heap over himself.

He somehow heard the door open moments later, and heard himself stammer "Armed officer..." before dropping his weapon on the ground.

He awoke thirty seconds later, his body dripping in sweat as if someone had dumped a bucket of water on him. His head spun as he tried to listen. "Call the police," a female voice said distantly, and then another, "No, he's with the FBI," and then a shocked comment, "What *are* these things?!"

"This is Thomas, uh, Fredericks?" Jackie stammered, shocked at what she saw, but recognizing the man collapsed on her deck. "He's a friend of Steve's!" She could see the disbelief in her parents' faces. How was this old man a friend of Steve Brodie?

"No," Thomas choked out the words. "Don't call the police." There was no way to explain what had happened, and Thomas knew that he can't involve the local deputy.

Thomas must have passed out again. He woke up to a mix of a nagging, crawling pain in his arm, as if maggots ate at his flesh, as well as a horrifying shake to his spine. Something was shaking the house from below.

He was able to regain consciousness enough to focus on the steps from the porch. The light from the porch lit only to the end of the deck. Something else was coming up the steps. He tried to look, to focus, to make his mouth and mind work, but the pain was intense.

All four people, Jackie, her parents, and Thomas, saw the shape arise up the steps, as if it crawled on long spindly legs. Hairy and naked, covered in blood and gore, it staggered and then stood at the end of the steps.

Jackie was horrified by the monster that appeared only feet from her. She heard her mother scream as her father, responding the only way he could, pushed her behind his back. "Jackie!" he cried, he couldn't protect both of them, "get inside, please!"

Jackie looked at the thing, then at the dead and broken revenants, and the bleeding wound in Thomas' shoulder. Instead of running, she picked up the abandoned pistol. She held it at arm's length from her, squinting in trepidation at the sound that would come out as she squeezed the trigger.

Thomas tried to yell, "No! It's…" but nothing happened. Thomas had discharged his entire magazine full of bullets. Jackie pulled on the open slide, then tried working the hammer, imitating the old cowboy movies while raking her thumb roughly across the lever. With no bullets left, the pistol would not fire. The trigger would not even engage.

"That's Steve!" Thomas was able to gather enough wits and strength to call out, as the thing collapsed on the top of the steps. When it looked up, Jackie could finally see the human face behind the mask of pain and wispy hair. Clumps fell off as it, as he, struggled to his feet, clutching his side.

They watched as the creature changed back, metamorphosed into the human they had known. Steve became Steve again, but now naked and torn.

"That," he panted, "would not have helped." Steve pointed a shaking finger at the pistol still pointed at him by Jackie. She sheepishly put it down, still staring, incoherently at what, and who she was seeing.

Her parents thought she was looking at Steve's naked body, but she was stunned instead, realizing that all he had told her was true. It had to be. She watched him change. Change back. Something had attacked him, something like the things lying dead and decomposing on her back porch, and he had survived. She moved from Thomas to Steve's side as she tried to help him up.

"I'll be okay," he winced, holding his side. The wound normally would heal quickly, but the silver from the decorative part of the steel blade had done its damage. That would take time, and it would hurt. "How is Thomas?"

"One of those things bit him," Jackie pointed. "He seems sick."

"He's infected," Steve said,

"Will he turn into one of… those?" Jackie pointed at the dead revenants.

"No," Steve answered, "He's infected, like you and I," not like me, Steve thought, "would be. It's from the bite. He's got an infection. It's old, and it will spread fast. We need to get him treatment."

Steve looked at Dr. Wood pleadingly, "Can you take us to my house?" he asked. He knew it was a lot to ask from the man. It was so much to take in, but they needed to hurry. "I can help him there."

The five of them piled unceremoniously into Dr. Woods' truck, and he raced to Steve's house. Even with Steve's home just across the road from them, there was no link but some boards over a ditch. The drive seemed long and full of effort. Steve found a towel in the car to cover up, more aware than ever that people were seeing him. They were unused to such an event, a personal vision that had shaken others, shaken them too far. This was the worst moment to have a crisis, he knew.

Once inside, Steve lay Thomas on the sofa. Still just in a towel, he found the bowl that sat on the windowsill, full of strange vials and bottles. "What is that?" Jackie had seen it and wondered, but never had the time to ask when she had been in Steve's home.

Steve was quiet for a moment, as he rummaged through the myriad collection. "Pain," he said mysteriously, "Death, life, the world, darkness," it seemed as if he was labeling the strange vials of powder and liquid. He gathered two in his hands. As he held the bottles, he watched to see if his hand was still shaking.

Steve went over to Thomas' prone body, which was covered in sweat. "What…" was all that Thomas got out before Steve stuck him with a needle protruding from a vial with a red label. Thomas almost immediately reacted, a mix of disappointment and then calm relaxation.

Steve looked at the other bottle in his hand. "What did you do to him?" Dr. Wood asked. It looked as if Thomas had fainted, passed out. Instead of answering, Steve looked at Mrs. Wood. Her concern was on her face. Steve hoped she would respond with action. "Go to my bathroom. There are syringes in there, in paper. Get me one, and look in a black bag under the sink. Find a tube with a red label that says 'Antibiotic ointment' on it. Bring them both back to me."

He turned to Jackie. "Go get a bag of frozen vegetables out of my freezer. Put it on his neck."

As the two rushed out of the room, Steve finally answered Dr. Wood. "Be careful with that vial," he pointed at the little bottle with the needle on top. "Put that plastic over the needle. Then go to the kitchen and stick it into a potato or something. Make sure the needle doesn't stick out."

Dr. Wood picked up the vial as if it were poison. He read the label, red and white, Morphine Titrate May Be Addictive.

When Mrs. Wood arrived with a paper sleeve that held a sterile syringe, Steve immediately tore it open, withdrew an amount of liquid from a vial, and injected it into Thomas' wounded arm. He neither measured nor cleaned the area, figuring there was nothing worse that could get in.

"You have to take him to a hospital," Steve explained. "Take both vials, tell the doctor he has a rapid infection, and received morphine and penicillin." Steve attempted to spread a layer of white goo from the tube Mrs. Wood brought onto the wound. "He will need multiple rounds of antibiotics and fever reducers." Steve felt around in Thomas' pocket, then into his wallet. He found a worn business card. "You need to call that number, tell them Thomas' name, it's on the card, and tell them I sent you. Say 'Steve Brodie.' Whoever answers may not know what that means, but make sure they hear it, that they write it down. You'll get help for him quickly."

"Shouldn't we call an ambulance?" Mrs. Wood asked. "They have a Lifeflight helicopter in Nags Head."

Steve had no time to explain the need to get them away from here. "Take him to Rodanthe, or to Oregon Inlet, just not here. You can't be here." He looked specifically at Jackie. "None of you can be here."

"Why?" Jackie asked. "What is happening?!" She almost started to cry. Again she felt the helplessness, like the time she was attacked. Only this time it seemed worse. Monsters were crawling up to her, to kill her family. None of this was real.

"There are things happening here," Steve just couldn't explain it all. There was no time. "I told you about me. This is why I came. I was drawn here, to stop this, I think." It seemed all too mystical and messianic, but Steve had felt this change from the first day he arrived, even before he discovered that poor girl's body.

And now he had to end it.

"I have to make sure that this doesn't happen anymore," he pointed at Thomas, but let his gesture travel to her parents, and then a deep glare at Jackie. "I'm the one to stop it. It's what I am supposed to do."

"No, wait," Jackie saw Steve and Dr. Wood lift a limp and tired man from the sofa to carry him outside. "What's going to happen to you?" she cried.

Steve didn't answer. He needed to get his friend safe. All his friends. "You have to go," he finally said to Jackie. "You're a weakness. You're my weakness. Whoever is doing this, they will come for you because you are a better target than me." He put his hand on his wound, now caked and dry with blood. "You would hurt more," he said simply.

Jackie was taken aback, thinking he was calling her weak, but then she realized. Steve meant that if something happened to her, it would hurt him more than his own wounds.

"Jackie," her mother pleaded, "we have to go!"

Jackie saw Thomas in the back seat, almost asleep and peaceful, except for the vague outlines of his face sagging in exhaustion, and the terrible wound torn through his clothes. Her mother climbed in the back seat with the man.

"Jackie," her father spoke now, knowing the words he had to say, "We need your help."

Knowing she could do no good with what Steve was going to face, but terrified that this was the last time she would see him, Jackie held back tears. She wanted to hug Steve close, not let go, not let him go to what might be his death, whatever it was he would face, but she was afraid that if she did, she would never leave.

But she had to.

"Come back," she said quietly, "You have to."

She closed the car door, and it sped off into the night.

43

Harrison Boarman, born of the death of Linda Patterson, who gave her blood and her life to let him become young again, born from himself, Greg Boarman, Gregor Boarman, Gregor Eberhard, the former Nazi, former of many things, so many that he barely remembered his first name, born five hundred years ago as Juraj Branimir. Juraj was a bastard child who took his revenge first on the people who ostracized his mother, killing them in the dark Croatian night. Then he found his father, his uncle, his mother's brother, all one, and killed him. Then his mother, who didn't understand who he was, what he had become. He killed her, too.

The Croatians called him *pijavica*, the leech, the bloodsucker, a cold blooded killer who took revenge in the night, while he sinned in the day. It turned into a curse, but only a curse if they saw it that way.

To Harrison, né Branimir, he saw it as a blessing. He would live forever, forever changing, growing old, then young again, as long as he fed. He gathered wealth, feeding on the worthless rich, taking advantage of them. He fed off of the gullible poor, just taking from them. His bloodthirst gave him a penchant for war, with his skill, and taste, at killing, as well as his near invulnerability to most injury.

He had delighted in war, and found his niche. His family name became synonymous with a callous ability to kill without concern. He saw the growth of a powerful and united Prussia, and knew that he would find a home there, not in the unwelcoming Balkans of central Europe. His family grew, new names created as he was born and reborn. When the Nazis arose, with their own form of killing and hate, Boarman finally felt his place in his world. A place where he could kill and take without reason, only with power and control.

But no matter what, he aged, he changed, he had to take to grow young.

"This *pricolici* will change that," he knew.

If he could entice the wolf into his home, Boarman could take its blood.

His people in Croatia had hunted the *pricolici*, the werewolf. They had feared the *pijavica*.

The vampire.

He had little hope that his revenants would defeat the pricolici. Boarman only hoped they would weaken it, and then drive it to him, where he could take what was left.

Boarman waited in the church. *His* church. The fools that followed that idiot Darrow thought they would become wealthy, to reach a heaven paved in gold that was on earth. The prosperity of greed. Yet he took from them all that they gave. The money wasn't the goal. He had all of that. He wanted their souls, their lives.

Boarman looked at the central decoration in the church, a giant glass mirror cross. It was made with old glass, streaked and veined. The power of the mirror radiated to him. The fools all had a piece of the mirror in their homes, allowing Boarman to be inside. He didn't need to see in their houses. They had nothing he wanted to view. But when they looked into it, just as they had been indoctrinated in the church, to look at themselves as better, more beautiful, more appropriate, more right, than others, all it did was feed power and control to Boarman, in his tabernacle.

He had no fear or discomfort at the supposedly Christian symbol. There was nothing Christian at all in this church. "If any of them ever read the Bibles in the pews," he thought, "they wouldn't believe the words inside. They would rather believe what they think than know what the words meant."

They were all idiots, he knew, moronic devotees that had nothing of value except their pathetic lives. When he took from the *pricolici*, he would leave this place. He could blame Darrow for the deaths, for the destruction. He probably would have to burn the church, but the building was worthless. As was Darrow. "He is an idiot, as well," thought Boarman, "easily manipulated with money or sex with a young girl or boy. That's the one problem with useful idiots. Once they are no longer useful, they are still idiots."

But that would come soon enough. It was still dark, and the *pricolici* was close.

44

Steve drove up to the front door of the new Island Legacy Church. Still hurt from his wound and still over sensitized by his metamorphosis, he could feel and smell everything. The monkshood, the wolfbane was far enough away that it did not affect him, but the scent was there. As was the reek of the recent dead.

The revenants had rested here, and been revived from their death. But one scent permeated the the church and the land. Steve knew it well. It was the same odor he remembered from decades ago. The smell of the remnants of the Nazi war machine, the killings, the mass murder, the torture. All those that had been killed to protect their secrets, all those that did the killings. They had a unique and peculiar rotten stench. Hate does that. It sticks to a person.

The worst of it came from inside. The door was open. He was expected.

Dressed only in athletic tights and a loose white shirt, stained with the last of his blood that leaked from his wound, Steve entered the dark nave. He had no idea who he would find. There was someone there, hiding in the shadows, a blood drinker, a nightwalker, a monster of some kind. He had seen them before. Whoever it was may know who he was, but they had no idea who they were dealing with.

"You can come out, Nazi," Steve called out. "I know you are here. I know your stench." Steve brandished his knife in the filtered light that made its way through the tall clear glass. There were no depictions of saints or apostles committing good deeds in stained glass in this church, Steve noted.

Steve walked to the sanctuary. He wanted to keep a wall to his back in the darkness, and make his threat come to him. "Whatever you are, you won't be the first one I've killed."

A soft voice came from the ether. "There is no need to fight, *wolf.*" The voice said the word as *volfe*, in a soft, almost condescending tone, as if speaking to a pet. There was no need to hide the Germanic origin. "I can give you what you want."

Steve tried not to show it, but the detatched voice uneased him. It came from above and behind, even though he knew there was nothing there. Whoever it was, they were trying to scare him. They didn't need to try. He had no problem admitting he was scared. He just wasn't going to admit it to them.

And just because he was scared didn't mean he still wasn't going to kill this thing.

"And what do you think I want?" Steve called out. He hoped to figure out where the monster, the vampire, the Nazi, whatever it was, would be hiding. "Why don't you come out and tell me. Nazi."

"I know what you want.

"You want to grow old. You want… to be with the girl. You want to be more than the wolf, more than the boy. You want power to be who was always inside you.

"I can give it to you. I can give it all to you. You can be the hero.

"Be a god. Like me…" those last words seemed to linger in the sickening and deep air of the church. The door let in the humid salt air, carrying a thick odor of dampness and death for Steve.

"Whatever god you think made you is long dead," Steve said, "and your unholy church won't stand for much longer. Whatever devil you worshiped isn't around to come to save you."

Deep in the darkness, Boarman felt the words reach him. He was used to fear, the joy of torture, when they don't fight back. Sometimes the bravado made the death better. But this time, the *wolf* believed what it said. Boarman just didn't know to be afraid.

"I can give you an eternity, with the little girl, with any girl or woman you want. I can give you money, control.

"Love."

Steve was quiet. He knew that the temptation was being sold to him, but it was all false. Not that it mattered. "I already have that. Everything. Money, power, people who follow me. Love, I have love. I've known more love than you ever will.

"I have no need for power, and no desire for eternity. Now, come and meet your end." Steve gnashed growing canines and twisted the knife in his right hand. The tear in his side remarkably felt no pain. Steve closed his eyes and felt the hair stand up on his neck. He let the feeling pour over him as his blood poured and boiled inside, a delightful rush of heat.

"As you wish," whispered the voice in his ear.

A dark cloud, a shape of nothing but gossamer and smoke, fell from the side of the church ceiling, coming for Steve's right flank. All the time they talked, Boarman had distracted the pricolici with his words. He had no intention of fulfilling any promise to the wolf. Boarman was going to kill it, drain it of its blood, take its power, too, live forever, young, powerful, perfect.

Between the last word that Boarman spoke and his silent launch at the wolf, Steve had changed completely. He had followed the darkness, the words, as they moved across the church. He knew exactly where the Nazi was before it had begun the attack. The pricolici stepped one step back, a grace that belied its giant size, and slashed with the large knife at the flowing vampire.

The knife tore across the face and body of the vampire. Boarman felt the cut, felt a strange and horrible burn. First a gasp, then a scream. Boarman crumbled in a heap, then rolled himself into a ball before standing up. He tried to pat at the scar across his face and down his chest. It was a reaction to the wound, and he expected the pricolici to fight like a duel, to let him recover.

The pricolici was no longer fully human; it could choose to fight like the animal it was, an eight foot tall monstrous wolf with black claws and spike teeth. It leapt at the wounded prey immediately, raising its back paws, raking and kicking, attempting to gut Boarman. Only by a swift twist and a rush of fear did Boarman avoid a crushing blow. He leapt away, falling behind the pews twenty feet from him.

"You have killing passion in you," Boarman tried to recover from the attack. He was used to antagonizing his victims. This one wasn't responding. Not the way he hoped, at least. "If you don't have desires, then you have fears."

Boarman leapt at the the pricolici, aiming for the center of its towering body. Again the wolf parried, but Boarman struck out with long, cold fingers, gripping at the fur, digging into its wound. Boarman felt the big gash open as he wrapped his arms around the beast. Boarman didn't care what it did to him. He would heal, recover, but he had to bring the pricolici down.

And Boarman had to taste it before he killed it.

Boarman spun behind the creature, gripping it from its back, and dove an oversized stretched mouth, cold, pale, as he bit into the torn and drying wound. Blood spurted, hot, sick, dark red.

Delicious.

The pricolici howled in pain. Boarman knew he had left his mark. It was torn open now, bleeding again, hurt, and it would weaken, he was sure. So delighted in his torment, Boarman didn't care when the wolf gripped him awkwardly from behind. A giant arm with a crushing claw squeezed and pulled Boarman off, then flung him into the pews with a crash.

The pricolici spun as it tried to find the wound under its arm. This time, the open cut continued to bleed and hurt. The pelt and fur were torn, exposing a ragged gray flesh, a thin layer above the last rib.

Deep within, Steve Brodie felt the pain. He felt himself return, unwillingly but necessary. He needed to think. He needed his brain, not the animal instinct. This was not a mindless battle. He needed more than just the scent of the evil, but also the thought of the Nazi, the demon man, the person behind the attack. He willed the pricolici, the wolf inside him, to obey. It was a self taught lesson over decades of loss of control.

"There you are," came the call. Still hiding in the dark, Boarman could see the slight change, the return of thought, which meant the man was there that could be reasoned with, or controlled, or tricked.

"You may be strong," Boarman called, "but you still have weakness. If you do not want to submit, I will take you anyway. And then I will take your girl. I'll kill you of course, but I may keep her."

The pricolici would have only felt the passion and hate, and attacked. Steve, as angered as he was, sickened by the threat to Jackie, had heard the words before. He knew the Nazi meant it. If he didn't stop him, the words would become deeds. But it wouldn't help to lash out. He knew the man was trying to goad him into a mistake. The words were just that, words, meant to incite fear.
Steve may have been injured, but he was no longer afraid.

He slid down, onto all fours, tensing, but waiting in the dark. He felt his side, blood dripping from his wound. The Nazi, cowering in the dark, could not wait, he knew. The longer it took, the better the odds for Steve. The sun would come up, people would see, would see it all. The Nazi had to hide in the dark, and act when no one was looking.

Boarman thought the same thing. He had seen the pricolici change. It went back to a more human form, though still gigantic, but not the feral wolf. Then it disappeared. The moments stretched. Boarman felt his own wound, one he thought impossible only moments before. The slash from the knife had torn him open from the face down his chest. A wet and black blood, long dead, had seeped out the wound, which burned like an unnatural acid. He drew inward, looking for help, power, repair.

In the silence of the church, in the dark, the sacrilegious cross made of the mirrors tinkled and began to crack. The thin mercury black veins crinkled and grew. Across the island, in their sleep, all the members of the church that had their mirrors felt their minds being twisted with nightmares of their own victimization. All their wishes and desires of the hurt they put on others began to crawl into their own bodies, taking their perversions and sicknesses and turning them against themselves, their spouses, and their children.

But Boarman felt the power heal him. He delighted in their pain. He felt his strength grow.

Steve hid in the darkness, moving silently. He, too, could hear the crackle of the large cross. In his decades of searches for cures, for ways to become whole, or even to finally die, he knew of the many ways that people gathered to do evil. He felt the tense power move to the cross, then across the church. It never touched him, unwelcome in his body. A wave of nausea and hate rushed over him, making him double over. Then it was gone, moved into a more welcoming target. He knew that the Nazi was gathering his power. But he also knew where it came from.

As soon as Boarman leapt up, hoping to pounce onto the pricolici in the dark and pin it to the ground with a demon's strength, Steve jumped forward. The two met at the front of the sanctuary in a horrid embrace of two inhuman creatures. Boarman grasped at the pricolici and sunk his teeth into its neck, tasting human and animal blood.

Steve gripped Boarman in his giant arms and suffered the pains of the attack on him. Then Steve raised his blade, a much sharper and larger weapon than the Nazi vampire's teeth. He stabbed deep, plunging the knife into the Nazi's back. It went so deep that the point came through his chest. Steve felt the burn of the tip of the blade on his own body.

The pain the two felt made them release their embrace. Steve fell backwards, pulling the knife out roughly. His shoulder and side hurt from his own wounds.

Boarman lat on his back as well, the big gash on him as his lifeless blood tried to leak out like a sickening and odoriferous syrup. He coughed at the intense pain, as both the blood of his own and the pricolici's spurted out of his mouth.

Steve held the knife menacingly, the steel and silver showing a gleaming counterpoint to the ebony black wood that ran down the top of the blade.

Boarman tried to laugh, but all that came out was a phlegmy cough. "Do you actually believe those foolish legends?! That a wooden stake can kill me?"

Steve had no such belief. He threatened with the knife as he lunged at Boarman, who turned aside the thrust easily, which was exactly what Steve wanted him to do. He reached out at the fast moving Boarman, grasping at where the vampire would be as he moved. Steve's giant claws grasped at Boarman's body. Steve picked Boarman up into the air and heaved him across the sanctuary. Boarman's body crashed into the mirrored cross, shattering it.

Throughout the island, where the blasphemous followers of the church slept in tumultuous dreams, they awoke en masse, screaming in pain as the veins of the mirror broke into their own skin. Creases and wrinkles formed, then skin broke, and faces bled. They suffered in their long earned sacrilegious crapulence. Unable to determine the cause of their pain, they rolled in pools of their own blood and excrement, whimpering and vomiting as their children cried. All the sins they wished into their mirrors for others had been gathered to power Boarman's authority, and now it had all been freed, returned to the owners, all at once.

Boarman felt his strength leave him as he fell. He lost his power as all his followers received all the pain they had wished on others for years. He tried to rise up, but was weakened by the sudden loss. He saw the wolf, the pricolici, and the man, all in one, as it stalked to him to stand over his body, the shining knife in a great hairy hand.

Boarman coughed, and laughed. "I told you, a stake through the heart won't stop me!"

Steve raised the knife and plunged it forcefully into Boarman's heart. He felt the knife part the skin, then break the sternum. The bones in Boarman's chest chipped and broke. The blade scraped horribly across a rib, then bent and snapped the bone. Steve continued to push, forcing the blade through the already open wound. The tip of the blade made its way through Boarman's heart and into his spine. Steve twisted the blade, finding the gaps, cutting through the nerves before feeling a distinct and atrocious snap. With a final push, the blade made its way through Boarman's body.

Steve never stopped. He gripped the knife and shoved on the silver pommel, feeling its burn in his calloused hand/paw. The hilt guard crushed into the broken ribs, going deeper into Boarman's chest. The blade went through, pinning Boarman to the cheap carpet and wood floor underneath.

Stakes had been long used as lore to kill a vampire. A wooden stake through an unbeating, uncaring heart was one way to end the reign of terrors in days long ago. But in reality, that was a myth. Townspeople had found dead bodies, quickly buried before they could rot, in coffins where the dead had not been dead, only comatose. The victims would struggle and twist in the coffin, scratching to get out until their fingers were shredded to bone. It was only assumed that they came back from the dead. So a stake through the heart would not only ensure a permanent death, but it would pin the dead to their coffin, never to rise and attack the living.

Steve knew the legend well, as he finally rose up from Boarman's speared and broken body. The vampire coughed and spat blood on Steve, reaching out with cold, bony arms.

"I know," Steve growled. The pricolici in him still lusted for the hunt and the kill. He tamed it with his thoughts, just enough so as not to respond too easily. "There's only one way to kill you. Leech. Nazi. *Pijavica.*

"I know what you are."

Boarman stared, wide eyed, blood staining his face, his own blood, black and thick, more than the warm blood of the pricolici he had tasted. He tried to rise, but found the knife pinned him down.

Boarman tried to reach for the knife to pull it out, but his own bones were unstitched, and didn't allow him to move his arms to his chest.

Seeing the attempt, Steve grappled for one arm, holding it in two fists at the shoulder, and twisted. The bones, tendons, ligaments, and muscles all gave way with a tense crackle, as if someone twisted the drumstick off a turkey.

Boarman tried in vain to reach out and strike the face of his tormentor with his left fist, but the blow was so slow, so weak now, it was caught in the teeth of the pricolici. Canines sank into the bony flesh, little peanuts of bones in the wrist popping through the skin. Steve reached for the left arm, while holding the wrist in his mouth, a sour and horrid taste from the long dead blood pouring out. He twisted and pulled again, this time separating the arm from the shoulder with a disgusting pop as the ball came out of the socket. He continued to pull until the skin separated and tore, with a final rushing gasp as the arm came off the body in a pool of diseased blood.

Boarman was now pinned down, weakened, and finally realizing his work and his life had been for nothing. He had worked to build wealth and power, to take and control. He had money, manipulation, a following, and it all was for nothing.

Steve saw the look in Boarman's eyes in the darkness. And he smelled the fear. It was a horrid, animal fear, a fear of knowing. The final fear of finally knowing that death was coming for them, and nothing could stop it. The scent of fear drifted out of the church and mingled with the other fears and pains that were wafting across all of Hatteras. Steve knew that for some, the fear would last forever, but for most, what he did would bring an end to their fear.

He reached for one of the shards of mirrored glass, and began to carve open the body of Harrison Boarman.

Steve gutted the creature, splitting him from neck to navel, then used the sharp pointed glass to cut away the organs. As he removed them, they turned black and rotten, mimicking the life Boarman had led. Steve struggled with the vampire's pants, trying to undo them until he just gave in with animal instinct and plunged the sharp point through Boarmans' abdomen and raked it down.

Boarman scream reached a high pitched cry. Of all the violence feasted upon his body, this was the worst. He felt the sharp shard of glass disembowel him from the inside. All the glorious terror he had inflicted, all the women and children he had tormented and raped, all that came flooding into a perfect memory of pain. Yet he was stuck, unable to fight back. Death was waiting for him, and he minded that less than the thought of being castrated.

Steve left the mirror stuck inside Boarman. He had only one task left. There was only one way to kill a vampire like this, and that was to cut it apart. He had one more hideous cut to make. Steve pulled the knife out of Boarman's open chest with a horrid rasp. It dripped black blood as Steve moved it slowly up, up, to Boarman's head. While Boarman watched, Steve placed the point into Boarman's clenched teeth to pry his mouth open. There would be no severing at the neck for this one, Steve thought. He pried open the mouth, seeing one, then two teeth pop and fly from the blade. With a firm and determined push, the knife slipped over Boarman's tongue, through his soft throat and across the top of his spine. Steve placed both hands on the hilt and pressed sideways, like a guillotine cutter, severing the spine and half the face off.

Boarman's head flopped, attached only by some remaining muscle and tendon to his lower jaw. A giant hand came down and squeezed the skull, pulling it, as the knife cut a diabolical fillet out of the remaining tissue. Boarman's head separated from the lower jaw and neck.

Steve saw the eyes roll back, a moment of delicious pain in their last sight, then nothing.

Whoever it was, Steve knew it was dead. He still smelled the Nazi stench on the body, but it mixed with decomposition, the offal of a deceased body, the rotten blood and organs spilled out on the floor. Whatever devil these people worshiped, whatever turned this man to a demon vampire, it just got its last sacrifice.

Steve felt himself changing. He rested, breathed, let it come, forcing the body to come back fully to obey his mind, as he had learned to do long ago. He stood naked and covered in gore, along with his own blood, weeping from the side, but trying its best to clot and stay in.

There was going to be nothing left of this man or this place, Steve decided. It was still dark, not quite sunrise even for late summer, but he had to hurry. He soaked the remains in gasoline from his Jeep's spare tank. He found a book of matches and a pack of cigarettes in a front office, "Of course they smoke in church," he almost laughed. He lit a cigarette and placed it inside the matchbook. It was a simple improvised fuse that he had used during his work in the war. But it gave him time to leave and be well away before the matches ignited and caught the gasoline on fire. The church would burn to cinders before anyone would know it was even on fire.

By the time Steve was drying off from his outdoor shower, he finally heard the siren from the first fire truck.

Analepsis III

Off the coast of Bodie Island
April 14, 1942

Oberleutnant zur See Gregor Eberhard heard the sounds of machine gun fire hitting his boat. The U-85 had surfaced in order to bring its 8.8cm deck gun to bear on its target. He couldn't bring himself to think that he was the hunted. It had been too dark to identify the American ship, but Eberhard was certain it was another of the near obsolete destroyers that the Americans had thrown into defending the coastline. "zu spät klug," he had muttered. "Too late smart."

Eberhard had at first run to the darkness, releasing a torpedo from his stern tubes, only to see the fish miss to the ship's starboard. With his position revealed, the surface ship had put on speed and began searching in earnest for him. The two ships began a circular chase, where his U-boat could turn tighter but at a slower speed than the chasing destroyer. He had ordered his crew on deck to engage the 8.8, but they could not accurately track the fast steaming ship. Eberhard had only moments to wonder why the destroyer hadn't engaged its large deck guns when a rattling sound of one of the destroyer's anti-aircraft weapons must have fired on his crew. It sounded as if an angry god had hurled rocks at his boat.

Then the U-boat was rocked by a deep shuddering blast, turning the boat sideways. Eberhard knew he had been hit by one of the big guns. Damage would be bad. One crew member reported all hands lost on the deck, either torn by the bullets or shredded by the big shell that had just hit.

Not that it mattered.

The U-boat began to tip, stern down. It took only moments to first hear the screams and yells, *"Schiff verlassen!"* Eberhard knew U-85 was lost. When he saw the cold waterfall of the Atlantic pouring down toward him, he further realized he was not getting out. Not that he wanted to. The notion of the captain going down with his ship was not lost on him, but he had no desire to be killed in the cold water. Nor did he want to be dragged out by the avenging Americans in their obsolete tin ship. While the rest of the crew struggled to find a way out and fail, Captain Eberhart locked himself in his cabin.

The U-boat sank in shallow water, only about 100 feet deep. Eberhard looked at his compass and determined east compared to the direction of his bow, almost the same, good enough for him. He was 14 miles off the coast of Cape Hatteras, a nearly empty land that he had only seen by periscope. Then the lights went out, all power gone. He had hoped that now that the U-boat was sunk, the destroyer would move on, but he could still hear the incessant sonar lashing. They were still looking for him topside. The Americans thought he had submerged to attack with torpedoes. It took about five minutes for the destroyer to circle around, then the depth charges began to wreak havoc in the shallow water. All those men who had struggled to get free of their tomb inside the U-boat were being blown to bits in the cold water above.

Eberhard waited and listened. It seemed to take forever, a likely feeling for the sailors who measure seconds as minutes and minutes as hours and hours as days. Time didn't measure the same to him. He had all the time in the world.

Once the water outside was silent, hours, days, it didn't matter, Eberhard cracked his watertight door open and the ocean flooded in, cold, heartless. It felt… familiar to him.

He struggled in the dark, but knew his way well. Long ago, ages, centuries, he had breathed water in his lungs for months. This time it merely filled him. It took time to get used to the cold and the weight, but he had more than enough experience in pain and suffering. This was an inconvenience at best. Weighted down by the water inside him, he began the long struggle to the coast. He walked the length of his ship, the bow pointing toward land. It would take days, cold, horrible days.

Eberhard walked ashore on a nearly abandoned coast, somewhere south of the little blinking light of a lighthouse. He remembered from his maps that this was probably what the Americans called Bodie Island. He was far to the south, past a small inlet. He stripped himself of his uniform markings and buried his coat. The setting sun led Eberhard to predict a cold April evening. He kept his cap over his head to block the bright light. A warm evening breeze surprised the captain. He wandered slowly to the dunes in hope of finding a road or a town. He knew there were villages interspersed along the islands here, and there were the occasional patrols. To the north were the more populous towns, and farther was the naval base at Norfolk. He needed to avoid that area.

He saw two men walking the beach, almost in the shadow of the dunes as the sun set. Eberhard quickly tucked his hat into his pocket. He should have gotten rid of it with the rest of his uniform. "Es ist schwer, die Vergangenheit loszulassen," he thought , then corrected himself into English.

The past is hard to let go.

The two men began to run toward him, but they were still a mile away, and quickly tired, settling to a trot. Eberhard didn't bother to run toward them. Let the others do the hard work. He was nothing but *Strandgut*, jetsam… "Think in English," he reminded himself. They didn't care who he was, as long as he wasn't the enemy.

Eberhard was surprised when the two men finally got closer. They were armed, with rifles pointed, somewhat menacingly, at him. As if they would do any good. The two, sailors? Soldiers? He saw the anchor markings on their uniforms. But what really surprised him was the color of their skin. The two were both dark skinned, well past the tanned and burned sailors he had seen that spent too much time in tropical sun. They looked African. "Neger?"

he thought, again in German. Eberhard was surprised the Americans had dark skinned people on their ships.

The beach is not actually a ship, he thought.

"Who are you?" It was a simple command from one man. His voice was both twangy, a strange lilt, almost Irish, or British, but thicker, a strange length to each sound.

Eberhard raised his hands weakly. He was the survivor of a shipwreck of course. In English, with what passed for a Norwegian accent to these two dark skinned men, he thought quickly…

"My name is Gregory Boarman. I was traveling on the ship *Benson* when we were torpedoed. I was fortunate to make it to shore."

The two men immediately lowered their weapons. "Can you walk?" one asked. "We can get you to the lifesaving station. It is about four miles that way." He pointed to the south. The other said, "We can call Hatteras to see if we can get a doctor. Or better yet, let's get you taken down there. Are you injured?"

Eberhard, now Boarman, the anglicized version of his name, his new name now, smiled at his good fortune. He waved off the offered hands, not wanting them to touch him. "No. I am well. Thank you for rescuing me."

45

Steve slept through the day. His body wouldn't let him wake up, even if he had wanted to. Even when the knocks came on the door, he slept through them. He would have to answer to what had happened the night before, sometime, but not to the people asking right now. They could wait. Let them figure out their own answers first, and then see what he needed to change.

The town would probably flood with state police, and SBI. The NC State Bureau of Investigation would always be called in when there was arson. And there would be no doubt that there was arson. A carpet soaked in gasoline would be a dead giveaway.

The FBI would be around, too. An agent had been injured, and the Bureau did not take those things lightly. But Agent Thomas Fredericks would have a rather special dispensation. Any issues would be kept secret. Higher ups would make quiet orders, with quiet mentions of grave consequences that would be understood by grave and serious agents. Steve's name would not likely come up, nor would his original name. Not unless it was necessary, and it had not as of yet ever been necessary. The last thing the federal government wanted was to expose Steve's rather dark secret and his past.

To everyone else, he was just one of many targets of a hatefilled group of people. He had been at the radio station all night, and had come home and slept all day.

Steve woke up, rested, wounded still, but healing. Normally his wounds would heal and scar over in hours or days at worst, but the diseased scratches, bites, and stabs, they took longer. Sometimes they stayed. Two shiny scars, small puncture wounds, were hidden by the dark downy hair on his right arm.

By four o'clock, Steve finally was fully awake. Sooner or later, he knew, another vehicle would pull up. He just wasn't sure who it would be. He expected the FBI to roll in on one of their black sedans, or a simple rental Oldsmobile, so plain as to stand out in its simplicity. Someone needed to come by, to tell him how Thomas was. Steve didn't even know where the man was.

The truck that pulled up wasn't the one he expected. Nor wanted.

Jackie's father, Andy Wood, got out of the truck that he and his wife had used to transport Thomas away from Hatteras, hopefully to get medical attention. His appearance back at Steve's house set a shade of gloom over the afternoon.

As if on cue, a green Oldsmobile pulled up the sand and shell road, but no one got out. Steve didn't know if this was a good or bad thing. He opened the door and went out to meet Dr. Wood.

"How is Thomas?" Steve said, an unfortunate anxiousness rushing his words. He quickly realized how he sounded. "I'm sorry, it's just..." he didn't need to make excuses. "How is Jackie? And both of you?" That should have been his first concern. Thomas has been a good friend, a mentor, his commander, but he also was a soldier and agent. Risk and the acceptance of that risk were part and parcel of their lives.

Dr. Wood waved it off. "Your friend is, well, okay, I guess would be the best way to say it. I know, you're concerned, he's someone close to you. He's going to be moved to a hospital in Washington, to Johns Hopkins, I believe. He's in Norfolk right now, but he was responding to antibiotics. He came out of that stupor you put him in, by the way."

Steve and Andy Wood looked at each other, both serious men with serious concerns. Steve looked at the FBI agents waiting in the car. They must have come with Dr. Wood, but let him have a moment alone. Steve was sure this wasn't about Thomas. "Come inside," he said with a dismissal wave to the car and the agents.

"Jackie, and your friend, and well," Dr. Wood jerked a thumb at the car outside the house once they closed the door behind them, "your *other* friends there, they pretty much explained things to me and my wife." Dr. Wood looked more crestfallen than angry. "I have to say, even though I saw it with my own eyes, I still don't quite believe it."

"I'm sure that's what they want you to say, isn't it?"

Dr. Wood nodded softly. "Yes, pretty much." He said that and was quiet.

Steve knew there was more, but Dr. Wood didn't know how to start. "Go ahead," he said, "It isn't like I haven't heard this before. I can do it for you, if you like."

"No, no," Dr. Wood shook his head. It was difficult for him to stand in front of this boy, and have to believe Steve was older than he was. And to know what kind of creature, a wild monster, that was inside him. For a moment, Dr. Wood fought back panic, as he was inside and alone, confronting something he feared.

Steve saw the look, one he had seen before. He sat down, far away, and tried to relax. "You can say it. I already know some version."

"I don't know who you are," Dr. Wood started, and then the words flowed out, angry and scared, "but you need to stay away from us. I don't want Jackie near you. I don't want you near my family. Not now. I don't know for how long, but not now. Not until I at least figure this out."

Steve felt hurt, but not the wounded, angry kind. Dr. Wood was telling the truth. He had heard the same words before, a few times, especially one time, long ago. He looked around the room, at the few mementos of his life, the bowl of poisons and cures he had tried, the things that ended up saving Thomas that he had used to try to kill himself or cure himself. Next to it was the little box, his box of dreams, with tokens of lost love, all aged away when he stayed young.

He wanted to explain to Dr. Wood that he had no interest in Jackie. Steve felt the worst sting of his curse, that no matter how old he got, he would forever be a nineteen year old boy. A man, yes. That, too. How to look at this man, a father, something Steve was not, and explain that he never got to be a teenager, that he was thrust into killing and seeing death at 18, trained as a soldier in high school at sixteen, never having a first love or teenage crush. Then forced to be a man, a killer. Then tormented and frozen in time to look like he did, his reflection a continual reminder that he will never move on.

To Dr. Wood, his daughter looked like just another target for another teen boy, and here was this teen, but also old, but also a monster, all rolled into one.

But Steve had been a protector, too. Steve had said the words he knew would help, because he had heard them said to him. And Steve had fought and ultimately killed for Jackie. Those were things that Dr. Wood, no matter how much he thought of himself as a father who would sacrifice everything for his girl, could never do. Fathers wish they were bulletproof, could suck the poison from blood, breathe in the sicknesses, and snuggle away a broken heart. In Dr. Wood's eyes, Steve could do all those things that he can't.

And Steve could also kill them all.

But explaining all that would take time, and Dr. Wood had no interest in excuses.

"I understand," Steve said. He almost started to say, "Don't worry," something he had learned long ago not to say. People were going to worry. "I'll do as you wish." I'll be the bad guy, he thought.

The room was silent for a moment. Dr. Wood had nothing else to say. Steve wasn't going to defend himself or argue, just acquiesce. It took the wind out of the sails. From long practice of saying the same thing.

Dr. Wood was decent enough not to try to get the last word. He simply opened the door and left.

Steve sat in silence. He wanted to cry, just a little. Just to see if it would help. It never had in the past.

The FBI gave him a moment, at least. The two that came to do the necessary visit were new. He didn't recognize them. Young, dark haired, tall man, and tense, severe woman. "In with the new," Steve said. It wasn't the first time. Or probably the tenth time for him to get new case handlers.

They stood at more than arm's length, of course. The man kept his jacket unbuttoned and the woman had an open purse. Steve thought evilly for a moment, "You need to be faster than that." He wondered if they had silver bullets. The thought made him chuckle inwardly. It took the sting off, a little.

Mostly it was the usual, a debrief, explaining that Thomas was in treatment, but awake, and would likely recover after a rather potent bout of antibiotics. "You probably saved his life," Severe said. She seemed slightly impressed, hiding it behind a veneer of nonchalance and nonplus.

"That's good to hear, at least." Steve suddenly felt tired again. As if he carried the weight of his friend for a moment, an onrush of empathy for a man that had been something of a dad, and maybe a crazy uncle. "Tell him he needs to retire. To go fishing. Fishing is good here." He wondered if Thomas would want to come back down, or even be allowed.

"I'm pretty sure the Bureau is going to insist on that," said Dark Hair. I probably should learn their names, Steve thought. Severe didn't seem to believe in what she was seeing. "Yeah, well, neither did I, until I got bit," Steve thought to himself.

The rest was revealed by the agents in a blur. The church was burned to ash. The fire department got there too late and only prevented the fire from spreading. The building was built cheaply and fast. It had gone down the same way. Darrow had been arrested almost immediately. His protests that he didn't remember any of what happened that night didn't go anywhere to create an alibi. Finding his secretary's lingerie and Polaroid photos in his home were somewhat damning, morally, but then finding Darla's body in a shallow grave put the nail in his coffin. The state police were also curious as to what might be under the basketball court.

It was a nice, tight case. Darrow would take the fall for the fire, and the deaths of both women and the sheriff, explained the agents.

No one even bothered to look for Boarman.

So many of the parishioners to the Island Legacy Church were left scarred and tormented by the strange scrying mirror that many had either gone into hiding or just left. They would be forced to wear the scars of their sins on their faces. It was assumed that Boarman was just one of many who took their money and ran. The FBI knew better, and did not bather to look. They knew exactly where he was.

There was nothing else to discuss. The agents took their time, knowing that they could not attempt to bring Steve up for any charges. What would they prosecute him for? Killing already dead Nazis? Dark Hair had impressed upon Steve the same message that was impressed upon them in Washington. "No good would come of it. We would look like a laughingstock."

Steve didn't bother to show them the door. Severe was strangely nice enough to ask, "Is there anything we can do for you?" Steve simply shook his head. It was close to 5:00 pm. He would have to go to work soon. He needed to make things look normal.

It was a grim evening at the radio station. Tim wanted to talk about everything that had happened the night before. He blamed Brin Darrow for Ellen Gaines' death in the car explosion. "He even burned his own church down to cover it all up. The man is a psycho!" Tim was irate. He needed to vent his frustration to a silent Steve Brodie, who could only nod and pretend to agree. Darrow may very well have arranged Ellen's death, though Steve still suspected Boarman sent a local toady to try to kill Tim, instead, and poor Ellen had just been in the wrong place.

"They won't even investigate it!" Tim just kept playing music and commercials, never taking to the mic, for fear of what he might say out loud.

Steve understood the frustration. He knew that the FBI and the state bureau probably also knew it was Darrow or someone associated with him. If it turned out to be someone else from their defiled "church," they would be found out. But most likely, they saw a person to blame that they already had in custody, and it was an easy way to wrap everything up and keep everything else secret.

After about an hour, Steve finally saw Tim crash. It was expected. Steve had seen it before, the exhaustion of being angry all the time. At some time, the body gives up. Tim looked at Steve, showing his sagging face, dark eyes, thick and puffy, with bright red rings on his lids. "I'm just so tired," Tim finally confessed. "I don't know how you are doing, but I need to go home. Can you take over early? Or if you want, I can just sign off and we can all get some sleep."

Steve waved Tim off. "I can run it, don't worry. I'll just do what you're doing. Then I'll do my show tonight like usual. They won't know the difference."

"I wonder if anyone is even listening," Tim confessed his thoughts. "I wonder if anyone would even notice if we were off right now."

Steve sighed. "Maybe not, but they still need music. Even in the background. Just a little something, some noise, to keep all the thoughts in the back of our minds at bay. You know how, when you feel bad, and somehow the radio knows just how you feel, and plays that one song, well, that's what we gotta do now."

The words put a slight smile on Tim's worn face. He knew Steve was right.

"Thanks, Morty," Tim said, a reminder of an old joke from long ago. Tim looked around, found nothing he needed to pick up, shook his pocket for the keys to his new car, and walked out into the hot evening.

Steve did just what he said, played records and commercials, then went on at ten for his late night show. He played happy, mournful music, setting the tone for the kids that stayed up late in the summer who hoped for better days.

He would sign off at 1:00am, then turn off the power. He left one light on, just to light the office, as he left.

It was a long, slow, silent drive back to Buxton from far down in Hatteras. This time, the bushes and shrubs hid nothing. It was just dark. A thin waxing moon came up an hour later, promising light but not quite getting there. As he neared Buxton, he could see the intermittent pulse of Cape Hatteras Lighthouse flashing over the trees of Trent Woods. Nothing felt bad, or scary, no more hidden monsters, no more worries in his head. It was just empty. Empty. No more enemies. Nothing to fight.

Empty.

No more friends.

Empty.

He pulled up to his house, dark in the shadows of creeping oak trees. Empty.

He looked through the trees to the south. No lights shown through from the new neighborhood.

Empty.

Steve walked up to his door. He had left it unlocked and didn't bother with the keys. The house would be empty.

Taped to the door was a small folded note. He took it off and opened the paper. It smelled lightly of sweetness and flowers.

Inside was a simple scribbled heart shape, an attempt that didn't quite open up completely, the lines closed and overlapped. The heart had tried and not quite succeeded in surrounding the words.

"Thank you"

Postlude

May 21ˢᵗ, 1989

It was incredibly sunny, almost burning down even though it wasn't even noon yet. A surprisingly hot day for mid-May. Steve sat on the beach, on a big old towel. It was slightly torn at one end. The strange purple, yellow, and blue pattern, signifying nothing more than a strange 1980s penchant for splatter and flash, was starting to wear and fade. But it was soft and familiar to Steve. It had been a gift two years ago from Thomas's grandson, who explained that everyone needed a good towel.

The kid had been right, Steve thought.

A surfboard sat on the sand next to him. The waves weren't really up, but Steve brought it anyway. The water was still cool, and he wore a short spring suit, unzipped and pulled down to his waist, even though the icy ocean in May didn't bother him much. He would watch for a while, then float out and do nothing, just to cool off from the solar heat.

Steve lay back onto the towel, nestling his head into the sand. "Just a few more minutes," he told himself. He closed his eyes and listened to the sound of the beach. He could hear the ocean waves rush up the shore in tiny rivulets only a foot high. Somewhere far off, some high school kids squealed and screamed as they tried to throw a Frisbee without much luck. He could hear the occasional scratch of cars and trucks in the parking lot as their tires scraped over the sand blown onto the gray asphalt. It was good background noise, a happy music that was familiar to him.

Steve heard more footsteps in the sand. People walked funny in the sand. It shifted and made them lose balance as they tried to dig the lateral side of their feet in to counter their weight. No one noticed they did that, but they all did. The footsteps got closer. The footsteps were closing, but Steve didn't want to open his eyes, not yet. "Please just pass by," he hoped.

But the footsteps stopped, right next to him.

"How come you didn't come to my graduation?"

Steve opened one eye. Towering above him, long brown hair, quickly turning to golden blonde, and a bright white smile.

"Hi, Jackie."

"Hi.

"How come you didn't come to my graduation?" Jackie had finished college at the University of North Carolina the week before.

"I did," Steve said. "I was six rows from the top. I saw you get your diploma with binoculars." Commencement was held at the university's football stadium. "Congratulations. I'm proud of you." He tried to make it sound genuine, but it came out slightly sarcastic.

Jackie had written him, on occasion, over the last four years. Her father had not only demanded that Steve not be around Jackie, but that Jackie couldn't talk to Steve, either. Steve had felt mostly sad for the girl, "Girl," he thought, looking up at her, "she looks older than me. She *is* older than me," but it wasn't as if he had ever pursued Jackie. She had just been kind to him, accepted him as part of the island, unlike so many others when he had first moved here.

"Thanks," she said back, with the same level of smarm. "I loved my graduation gift, by the way. The pen and pencil set was really nice."

"Oh, you knew that was from me?" It had been a bit of a gag. Steve had mentioned the rather useless but traditional gift that so many adults gave graduating students.

Steve had written her back, pointedly, twice a year, typed, no name, with nothing specific ever included in his letters. It was just a way to let her know he still knew she was there.

Jackie sat down next to him. "You finally took up surfing, huh?" She stared at the board.

"Last year," Steve answered. "You weren't here that summer."

"You noticed." It was a statement, not a question.

All of Jackie's friends, in one way or another, drifted over the last four years. Not drifted away, though some did, somewhat, but they grew up, took jobs, went to college, and some were not moving back. Steve noticed the change in the beach as they were replaced by younger versions. He wondered if Jackie still felt like she ruled the shore like she did when he first met her.

Jackie looked at Steve, still young, with shorter hair now. But still handsome, cute, bright, and fit. Except now he was tanned, a smooth creamy skin instead of his soft paleness that he had carried from so many nights at work. "The beach looks good on you, kid."

"Yeah, I gave in and embraced it. I cut my hair, of course. It was easier for the barber."

"No more Jon Bon Jovi, huh?"

"No more Jon Bon Jovi."

Jackie looked at Steve, closely. She was not admiring him, just looking. His side still had some slight scarring from long ago. "Does that still hurt?"

No one would normally bring up the thin pale cut on his ribs. It was barely visible, unnoticeable unless he had his shirt off and lifted his arm. "No," he said simply, "not any more. It should disappear. I'm surprised it's still there."

"Just as good a reminder for no one to fuck with Steve Brodie." The swear word was a surprise to Steve. He had heard it time and time over his life, but didn't know if he had ever heard it from Jackie before.

"You know," she said, "If you see me around town, you can talk to me. My dad has kinda come to terms with you."

"Did the fact that no one has been attacked by a wolf in the past four years help in his decision?" Steve joked. He had seen Jackie's parents at the Red and White, it was a small island, there was no doubt about that. And Steve's voice still covered the airwaves at night.

"Okay," he said, "I'll say hi.

"Hi."

He smiled his white smile at Jackie, who finally felt like she could genuinely smile back. She bumped him in the shoulder with hers.

"So, are you any good on that?" Jackie pointed at the board.

Steve looked out at the strangely flat Atlantic of Hatteras Island. "Today?" he laughed. "Not likely. All I could do is just float." Not a wave over one foot appeared anywhere along the horizon.

They sat quietly, Jackie clenching her knees to her chest, Steve with one eye closed, the other squinting at the ocean while he lay supine, lifting only his head. They watched the ocean, listened to the soft waves. It was a pleasant sound, one that both could enjoy on end, without speaking. It was a talent few had.

"My father got me a job in Manteo. At the aquarium." It wasn't the dream job a marine biologist desired, but it paid well, well enough. "He wants me to move up there."

Steve said nothing at first. Then, "That's a pretty cool place. Dark, quiet. I like going there. I like the Elizabethan Gardens, too. Manteo is pretty. A little crowded for me, but pretty."

"You know they have radio stations up there, too." Jackie said softly, with a hint in her voice. "There's one in Wanchese, and one downtown."

Steve knew the two stations. Both were, well, adequate, but didn't play his style of music, and didn't have the recording studio he needed. Not that he couldn't build it himself. And he would be an hour closer to shipping his show off to Norfolk…

"Tim would have my head if I left him," Steve came to his senses. He was content here. Safe.

"I'm just saying, you can think about it. The beach is nice there. Not waves like this," Jackie mockingly waved her hand at the flat slick calm of the Atlantic. "But still, nice."

Behind them, loud voices chimed in from the parking lot. A group of young women came storming out to the beach. Jackie looked up and recognized her old friends, all home to meet up.

"Your friends are here," Steve said, with his one eye squint on the approaching squall of women.

Jackie got up and waved. "Yes," she said. "I know they are."

That night, Steve took over his show as usual, planning a new lineup of songs, as he looked at the just released Hot 100 from Billboard. "Damn..." he swore softly, making sure the mic was truly off. That would be bad. After lining out the softer ballads, the remaining titles seemed to be saying something to him from the mix of fun pop and rock songs. "I gotta go with something." He avoided his favorite, a near chart topper by Guns N' Roses, as being too slow to start the show. And he didn't need a lesson in patience at the moment. "Bon Jovi it is," he said as he slipped in the CD.

He came out of his commercials, turned on his mic, and slipped into his persona. "Welcome back home, Hatteras. Summer is here by the feel of the air, and we've been waiting for you, all year long. It's good to have you back.

"I'm Steve Brodie, and this is Midnight Radio."

A NOTE ON THE EVENTS

On April 14, 1942, the German U-boat U-85 was sunk about 15 miles off the coast of Bodie Island. Almost all guns on the USS *Roper* had jammed due to the corrosive salt air, even though the crews had been diligent in their care and practice. The *Roper* was simply a very old ship. Chief Boatswain's Mate Jack Edwin Wright opened fire with a .50 caliber machine gun on the sailors aboard the deck of the U-85 to keep them from firing their main deck gun. Coxswain Harry Hayman was then able to engage with the *Roper*'s 3 inch main gun, landing several shots under the waterline. The U-85 was unable to submerge, but then began to flood and sink. The *Roper* continued the attack out of fear that the U-boat was below the surface and would launch a torpedo. The *Roper* continued its attack until it was sure it had sunk the U-boat. It then left the area until the next morning when daylight and aerial patrols could help confirm there were no other threats. All sailors on board the U-85, including its skipper, Eberhard Greger, were lost.

Radio Hatteras is a community run radio station, going live on March 14, 2013. Broadcasting on 99.5 and 101.5 as WHDX and WHDZ for music and community news.

In the summer of 1942, a couple with heavy German accents spent several days at Maude White's boarding house, sketching the area and sending letters from the local post office, run by Maude. They asked several questions about the lighthouse and other areas, drawing pictures and rolling them up to be mailed off. While no one knew if they truly were spies, years later, a certificate from the Intelligence Office of the Fifth Naval District was found acknowledging Maude White for her patriotic services during the war.

The legend of the ten or twelve men who showed up to render help along the coast has been quietly told over the decades. Locals knew they were not native to the islands, and allegedly took matters into their own hands. There is no evidence of this actually happening, though.

About The Author

John Martell grew up on the coast of North Carolina, swimming and sailing along the shores, exploring the beaches and shipwrecks of the Carolinas. He spent his adult life exploring both the Atlantic and Pacific coasts, going up and down both the west and east coasts for bits of history.

He currently spends his summers at the beach with his family when he is not writing. He penned his first horror novel, *The Unmerciful Sea*, as an homage to the great pulp horror novels and zombie flicks of the 1980s he saw as a kid.